Skullduggery at Golgotha

The Untold Story of Christ's Crucifixion

A NOVEL BY

PASTOR BLAINE MacNEIL

THE TRILOGY OF THE CROSS PART TWO

1

Skullduggery at Golgotha
The Untold Story of Christ's Crucifixion
The Trilogy of the Cross Part Two

Meet Me on Facebook

A Novel by
Pastor Blaine MacNeil
pastorblainemacneil.com
Copyright © 2018 Blaine MacNeil
MacNeil Publishing

Skullduggery at Golgotha

Pastor MacNeil's Bio	8
Thanks	10
Introduction	11
Chapter One Conspirators at the Palace	12
Chapter Two Pilate's Soldiers	18
Chapter Three Claudia and Pilate	24
Chapter Four Judas, Lead Us	28
Chapter Five Into the Hands of Sinners	33
Chapter Six The March to Jerusalem	43
Chapter Seven For Peter's Shame	48
Chapter Eight Abuse from The Temple Guards	52

Chapter Nine   55
Pretrial Before Annas

Chapter Ten   64
Annas And Caiaphas

Chapter Eleven   68
Law Without the Law

Chapter Twelve   71
The Lesser Court

Chapter Thirteen   87
The Judgement Hall of Hewn Stones

Chapter Fourteen   97
Silver Regret

Chapter Fifteen   103
From One Courtroom to the Next

Chapter Sixteen   108
Pilate's Courtroom

Chapter Seventeen   121
High Priestly Garments

Chapter Eighteen   129
Death on the Desert Tree

Chapter Nineteen   139
Before Herod

Chapter Twenty   149
A New Trial Granted

Chapter Twenty-One   144
Jesus of Nazareth or Jesus Bar-Abbas

Chapter Twenty-Two   171
Preponderance of The Evidence

Chapter Twenty-Three   182
The High Priest's Garments

Chapter Twenty-Four   185
The Thrashing

Chapter Twenty-Five   197
Behold the Man

Chapter Twenty-Six   207
The Judgement Seat

Chapter Twenty-Seven   214
Their Voices Prevailed

Chapter Twenty-Eight   222
Behold the Passover Lamb

Chapter Twenty-Nine   225
To the Place of the Skull

Chapter Thirty   230
Mary, Your Son

Chapter Thirty-One   242
Nails Shall Pierce You Through

Chapter Thirty-Two   252
Mock the King

Chapter Thirty-Three   257
At the Cross, At His Feet

Chapter Thirty-Four   268
Jesus, Remember Me

Chapter Thirty-Five   272
Into Your Hands

Chapter Thirty-Six   279
Sacrifice Synchronicity

Chapter Thirty-Seven   283
This is My Body, Given for You

Chapter Thirty-Eight   287
In A Rich Man's Tomb

Chapter Thirty-Nine   294
Sabbath Unrest

Chapter Forty   299
Pilate's Imperial Seal

Chapter Forty-One   307
The day of the Sabbath

Chapter Forty-Two   322
Sun Fall to Sun Up

Pastor MacNeil's Bio

Pastor Blaine MacNeil has specialized in small town and rural church ministry. He spent his career in parish ministry including seven years working as an interim pastor for churches throughout his home state of Minnesota. He has also worked as a hospice chaplain, helping others to prepare for their journey home to heaven.

Pastor MacNeil holds a Master's degree (2001) in Counseling Psychology from the Adler Graduate School in Richfield, Minnesota. He graduated from Luther Seminary in St. Paul, Minnesota with a Master's in Divinity degree (2004). He furthered his educational experiences by completing the chaplain residency program at the Veterans Administration Hospital in St. Cloud, Minnesota (2013-14).

He also served as a Major in the United States Air Force Auxiliary/Civil Air Patrol as the chaplain of squadrons in the Minnesota and Wisconsin wings. In his service to our nation he has earned two Commander's Commendation awards for his service. He has served in search and rescue missions as a ground team member, and as a flight crew member. He is a graduate of the North Central Region Chaplain's Corp College and was the Minnesota Wing and North Central Region Chaplain of the year in 2012.

He and his wife Melanie love spending time with their grandchildren.

Thanks

A great word of thanks is due to those three people who have helped along the way to make this book possible. Thanks to my proofreader, my wife Melanie MacNeil. Her technical expertise completed what my creative writing skills lacked. Her help and encouragement has gone a long way to help me in the completion of this novel.

Introduction

It is from my heritage as a Scotsman and my faith as a Celtic Christian that I have name this book. Skullduggery is a word that in ancient Scotland meant to do something offensive. However, its modern use has evolved to mean trickery and in particular to be politically deceitful. Skullduggery was certainly the word of the day when our Lord was betrayed, arrested, criminally tried and condemned unto death.

In this second book in the series Trilogy of the Cross I have endeavored to write a story that is true to the biblical witness as a historical fiction novel. I have also worked hard to bring to the light many of the other events that occurred during those hours as well. The people of that first century would have already known many of these things but with the passage of time they are no longer common knowledge to most of us.

I have also included much of my personal theology with my own beliefs and insights about what happened. I did not want to write these things out as biblical commentary that matter-of-factly focused on the dry data. I wanted to write these things out in a plausible historical fiction story that brings to light and life what happened. This was so that I could stir the imaginations of my readers by putting things into terms of what it actually may have been like.

My hopes for you as you read this story is that you grow in faith and in your personal relationship that you have with God our Father through our Savior Jesus Christ our Lord.

Pastor Blaine MacNeil

Chapter One
Conspirators in the Palace

Having been dismissed from the Passover meal by the Lord, Judas made his way out the door and down the high and steep staircase. There he found himself alone and standing in the night darkened street below. He was having trouble breathing; it was the stress. He could fill his lungs, but it was very hard to exhale. He tried to overcome this and found that if he forcefully made himself breathe out, then he could take in a breath of air. He concentrated hard on doing this, forcing the air out by making his tense muscles work at it. He bent over, hoping that the weight of his hanging arms would help ease the tension in his shoulder. As his arms dangled he imagined that he must look like a child's lifeless puppet to anyone who might be watching. He felt panicky, fearing that he was near to passing out from oxygen starvation. This laborious effort did not end for him, but he did adjust to this difficult way of breathing, strange as it was.

He looked at the Temple in the near distance. The lessor light of the moon that ruled over the night hours now cast only a dim and darkened light on it. With the pitch-black night sky behind it, all that remained to be seen was the mere silhouette of its outline. It was minimally lit by a couple of outdoor braziers burning at its entrances. Untold numbers of people of faith had visited there that day, but now it was a quiet and desolate place, void of anyone other than a few staff that kept watch over it by night. He recalled its former beauty, how in the sunlight by day its pure white marble shone brightly against a heavenly blue sky. But now it was night and that time was ruled by the hours of darkness. He stood and gave thought to what he must now do. He began walking to the palace of the high priest because that was the arrangement. He had already been given thirty pieces of silver and now he must tell Caiaphas where Jesus could be found.

He made his way down the quiet streets of the Holy City. He hoped the colder night air would bring him relief for his fears that had overcome him during the Passover meal. It was there that Rabbi Jesus had announced to his disciples that one of them would betray him. He wondered how could the Lord have possibly known this? Worse, how did the Rabbi know it was him? Yet, it was Jesus himself who told him to leave the meal and do what he had planned to do. Judas laughed a little to himself and took a twisted sense of comfort in knowing that he was sent to fulfill this plan of his. He told himself that because the Rabbi told him to go and do it, that it would, in the end, all work out somehow. With that for his reasoning, he continued on his way. Even still, he did not find any relief for his tension. Instead he had a growing sense of torment in the thoughts of his mind and in the emotions of his heart. This drove him to go faster until he found that he was running hard and nearly out of breath. His side, his collar bones and his lungs all hurt from breathing so hard. He stopped for a moment to catch his breath and tend to his aching body.

As he continued walking he found that he was again quickening his pace. He looked behind to see if he was being followed. Then he realized that he did this because he was feeling guilty about what he was doing. He heard the distant bark of a several of dogs and imagined that they were alerting their owner to a nighttime thief. He quickened his pace once again thinking that there might be someone in hiding just waiting to rob him of his silver. If there was, he did not want to run into him and be robbed of his precious wealth. He grew increasingly suspicious about being followed and the sound of the barking dogs behind him grew louder. Again, he looked back but there were no dogs, and no one was following him even though he would have sworn someone was there. Yet the suspicious feeling persisted. As the dogs continued to bark he felt at moments like his ankles were being touched by their wet noses and he jumped forward to escape them.

As he arrived at the entrance to the palace there was a guard and a servant girl stationed there. She knew who Judas was and so she waved him in immediately. As he approached the door to Caiaphas' residence a guard met him and ushered him into a side entrance of the palace. That was where the high priest's administrative offices were located. Caiaphas was already waiting for him there and he was very glad to see him.

Judas was still huffing and puffing, half from rushing to get there and half from the excitement of the moment of being in the presence of the high priest. He opened his mouth to speak, but instead he hesitated before stumbling to say, "I, I, I... I know where he is right now, and I know where he will be spending the night."

Caiaphas' eyes widened with a keen sense of interest and then they grew sharp as his excitement grew. "Where is he right now, my friend?"

Judas found himself in distress because he was still having difficulty breathing and speaking. He had to concentrate and force the air out of his lungs. It was with some difficulty that he was able to say, "There is a man named Zechariah who lives not far from here. He is a patron of the Rabbi and he offered Jesus and his disciples the use of an upper room."

Caiaphas' face grew disappointed, "I know this man. He is wealthy, well known and influential. It would be too great a risk to arrest the Rabbi there. Word of it would spread immediately and there could be an uprising by his followers." The high priest thought for a moment before saying, "Is that where he will be spending the night?"

Judas worried he had disappointed the high priest and hoped now that he could please him by answering that question too. "He will be spending the night on the Mount of Olives in the Garden of Gethsemane. I know the exact place. I can tell you where you can find him there."

Caiaphas' face grew angered, "Find him myself? Oh, no, that I will never do. The location you are referring to is of no help to me at all. There are thousands of pilgrims camping there tonight. How can we find him among so many and in the dark no less?" He expected a helpful answer from Judas but received none. Now the high priest giggled with near joy as he said, "Ah, you will lead my Temple guards to the place and point out the Rabbi to them."

Judas did not like hearing the idea of him being involved in this addition to the plan to arrest the Rabbi and he grew fearful of the idea. He did not want to be directly involved in the arrest. This was especially true because it held certain inherit risks.

Caiaphas' face grew intensely focused and he smiled widely, "This is all good, so very good. Now, tell me, how many of his disciples will be with him?"

"Well, all of them." He hesitated and gave a moment's thought to the number that he would say, which was no longer twelve. He was no longer a part of them and he nodded as he confidently replied, "Eleven in all."

Judas' mind was still nervously pondering the idea that he would have to go and identify the Rabbi. Yet he knew he was in it too deep to back out now. Neither was he about to give up his silver, that money meant too much to him. He knew that he was obligated to the high priest to follow through on this. Even still, he thought about trying to flee from the palace, or maybe later, escaping on the way to the garden. But he knew he would be stopped by the guards and that would worsen everything. Still, he hoped that somehow, he might escape having to point out the Rabbi to them.

Caiaphas waited to hear more from Judas, but he was silent. So, he spoke to him, "I imagine that you are worried for your own safety in this. I can assure you, you are in no danger, no, none at all. My personal guards, the palace guards, will surround you. Added to that will be a squad of Temple guards as well as a squad of Roman soldiers there to protect everyone."

Still Judas said nothing, nor did he even offer so much as a nod or give a look of his eyes to show some kind of acknowledgement of what was said to him.

Caiaphas bent forward and looked straight into Judas' face hoping to make eye contact with him, but that didn't happen. He waited a moment for some reaction. Still no response came, so he said, "I will assume by your silence that you are in full agreement with me about this night's plan. So, you will wait here until I assemble everyone that will be part of the arresting party. Then you will lead them to the Rabbi for me."

The high priest stepped out of the room and summoned a guard. Judas could not hear what was said but he assumed that Caiaphas told the guard to hold him there. Judas sat down in an unhappy huff and felt like a child who was being punished unfairly.

Caiaphas spoke to Judas again, "Can I offer you some wine or something to eat?"

He did not feel like sharing in the high priest's offer of hospitality. It reminded him of the bread that Jesus had hand fed him with earlier that night. In a bit of a stupor, he shook his head slowly side to side as he stared at the whitewashed wall before him.

As Caiaphas left he said, "Judas, please make yourself at home. If you need anything, anything at all, just ask my guard."

Somehow that gesture of generosity did not rest well with him. He resented the idea that he had to be watched over by a guard and was restricted to the room.

Chapter Two
Pilate's Soldiers

It was well into the night when the personal attendant of Claudia, Pontius Pilate's wife, entered the bedroom and stood more than two arm lengths away from the governor. She whispered hoping to gently wake him, "Sir, forgive me for waking you but there is an urgent matter at the gate."

At the sound of her voice, Pilate's eyes suddenly opened with alarm. He instinctively moved with the speed of lightning as he drew a dagger out from under his pillow. His arm coiled and was ready to strike at the silhouette of the women. As his eyes came to focus on her, he could see that it was only his wife's slave who had woken him and that she was no threat to him.

The slave repeated what she had said a moment ago, "Forgive me sir, but the officer of the night watch sent me to wake you. He says, 'There is an urgent matter at the gate.'"

Pilate nodded, and she bowed low as she walked away. The governor sat up on the side of his bed and looked over his shoulder to view his wife. She did not stir, instead her eyes were rapidly moving about and he was warmed to the heart knowing that his beloved was having a dream. Then he went into his dressing room where his household attendant was already waiting for him. "Let me guess, it is some of the chief priests again. That is why they are at the gate instead of inside the gate. They do hate the idea of defiling themselves by coming inside, don't' they?"

The slave nodded, "Yes sir, it is them."

Pilate donned portions of his uniform: his tunic, boots, a sword, his chest armor and with his helmet in hand he made his way out of the residence and into his headquarters where an officer met him. "Sir, Chief Priests Rabsaris, Elamadad and Kallahadad are here at the request of their high priest who is asking for a ..."

Pilate interrupted, "Which high priest?"

The officer continued on, "I believe they said Caiaphas, sir. They are requesting a squad of soldiers to assist them in an arrest."

Pilate was not pleased, "At this hour? On this night? It is their festival! I would have thought that their criminals were also celebrating instead of making trouble at this hour." He worried, sending out soldiers during the dark hours of the night was risky. They could be led into an ambush.

Even though they came with great regularity, Pilate had never become comfortable with any of the demands the priests made on him. They were a class of people who were inflexible and compulsive. Worse, they were dramatists who made everything seem bigger than real life, and for that reason he just didn't let himself get worked up over their theatrical performances anymore. However, this request did worry him because it was unusual for them to come at night, and it was especially unusual for them to come on the night of one of their festivals.

As he went to the gate, the officer of the night watch accompanied him with a lantern in hand. Rabsaris, Elamadad and Kallahadad were anxiously waiting there for him. He understood their reasons for not coming inside his headquarters, and he looked down on their ideas of ritualized, religious cleanliness. He was a soldier of Rome, and his hands were stained with blood, and he knew they would never really be clean again.

As he made his way there he thought to himself, *'I should just set up a table and chairs outside the gate for times like this so we could all sit down together and meet there. But then I suppose that they would consider that space unclean to them as well.'*

He spoke to the three men with a hint of cynicism in his voice, "Wouldn't you like to come in and sit? I can offer you some wine, some food and we can enjoy some conversation before we discuss your request." He took pleasure in his sarcastic offer to invite them in; it was his way of paying them back for waking him up at that hour of the night.

Rabsaris spoke half apolitically, half sarcastically, "We would, but no. In fact, we cannot come in."

Pilate expressed a false tone of disappointment, "Fine. Suit yourselves."

Rabsaris was direct, "Governor, this is most urgent."

"So, what is it that could not wait until morning?"

"We have uncovered the whereabouts of a notorious criminal and are prepared to arrest him with our Temple guards."

Pilate raised his hand to his chin and showed interest in their story. It was a rare event when they were involved in arresting one of their own troublemakers. Then he wondered why they wanted him to be involved. He chuckled as he spoke "So, good. But, why are you here instead of out there capturing this man?"

Elamadad explained as he made their request, "We would like a squad of your soldiers to join in with us in the arrest."

Pilate chuckled at their words and drove home his mockery of them saying, "Oh, your Temple guards are not up to the task? Or, did they have too much wine celebrating your festival?"

Rabsaris quickly snapped back defensively as he stood forward in a threatening gesture, "Our guards are up to the task. But this man has disciples and many followers. We want him arrested while the city sleeps, quickly, quietly and without incident. It is only if a problem arises that your soldiers will need to step in and help by simply backing us up, nothing more."

Pilate responded to the chief's threatening gesture by stepping forward and letting them see him put his hand to his sword. His voice deepened and took on an aristocratic tone as he spoke assertively to them, "My soldiers that you need have gone to bed. If I have to wake them up it will have to be for a very good reason. I have already had one uprising this week and that insurrectionist is in my prison awaiting crucifixion in the morning. Are you are telling me that there is another dangerous criminal lurking about in the city? I thought this festival was a time when your people would be content and celebrating, not committing crimes. I have to ask you, what in the world is going on in your city?" He paused for a moment and then spoke with contempt in his voice, "What is the likelihood of this trouble maker offering resistance?"

The chief priests impatiently waited in silence with sullen looks on their faces to see what the governor would do for them.

Pilate looked them over head to toe and gave their request some thought. He had already made up his mind to agree, but he didn't want to make it look as if it was that simple. He leaned over and motioned to his officer to come in closer as he whispered into his ear. Then he turned to the priests and said, "Very well." He yawned, partly because he was tired, but also to show the priests that he was bored with their company and did not consider their request to be of much concern. "The soldiers that you are requesting need to be waken and assembled. Where do you want them dispatched too?"

Rabsaris spoke quickly, "To the high priest's palace." Then he added an extra emphasis, a snobbish one, to his next words, "They will have to wait on the street outside the walls until we are ready to depart! They cannot come into the high priest's compound."

Pilate paused before answering, he did not want to appear as though he was simply agreeing to this because they asked for it. "Of course, as is your custom here. I understand that you don't want them defiling his residence any more than I want you defiling mine." Pilate was toying with their minds and taking a poke at their practices. "Oh, I'm tired, that isn't what I meant to say. I meant to say, any more than you would want to be defiled by coming into mine." Now he expressed his irritation with them saying in a sharp tone, "Is there anything else you need tonight before I go back to my bed?"

Elamadad was quick to jump in and say, "No." He did not want to let Rabsaris answer, he would have likely given an offensive response to the governor. He felt like he needed to prevent an insult from being said by acting like a buffer between the two rivals who did not care for each other in the least.

Pilate looked the priests over again with mild disgust, "What? No 'thank you, sir' for my services to you? Pity, those soldiers that you are inconveniencing may not like knowing that. And remember they are not under your command; they take their orders from my officers and they take their orders from me alone. Is that understood?"

As the priests shook their heads in agreement Pilate quickly turned his back on them and swiftly returned to his private residence in the Praetorium. As he walked away he gave the order to his officer, "Assemble a squad of soldiers. Tell the officer to work with the priests. Assist in the arrest only if the Temple guards are overwhelmed. When dismissed by them, return to the Praetorium where they may go back to sleep. If anything more than that happens, have me woken up immediately."

Chapter Three
Claudia and Pilate

The Roman Governor Pontius Pilate had married into what was considered to be the most prestigious family in all of the Roman Empire, the emperor's. His wife, the Princess Claudia Procula, was the granddaughter of the illustrious Cesar Augustus, who had ruled the empire at the time of Jesus' birth. This made her the niece of the reigning emperor, Caesar Tiberius. Though not his son by birth, he had been adopted by Augustus because he was the son of his wife from a prior marriage. Claudia was of royal blood, Pilate was not. She married him for love, and he married for love, and for advancement in the empire. This meant he was also married to his career.

Pilate's given name, Pontius, revealed that he was from an equestrian clan in the middle of the Italian peninsula. He was not of noble birth. He began his service in the empire as a cavalry soldier. He sought to improve himself by hard work and through his marriage, which gave him some great advantages. He rose from his humble station in life to become a nobleman and an aristocrat. It was because of his track record for success that Caesar had appointed him to be the governor of Judea, which also made him the military commander there. He was also given the title Prefect. This made him a ruler with great power so that he could carry out the will of Rome in the province where he reigned supremely.

Unfortunately, he was made governor over the most difficult of all the provinces in the empire. This people he ruled over believed in only one God, their God, Yahweh. They believed he was invisible and was everywhere. Most provinces had their local god, sometimes more than one, but they also accepted other people's gods as well. The pagan people who prevailed in that day believed that if a region had a god who ruled over the plains for example, that meant that their land would be fertile. If it came to war with them then you did not want to go to battle with them on a flat, fertile plain in their land. That was where their god was strongest and he would favor them, and oppose you in fight. In the land of Judea, their God was different. Their God was not limited to a fertile plain or a mountain, he was everywhere at once.

Their unique religion and their devotion to it created frequent problems for the governor. They believed that any other god, other than their own, was a false god. They had a religious fervor among them that was renown among the nations. Unlike all the other gods, there were no graven images or statues of their God, it was forbidden. You could call on him at anytime, anywhere, and he would hear you. He was all powerful, all knowing, and this frightened outsiders who worshiped a different god. But for the people of this land, their faith emboldened them to great extremes. Their strict devotion to their God and religion was without compare in all the empire. They would sooner die, and gladly so, then to go against the tenants of their faith. For these reasons they were very independent and there were frequent uprisings by them against the Roman occupation of their land. Because of this the governor had his hands full.

For Pilate, it was because of his ambition and past triumphs that he landed in Judea. If there was a man who could rule over these people, Rome believed it was him. He was known for his cruel and oppressive reign in his previous appointments. He was a firm and proven leader. His commission from Caesar and the Roman Senate was to ensure that the Roman tax was collected. He was to send a portion of the money to Rome and make local civic improvements with the rest of the money. He also had to keep the *Pax Romana*, the Roman Peace, in their land. This he did at the expense of many lives because he brutally put down every uprising against his rule.

Because his wife was of the royal household of the empire she was a pagan and a devout one at that. Pilate was a pagan, but he did not give much devotion to religion. The god they worshipped was Mars; he was the god of Rome. Within their religion, the Roman Imperial Cult, there were those who wanted to declare Claudia's grandfather, Augustus, to be a divine god while he lived. He refused to be declared a god, or even called a divine ruler. However, in death he was posthumously declared to be a divine god and that in effect made her uncle, Tiberius Caesar, the son of a god. But Claudia both knew better than most what the truth about that was, about how human and flawed both these Caesars were. After all she grew up as part of their family. In her mind, they would always be human, mortal, imperfect and flawed.

Though she had grown up in the first family of the Empire, she did not involve herself with his politics. Claudia's singular interest was in supporting her husband whom she loved, and she was devoted to him. She wanted to make him happy so that his life was made easier. She did not want to become a problem with all that her husband needed to consider as he tried to fulfill his duties. She genuinely cared for him with a deeply loving heart. Though she was also well versed in politics, she avoided any discussion of them in their home unless he brought them up first. She knew that his loyalties were torn in many directions which included his own self-interests, and in further advancing his career by bringing glory to Rome. She knew that he truly loved her, and she knew that she shared him with his other mistress, which was his career in the greatest empire that had ever risen. He loved her, but he was first devoted to his responsibilities as the governor.

For Pilate, it was a massive game of strategy and tactics, of suppressing their frequent uprisings, large and small, of pacifying their local leaders who were of a priestly cast, and their high priest Caiaphas. And all of this had to be done before several secretive and invisible audiences, the spies of Rome, both Caesar's and of the senate, and of the high priests. For any Roman politician, Judea was a demanding and dangerous appointment.

Pilate did not like bringing his work into their marriage. He did not want to compromise his wife in the chance that Rome might press her for information about his rule. What little he infrequently did share was of no consequence as far as Rome might be concerned. The difficulties he faced he kept to himself, and he like it that way. This kept his life simpler and he liked bearing the burden of ruling alone.

Chapter Four
Judas, Lead Us

It was ever so slowly for Judas that the dark hour of the night passed. He resented being under the watchful eye of the high priest's guard. He heard the voices of men out in the hallway and outside in the courtyard. There was much action underway and soon everything that was necessary had come into place. The guards under Caiaphas' command had been assembled. Just outside of the palace walls was a squad of Roman soldiers, two dozen men along with their officer, who had just arrived. All were ready to march up to the Mount of Olives and into the Garden Gethsemane. In charge of it all were several officials, the personal aides of the high priest, several chief priests and elders too. Lastly, there were the scribes. They were the expert lawyers. They were there to ensure that everything that happened would appear to be in compliance with the Law of Moses. Under the careful and scrutinizing eye of the former High Priest Annas, Caiaphas gave his final instructions to his officials and to the officer of his guards.

Lastly, Caiaphas came to the room where he had left Judas and knocked on the door as he entered in. He had expected to find the man sleeping because the hour was very late. Instead he saw a weary man, muttering unintelligibly to himself, and rubbing his ankles as if he was trying to relieve himself of some pain. The skin around where he had been rubbing was reddened and there were small abrasions on the surface of his skin from where he had scratched himself.

As Judas saw Caiaphas enter, he abruptly stood and stepped about uneasily because his feet were hurting.

Caiaphas spoke to him with a soft and soothing fatherly voice, "Judas, the time has come for you to do your duty for me. You must lead my guards to the Rabbi so that he can be brought here to meet with me. Do you understand?"

Judas childishly looked down and away as he barely moved his head and nodded in agreement.

The high priest assured him, "All you have to do is lead my trusted people to him. They will take care of the rest. Once you have done that, this will all be over for you. Then you can go wherever you want and enjoy your new wealth. There are enough guards to keep you and the others safe. But just in case they are needed, there is a squad of Roman soldiers that will accompany you. If anything happens they will help us too."

Judas made a half an effort to look up, smile and nod knowingly. Then the two of them went out to the courtyard where Chief Priests Rabsaris, Elamadad, and Kallahadad were waiting. They eagerly looked at Judas as though he was an honored guest among them and showed their approval to him for what he was helping them do. They were the ones who were with Judas when he was paid the thirty pieces of silver to conspire and lead them to Rabbi Jesus.

Caiaphas, with Judas in tow, walked over to his chief administrative official. He was standing alongside the captain of the guard. Caiaphas introduced Judas to them, "This is Malchus, my most trusted personal servant. He will be overseeing the arrest. And this is Jemel. He is the captain of my palace guards. I trust him with the safety of my family and my own life as well. He will see that you are kept safe tonight." But even with all the assurances that were made to Judas, he did not feel at all safe.

Malchus would lead the way to the Garden of Gethsemane with Jemel following behind him and he would have Judas at his side. Before they set out, another guard came and stood at Judas' other side. Jemel introduced him, "This is my First Sargent, Tishadin." Judas was suspicious about why he suddenly joined them. He wondered if he was there to protect him or to keep him from running off. Though nothing was said directly to him about it, he was right in his suspicions. They were concerned that he might run off if the opportunity presented itself. If he tried, they would stop him and force him to fulfill his service to them.

As they set out, Jemel had his Sargent call the guards to attention. They snapped to like an elite military unit. Then he ordered them to march. As they exited the palace grounds a squad of Temple guards fell in line behind them. Lastly, after they exited the gate, Pilate's soldiers also fell into line and marched in formation behind the rest.

Seeing them leave, Caiaphas took in a deep breath and let out what was meant to be a sigh of relief. Still, he was tense, He could not simply shrug off the great weight he was under and that did not rest well with him. He had much to worry about. He was not convinced that he could trust Judas. After all, the man was about to betray his former Master, therefore he had no honor. Nevertheless, the high priest had to hope that he would do exactly what he was paid to do because the entire plan hinged on the reliability of this fallen disciple.

Annas looked at his son-in-law and smartly said, "Shall we retire to your residence as we wait for them to return?" Caiaphas did not care for his way of inviting himself into his home, especially under these difficult circumstances, but he knew better than to refuse him. Together they walked to the door with Annas leading the way.

Inside they sat and began their time of waiting. Now that they were so close to having success in their clandestine affair it was easy for Annas to relax. But he was not the reigning high priest, Caiaphas was and as such he had little to lose if things turned out badly. This idle hour of the late night contributed to Caiaphas' restless soul. He was publicly responsible for everything that would take place. If things were to go as planned or if they failed, either way he would be the one that blame would fall on.

Annas spoke to him in a patronizing manner, "Son, you need to let yourself relax. It will all work out as I have foreseen."

Caiaphas defended his anxiety, "Easy for you to say. You do not have my responsibilities anymore. No one will blame you after all this is done."

Annas shrugged his shoulders and tried to lessen his son-in-law's stress, "Sure they will, we are in it together. First, they will blame you, and then they will blame me. We are both in it together."

Caiaphas remained anxious, "Yes, we are in it together up to our necks."

"You worry so: about the Romans, about Pontius, about our people, and about what they may say or do."

His worries were numerous, but they were also well founded, "There could be riots, Annas. This Galilean Rabbi's followers could storm the palace and stone us for what we are doing tonight."

Annas in his age gained wisdom and foresight spoke out, "Not likely, the people will be too busy with the festival to take notice. Then, they will celebrate and it will all be over before they can learn of it."

But Caiaphas was feeling deeply guilty and worried greatly about being discovered, "Someone is bound to see our guards and the soldiers marching through the city and entering Gethsemane."

"So! What if they do? Everyone knows that there are nighttime soldiers patrolling the city and others are patrolling outside the city too. It is for their own safety and protection. The people will not fear or think there is a problem. Instead, they will be glad for the night soldiers that keeps watch over them."

"You make it seem so simple."

"You make it seem so complex. Take this time to put your worries aside and relax. Enjoy this time. Don't give in to the temptation to worry. There is nothing more either of us can do during this hour anyway. They will return soon enough. Save your energy until then."

Caiaphas nodded and the two of them silently waited for the return of their guards.

Chapter Five
Into the Hands of Sinners

The streets of the Holy City were all but empty as they began their march. They left the peace and quiet of Jerusalem and climbed up the mountain road to the Garden of Gethsemane. The lanterns they carried did not give off much light, but then they did not want to attract attention to themselves either.

All the officials who were part of the conspiracy were glad to be there, but most of the guards and all the soldiers resented that they were ordered to do this. For them this was a very inconvenient hour to be pressed into service. The guards had homes and families that they should have been with, asleep and in their own beds. They all deeply resented the presence of the Roman soldiers. They knew that they were competent to make this arrest alone and if anything should happen beyond their control, they did not want to be subject to orders from a Roman officer. If a fight did break out they most certainly did not want to fight alongside those soldiers either. They believed this was their own internal affair. Therefore, they should be taking care of it themselves from start to finish.

The Romans soldiers did not want to be there either. Their officer believed that if a fight broke out he was the ultimate authority. He did not believe that the guards would be reliable in combat, and if he had to issue orders to them he did not trust that they would obey him. Neither he, nor his men, wanted to fight along-side the guards if it should come to that. Not a one of them trusted the guards. They looked down on them as inferiors in every way. They worried about what would happen if they had to assist them in a fight. Those guards would be just as likely to take a stab at them as they would a criminal. So, unless hostilities broke out, their objective was to present a professional appearance, coldhearted, impervious to fear and battle-hardened soldiers of the world's most powerful army.

There were three men who, more than anyone else, wanted to be there, Chief Priests Rabsaris, Elamadad and Kallahadad. It wasn't that they were glad to be doing it. They were angry men. They weren't happy about anything. They were motivated by what could best be described as an evil craving. One that ceaselessly gnawed away at their very souls. It was as if their entire world was solely focused on taking out all of their anger on Rabbi Jesus. As priests they were accustomed to taking the lives of innocent lambs in sacrifice at the Temple and this was not that different to them. As chief priests, they were still out for blood. They wanted the death of Rabbi Jesus who they held to be guilty of many crimes.

The march through the Holy City and up the Mount of Olives was done silently. Everyone stepped softy and moved quietly. Now they had reached the entrance to the Garden of Gethsemane. The garden was famous for its many olive trees and its great oil press. In the harvest the olives were crushed under the heavy weight of the great stone press that was rolled over them. This released the valuable oil from them which was bottled and sold. The oil was used in cooking, as a medicine, for perfumes and ointments, and for burning in lamps. Now the garden was very large, and thousands of pilgrims were camping there for the Festival of the Passover.

As they entered inside, Malchus told Judas, "You and I, along with Jemel and his Sargent, will go first. The guards and the soldiers will follow about twenty-five yards behind us. I will be only one step behind you. Now, Judas lead us to the Rabbi."

Judas knew exactly where to go among the thousands and thousands of campsites there. Before long he turned around and made eye contact with Malchus as he nodded. It had gone easier than he thought it would. He pointed his finger to the silhouette of a man who was praying on his knees with his arms outstretched into the night sky. Judas could just barely hear what he was saying, "My Abba, for your will to be fulfilled, and for the redemption of all your fallen children, I die to myself this night. Amen." This was Rabbi Jesus.

Jesus was quickly alerted to Judas' presence. It wasn't hard to see him moving about in the light of the moon, and behind him the many officials, guards and soldiers. He called out loudly to his sleeping disciples startling them, and they woke in a fright. They very quickly rushed and stood nearer to their Master wondering what his alarming call to them was over.

The Rabbi stood tall and with single sweeping motion of his right arm he pointed toward the arresting party and shouted loudly, "See what evil the darkness of this night has brought. The time of my trial now begins. Look, all of you! I am betrayed into the hands of evil men."

The arresting party's presence was no longer hidden by the darkness of the night. The guards and the soldiers all lit flaming bright torches from the lanterns and suddenly their light shone upon everything. Malchus and the chief priests moved in closely with the guards just behind them. Rabsaris demanded the fallen disciple fulfill his service to them as his voice cried out with a terrible shrieking sound, "Tell us which one he is Judas!"

With a guttural grunt from his belly he told him, "He is the one I will kiss." Suddenly Judas rushed toward Jesus' side. He did this because he wanted it to appear as though he wasn't part of the rest. Fearfully, Judas looked to his rear and felt assured that they would protect him if he needed it. Then he pressed onward to Jesus' side.

The disciples reacted to this intrusion. They were wide eyed and quickly gathered to Jesus and tightly surrounded him. A very tall disciple stood in the very front and to the right of his Master. Another one, an adolescent, stood to the front of him on the left. The disciples had effectively provided a shield for their Rabbi against those who were approaching.

Malchus anxiously called out, "Which one is he, Judas?"

Judas rushed toward Jesus, but the tall disciple in the front moved to stand in his way and Judas ran directly into his shoulder block and was hurt. Then he maneuvered in between the two disciples in front and reached out to hold Jesus by his shoulders. Then he stuck out his neck and offered him a hug and kissed him saying, "Hail Master!"

Suddenly, from inside Judas' sleeve, a slithering viper appeared, his tongue hissing, and his head bobbed about. It was coiled and ready to strike out and bite Rabbi Jesus. It quickly moved toward his arm, but the Rabbi instinctually reacted with great speed. Without taking his eyes off Judas he grabbed the viper by the neck and threw him down to the ground below with violent speed. Then he moved his eyes from Judas to the chief priests standing there behind him. With a sure and certain confidence, he stomped down hard on the vile being's head with his heel. Those standing nearby could hear the sound of its skull being crushed underfoot. Then he stepped back and looked at its flattened skull. Now he looked again at Judas and the chief priests who were behind him. They were shocked to see what had just happened and as Jesus' looked directly at them they felt as if he saw directly into their hearts and they feared.

Judas looked at Jesus with utter surprise over this and then stepped back placing his hand over his heart. He pretended to be offended but he was not a very good actor and did not put on much of a façade. As Jesus spoke to him he tried to listen to the words, but he could not understand them. It was as if it was nonsensical to his ears. Then he stepped back stumbling into that tall disciple who looked down on him with contempt as he put his hand to the sword that was hidden under his robe.

Judas saw it and feared for his life. He called out in a broken voice "Help me! He has a sword! Get me out of here!" Then he turned around and escaped by moving behind the guards and the soldiers.

The guards moved in closer. Their first row formed into a semicircle facing the disciples and they stood ready to fight if they needed to.

It was Malchus who was charged with making the actual arrest. So he looked past Peter and to the Rabbi as he prepared to speak. But before he could say a word, the Rabbi smiled and calmly said to him, "Who are you looking for?"

Malchus was surprised by this and he felt that it was a favorable sign of how things would now go. "We are looking for the man named Jesus of Nazareth."

The Rabbi appeared to be expecting this answer. Then he stepped past his tall disciple and to the front so that he could face Malchus directly. He gave them this answer. "I ..."

Now as Malchus and everyone with him heard this one word it became in their ears like the sound of a violent and harshly cracking whip. They felt a terrible crushing pressure on their ears that radiated down to their shoulders and left them reeling in pain everywhere. They stumbled forcefully backward and worried that they might fall to the ground. They looked at each other not understanding what had just happened to them.

Jesus continued, "I Am ..."

As before, their ears felt a hard-booming sound like a thousand powerful drums beating in unison. And again, they felt something shove their shoulders as if they had been kicked by a horse. The pain was nearly overwhelming and Malchus wondered if they could continue to make the arrest.

But before they could do a thing, Jesus finished what he was saying, "I Am he."

As they heard the sound of his voice it was as if a violent sea wave had come against them. They felt as if they were being crushed under by deep waters and were unable to breathe. They felt such pain that they longed to die rather than endure another second of it. They were suddenly knocked forcefully off their feet by this great power and they all landed hard on the ground below.

Malchus and the others with him gasped to breathe, but the wind had been knocked out of them. Fearfully, he looked about with twitching eyes and in a panic. He fought against the idea that he would suffocate in the darkness of the night. It took a moment before he or any of them could stand and resume their plans to arrest the Rabbi.

As the guards and soldiers stood again, they looked like ragtag toy soldiers. Their uniforms were disheveled and loose about their shoulders, their tunics uneven and torn, and many of their helmets were missing. They were in pain, and whatever fight they had in them when they left Jerusalem was gone. The arresting party reassembled themselves and faced Jesus.

Malchus stood in the front, speechless and worried about what they might suffer next. He saw the Rabbi open his mouth to speak again and he quivered in fear.

The Rabbi spoke in an unpresuming voice, "Who did you say that you're looking for?"

Malchus along with the entire company of people with him stepped back and braced themselves for another beating, but none came. Malchus hesitantly spoke, "Je... Je... Je... Jesus of Nazareth."

Jesus then looked directly into his eyes and said, "Then it is me you are looking for. As I have said, I Am Jesus. I surrender to you." Then he lifted his arms out so that they could bind his hands.

Malchus had heard what was said but he was frozen in fear. His eyes searched about as if he was looking for something, but he neither said nor did anything. He looked upward to Jesus' eyes and heard him say, "So, here I Am, you have found me. I surrender to your custody. But these other men here, let them be on their way."

Some of his disciples having heard this, stepped back and motioned as if they would leave. But the two in front stood boldly at their Master's sides.

Malchus chastened himself silently as his thoughts told him to remember why he was there. He moved cautiously as he motioned with his hands for the guards to come forward, "You there step forward and bind his hands. You, place those shackles on his feet."

The guards did not move though. They were still dazed and hurting. They did not want to suffer another blow like the ones before. They merely looked at Malchus in fear and whimpered.

Now the high priest's servant had regained enough of

his composure to assert himself better. "Get to it right now you two! Jemel order your men to obey me!"

Jemel having heard these words threw out his arm, pointed to the men and then to the Rabbi. He ordered his men saying, "You heard him! Get to it!"

Finally, the two guards moved in to bind Jesus as they were ordered too.

As the first shackle appeared, the tall disciple sprang into action and stepped forward putting himself between them and his Master. He had been emboldened by the display of power that he had seen when Jesus spoke to them. As he moved forward, the arresting party looked fearful as he shouted with a great and powerful voice, one like that of an archangel "Don't you touch him! None of you touch him!"

They feared for their lives as they saw his hand reach into his robe for the sword he had been hiding there. Now the guard standing closest to him reached for his sword, which was all that it took to get the fight started. That disciple suddenly rushed at him and stuck him hard with a body block that knocked him to the ground. Upon seeing that the other guard dropped the shackles and put his hand to his sword to draw it out. The next thing he saw was the butt end of the disciple's sword handle coming swiftly at him as it hit him in the face. He felt a searing hot pain in his cheek and he quickly collapsed to the ground.

Malchus feared that the disciples of this man would quickly overwhelm them. He looked at Jemel hoping that he would order his guards to draw their swords. He tried to speak but he was so fearful that he couldn't even take a breath in or out.

Now this one disciple called out fearlessly saying, "Disciples, arm yourselves to fight, the Kingdom of God has just begun its reign!" Fearlessly he stepped forward and threatened the guards by swinging his sword high in the air.

Then another disciple, the young one, shouted out and drew his sword as well. He held it high and swung it about. Seeing this the guards reacted, but very slowly. The First Sargent tried to draw his sword but as he looked down at it the blade of the tall disciple was already at his belly. All he could do was put his hands in the air and step back. Then the disciple shouted out, "Hands off my Master!" He raised his sword high and stood tall showing them that he was poised to strike.

The guards cowered, backed down and then backed up in fear.

Malchus tried to back away too, but the disciple grabbed his robe and pulled him in close, touching his sword to his neck. Malchus looked into his eyes with fear and heard him shout out angrily, "I will slice every last one of you from head to toe if I have to!" Malchus tried to pull back and get away but the disciple quickly sliced his ear off. He fell backward to the ground weeping and shouting for help, "I'm cut, I'm, cut. My ear! My neck! Is my neck cut!"

Then to everyone's utter surprise, both to the Rabbi's disciples and the arresting party, Jesus shouted with an almighty voice, "NO!" Then he ordered the two disciples by name, Peter and John, to stop the fighting.

Malchus found no help from all those who accompanied him. He looked at Jesus and heard what he had said, and he found great relief in it. He saw Jesus step toward him, and again feared greatly not knowing what might befall him. Jesus reached down and picked up his severed ear and came over to his side. He heard the Rabbi speak to him as he placed his ear to the side of his head and prayed, "Heavenly Father, mercifully bring healing to this man." The Rabbi helped him to his feet and Jesus spoke to him, "Please forgive the man who did this to you. And, so that you may know that I Am laying down my life, I surrender to you in peace. Neither I or my disciples will resist you any further."

Upon hearing that the Rabbi's disciples fearfully ran off into the darkness of the night and hid among the trees of Gethsemane, all but the two with swords. Seeing this the guards moved in once again to bind their prisoner, hands and feet, in shackles and chains. The other guards saw that the tide of things had changed to their favor. They ran toward the remaining two, the ones who had drawn their swords, and tried to capture them. The tall one who Jesus called Peter was too fast and got away. The younger, whose name was John, was caught by the coat as a guard tried to wrestle him to the ground. That disciple wiggled out of his coat and ran off into the darkness of the night.

Chapter Six
The March to Jerusalem

In the shadows of the night they made their arrest. Out of the garden, down from the Mount of Olives, down on the stony road they lead their prisoner. Jesus was heavy laden by the weight of the chains and shackles that bound his hands and feet. He was marched between the columns of guards on his right and left sides. In front of him and behind there were rows and rows of guards who were followed by the Roman soldiers. First to come was Malchus and with him Chief Priest Kallahadad. Then followed Elamadad and Rabsaris. They were the ones who had severely criticized Rabbi Jesus over how the people had praised him on that past Sunday when he made his triumphal entry into the Holy City of Jerusalem. It was then that he had ridden on the colt of a donkey to the cheers and praises of the people who adored him. They had come out in masses and filled the road. When he came near they stepped aside to make room for him and carpeted the way with their coats and palm branches.

Unlike his triumphal entry on the first day of that week this time coming down from the top of the mountain was not the same. On this night Jesus was being jeered and abusively shoved about by the guards who held him in their brutal custody. Those on his righthand side took turns shoving him into the guards on his left, who also roughly shoved him back again. They made a joke out of it, but for the Rabbi it was painful and humiliating. As he was thrown and shoved forcefully back and forth between the columns the guards took turns punching him and kicking him. From behind him they stepped on his heels and mockingly apologized as if it were an accident. They kicked him in the back of his knees which forced him to crash down hard onto the stony road below making his knees to bleed. One of the guards grabbed hold of his chains and stood him up again. Then he pulled him close to his face as he sprayed him with his spit shouting, "Walk tall if you are a man, not on all fours like an animal."

Other guards also abused him. They angerly shouted into his ears, "Where do you think you're running off to, hum?" They stomped with their heels onto the arches of his feet screaming, "You can try, but you aren't going be escaping from us!"

The guards were glad to use their positions of authority in the arrest, and now they were going beyond their authority and treating him terribly. They were going against Moses and the Law, but the scribes that accompanied them said nothing against it. They were merely there for a show of pretenses.

The Romans had limited the duties of the Temple guards severely. In the occupation they were not allowed to serve in the traditional roles they might have as soldiers of their national army. Their nation was not allowed to have an army for them to serve in. Though the guards were trained to fight as soldiers, they were at the same time forbidden to fight as soldiers. Their service was restricted to simply serving in their parade uniforms: as doorkeepers at the entrances to the Temple, to securing its treasury, to guarding keys to doors and little more. They were all Levites, members of the favored clan of Levi, Moses' brother. They were set aside for service in supporting the Temple's needs and assisting the priests who served there. For them, this opportunity was the closest they came to being soldiers and so they made the most out of it. They were taking the worst of their anger out on Rabbi Jesus because they knew the opportunity would not come to them again for a long time.

As they neared Jerusalem, the city was covered in the dark veil of the night. Their own torches and lanterns had long since burned out. They entered through the Golden Gate, the same gate that Rabbi Jesus had entered triumphally only six days prior. The Romans soldiers standing guard there made a half-hearted effort to come to attention as they curiously looked at the chief priests and the Temple guards marching past them. This was a rare sight, especially at this time of night and, of course, they allowed them to pass unhindered. As their prisoner was march past them they looked scornfully at him. They knew that whoever this was who was being brought into the city shackled in chains, was a wanted man and must be a dreadful criminal. To the soldiers, it was this kind of lawbreaker who made their lives difficult. When they had to capture someone like that, it was not without a fight where one of them could be injured or even killed. They remembered the capture of one of these kinds of men earlier that week. His name was Bar-Abbas. He had committed a murder and led others in a revolt. Following the Temple guards was a squad of Roman soldiers and their officer marching with them. The soldiers guarding the gate now quickly snapped to attention, standing tall and straight. Their faces grew serious. Once the procession had passed the soldiers at the gate simply relaxed and gave it little more thought.

Just a short distance behind the soldiers there followed Peter and John. The two disciples had already hidden their swords in the Garden of Gethsemane for fear that if they were searched it would quickly lead to their own arrest. They had been walking just a few yards behind the Romans and using them to visually block their presence from the chief priests and their guards. As they strolled into the city, they pretended to be so involved in a conversation that was so interesting to them that they didn't even notice the soldiers guarding the gate. They continued to follow but not so close as to bring suspicion upon themselves. They simply appeared to be two would be pilgrims who were coming into the city late at night. The streets that they walked on were deserted. All was quiet other than the muffled echoes of the rhythmic percussion of the marching of the guards and trailing soldiers. As their feet struck the stone pavement in unison, they gave off a certain cadence that told the silent city that they were on the march and their conquest would soon be fulfilled.

As the guards neared the palace of the high priest John spoke to Peter, "I know this woman who is at the gate and she will most likely let me in. Why don't you stay outside for now? You must keep your distance and not be seen in case they take me under arrest. If I'm able to get inside and if it is safe for me, I will return and try to bring you in too." Peter was in agreement with him.

John moved in close behind the Roman soldiers and continued to stand out of sight of the guards as they passed through the gate and assembled in the courtyard. The Romans knew they would not be granted access. Instead they stood at parade rest in the street just outside the compound's walls. Though the guards had nearly caught him in Gethsemane, John felt it was important that he remain as close as he could to his Master. He was bold in hiding from them in plain sight. Fortunately for him they never looked back to see if anyone was behind them, and he gave them no cause to worry about his presence there if they had looked.

Inside the palace compound the captain of the guard ordered his men to continue to stand in their ranks with their captive held in the middle. He looked at the palace where Caiaphas lived and then at Annas' home, which was a smaller home inside the walls. He wondered which one he should report to. Then he went to Annas' door and was greeted by the head servant who reported to him that Annas and Caiaphas were waiting for him in the high priest's residence.

John now approached the gate and he was admitted entrance without incidence. Peter remained in the shadows across the street from the palace walls for fear that he would be recognized and taken into custody. He strained to look into the compound to see what was taking place but could hardly see anything because of the darkness there. Soon there was a small crowd that had gathered outside the gate and so Peter moved up to mingle in with them even though he feared he might be recognized. There he waited for John's return.

Chapter Seven
For Peter's Shame

With the arrival of Rabbi Jesus, Caiaphas now sent out messengers with orders to awaken the Sanhedrin, who were members of their supreme court. He was asking them to come at once for the trial of the Rabbi. As the messengers passed out of the gate, John stepped outside with some of them to seek out Peter and then bring him back in. The two easily passed through the gate and mixed in with the growing number of people congregating in the courtyard.

As the long hours of the night passed on it grew particularly cold. A few guards lit a fire in an outdoor brazier to warm themselves. Before long John and Peter came near it and warmed themselves too. In the light of its flames a servant girl saw Peter and stared at him which made him very uncomfortable. He drew the hood of his robe over his head and low over his face in the hopes that it would conceal his identity. Though he felt vulnerable, he did not want to leave the warmth of the fire because of the cold. His curiosity also prevailed over his worries because he wanted to know what was happening to his Master.

The servant girl glanced at those around her. She stopped for a few extra seconds to study Peter's face. As time passed, she continued to look at him more frequently until she rose to her feet and made an accusation against him. Toying with him she spoke, "Do I know who you are?"

Peter looked to her and said, "No, I don't believe we have ever met or seen each other before."

"Maybe I do recognize you. You were with the Nazarene earlier tonight, weren't you?"

Peter tried to pay no attention to her as she pointed him out. He looked at her as if she was unimportant and simply said, "Whatever are you talking about woman? What Nazarene? I was with no one tonight. I am not who you are imaging me to be, that is certain!"

John casually moved away from Peter for fear he too might be recognized as a disciple of his Rabbi. He purposely avoided looking in Peter's direction. He acted as if the accusation against Peter was of no interest to him. Still, his heart pounded hard and his ears were quick to listen to every voice in the hopes that he might gain some news of what was happening to Jesus.

A little while later someone else spoke to Peter, "You, you are one of the Rabbi's disciples, aren't you?"

Peter pretended that he did not even hear their voice, but they asked him again, "Say, you there! You're one of his disciples, aren't you?"

"No, I am not a disciple of anyone."

Now the man spoke more assertively to him, "I know you are his disciple because you have the same Galilean accent as the Rabbi. You and he are from the north, I can hear it in your voice. Don't deny it. Why else would you be here at this hour of the night?"

Peter tried to act surprised as if he was innocent of the accusation. He shook his head as if the claim about him was irritating to him. He wanted to intimidate anyone who picked up on the idea that he had some connection to his Rabbi. Yet he did not want to make too great of a denial in the process. He acted as though he was disgusted with his accuser. As he asserted himself his ascent grew even more distinct, "Listen to me mister, I have no idea what you are talking about! None at all! I swear to you and everyone here that I have nothing to do with this man you are talking about. Nothing!" But his denial took on the appearance of an admission as he protested too strongly.

As Peter was robustly asserting himself, a roaster came out from his coop and strutted about in a show of moxie. It was the intensity of Peter's voice that had aroused him from his sleep. He too wanted to be a contestant in war of words being exchanged. As Peter ended his denial, the bird stretched out his chest in a vigorous show flapping his wings about and crowing loudly for all to hear. Peter was irritated by the dumb bird who didn't have enough sense to know that it was the middle of the night and he should be sleeping. According to the bird's reasoning, it was his roust and he was the chief bird in residence there. Therefore, he simply wanted to have the final word on the matter.

Sometime had now passed, and another servant looked at Peter. He was unaware that others had made accusations against Peter. This servant was a relative of Malchus, the man whose ear Peter had cut off during the arrest. He had also been there in the garden with them. He came close to Peter and stared at him for a few seconds. Then he stepped back as he recognized him and with a startled look on his face he spoke loudly. "You! I saw you in the garden with the prisoner! I am sure of it! You were there, weren't you!? Admit it!"

Peter looked at him, eye to eye, and in a hushed insistent voice told him in no uncertain terms, "Whatever in the world are you claiming of me? I am not whoever you think I am!"

As Peter began asserting his claim, the rooster came around again strutting about and making a show of himself, but Peter thought little of it. The bird listened in as if he was himself part of the conversation, quickly rotating his head as he looked about at those who were speaking.

Before Peter was done denying the man's claim, the rooster stuck out its chest, quickly flapped his wings and crowed so hard that it almost fell over. Now Peter did a double take as he looked at the bird and then fell into shock as he remembered. He felt the waves of time pass through him as his mind returned to earlier that night. He remembered with greatest sorrow how Jesus had forewarned him that he would do this very thing. That he would deny his Lord three times this very night. He looked about to see who else's eyes had fallen upon him.

At that very moment the guards that surrounded Jesus moved about and there was a clear view between the Rabbi and Peter and their eyes met. Jesus' expression was filled with compassion for his disciple whose human failings were now so painfully evident to himself. But Peter took this look to mean that his Rabbi now despised him for his denial even though nothing could have been further from the truth. Head strong Peter could see it no other way. He fell to his knees as he bent over at the waist and broke down in bitter weeping as he was overcome with guilt. He hands rose to hide his face and he knew there was no doubt left in anyone's mind. He was with the Rabbi in the garden. He quickly rose to his feet and swiftly walked, nearly running, to the palace gate and he made his way out into the darkness of the night.

Chapter Eight
Abuse from the Temple Guards

From the administrative wind of his palace, Caiaphas ordered the captain of his guard to bring the prisoner and hold him in one of the rooms there. This was where the Rabbi would be kept until the trial. The captain called on six of his men to bring the Rabbi and follow him inside. Now that there were just these few guards present with the Rabbi they took it upon themselves to bring about their own form of justice. They were angry for having to be on constant alert for the last few days so that they could assemble quickly and arrest this Rabbi on short notice. That became an exercise in frustration for them. Even though Caiaphas had given an arrest order it was the chief priests who worked directly with the guards. It was Rabsaris, Elamadad and Kallahadad who constantly hesitated about letting them make the arrest. That was because these chief priests feared it would start a riot among the people. Over the past few days the guards had grown very irritated over the situation that had placed them in harm's way and held them there with no clear end in sight. They were secretly angry with the priests but could not say anything against them. Their anger was redirected toward the Rabbi instead and now that no one was looking on they took their anger out on him.

One of the guards eyeballed the rest and then turned to Jesus. "I am not sure we have arrested the right man. It was dark out there and maybe we captured the wrong one. Here, let me get a good look at you!" He took the Rabbi by the beard and jerked his head about. Then with his fist, he hit him hard in the face.

As Jesus recoiled in pain another guard punched him in the stomach. Then he grabbed him by the hair and lifted his head up saying, "Maybe this is the Rabbi..." and he backhanded him in the face, so he could see the other side and said, "and maybe it is not him!"

Now another guard took Jesus by the beard and said, "I need to get a better look at him too." He struck Jesus with his fist over and over again. "There now I can see who you are, which is good, because for some reason your face is changing before my very eyes." Jesus' cheeks were swelling from being struck and one of his eyes was also swelling shut. In mocking laughter, the guard turned Jesus' head toward the others and said, "I don't know. What do you think? Is it really him? He doesn't look the same as when we first captured him."

Another guard said, "I'm not sure who this man is. Let me see him again." He struck Jesus and gave him a bloody nose. He spoke again as he roared in laughter, "There, that looks more like the Rabbi I saw teaching in the Temple."

Then their officer reluctantly spoke up, "We aren't supposed to be doing this. What if someone should see that he had been beaten? I don't want one of those scribes accusing us of being lawbreakers."

One of the guards placed a blindfold on the Rabbi and mockingly said, "There, now no one will see what we have done to you." He slugged Jesus twice in the stomach and laughed saying, "There, if you are a prophet tell us who it was that hit you? Tell me my name."

Now another guard stepped in and spun Jesus around and around on his feet until he became dizzy. As he stumbled to keep his balance the two guards and their officer repeatedly took turns slapping him.

The one guard heaped insults on Jesus saying, "There, now you hardly look like a man anymore, and soon you will be no one at all. You do know that they are going to put you to death, don't you?"

Then the other guard yelled loudly into his ear, "If it wasn't for you I would be home with my family tonight! If it wasn't for you I would be sleeping in my own bed right now. So, if I cannot enjoy the night then neither can you." He shoved the Rabbi into the wall. There Jesus fell to the floor and another guard kicked him in the stomach.

Another guard abused him saying, "Rabbi you are just upsetting everybody tonight, aren't you?" He also kicked him as he shouted, "How is it that some of the people love you and the rest of us here hate you so much? Did you know that you do that to people? Why don't you do something to protect yourself? Or is it that now you are in chains you have become powerless?"

Chapter Nine
Pretrial Before Annas

Annas sent an order to the captain of the guards to have Rabbi Jesus brought into his home. When the guards arrived at his door with their prisoner so did a scribal lawyer named Bacchus. He was among those who Caiaphas had urgently summoned during the night to come. This lawyer insisted that he speak to the high priest before Jesus was brought into his home.

Bacchus was very irate as he explained the Law to the Annas, "What are you doing having the Rabbi brought before you like this? Have you forgotten the requirements of our laws? It is forbidden that you or anyone should conduct a private interrogation of him. If he does tell you anything it cannot be admitted into the proceedings because our Law protects him from self-incrimination. Beyond that, you are one of the jurists who will sit in judgement of him. Therefore, you cannot meet with him like this. If you do this it could disqualify you from sitting in the judgement seat and hearing his case."

Annas looked directly into the eyes of the scribe and then coughed softly in his face before he spoke, "You know the Law so well but then that is your specialty." He paused before thoughtfully answering him on the finer points of the Law that he was explaining, "Yes, you are right. Thank you for your guidance. But then you are wrongly assuming that this is an interrogation that I am conducting. I have no intention of interrogating him. So, I am sure you will allow this for now."

The scribe was a little put off by this unexpected answer from Annas and as he thought about it he relaxed his posture. Then he inquired, "So then, what is it that you are planning to do with him?"

Annas answered him, "Thank you for your cooperation on this very delicate matter." Then he looked at the guards standing there with the prisoner. He gave them a look that conveyed the message that he was annoyed by Bacchus' presence. Annas put on a very calm exterior and told the scribe, "I believe that members of the Sanhedrin are already gathering for a meeting in the administrative wing of Caiaphas' palace. Don't you think that you should be joining them right now?"

Then one of the guards moved in between the lawyer and Annas and then he stepped back forcing Bacchus to step away. Annas motioned with his hand that the guards should bring their prisoner in. The last guard closed the door behind him leaving the scribe with the clear message that his objections were no longer going to be heard.

Annas was old, but he was far from feeble in his body or his mind on this night. It was as though he was thriving on the situation and at his best. He could be a very cunning man who, as the former high priest, had far reaching influence among the leaders of their nation. He had strong loyalties with powerful people that he had established over his lifetime of service. He had ruled over Judea as the high priest for ten years before Rome deposed him. However, the Law of Moses gave him the right to be high priest for a lifetime. None the less, he continued to be highly involved even after he was replaced by Caiaphas, who was in some, but not all respects, a bit of a figurehead in his role.

Inside Annas' home the guards stood by the wall and their officer remained at the Rabbi's side. Jesus was kept in shackles and was forced to stand in the middle of the large room. The lighting was poor because there was only one lamp burning so everything was seen in shadows.

In silence Annas walked at a leisurely pace in a counterclockwise circle around the Rabbi as he considered what he might say. He hoped that doing this in the dim light would have a unique effect on his prisoner. He hoped to either unwrap his secrets or to create in him the feeling that he was being wrapped into the web of his control.

Now, Annas employed his finest skills and cunning to try a probe into the heart and mind of the Rabbi. He came to a stop behind Jesus, paused and then spoke directly into his left ear. "So, Rabbi, if you haven't gathered by now I will tell you why you are here. You are to be tried as a criminal tonight. You will be found guilty and you will be condemned to death. What I can do for you is this, I can make this proceeding very simple and there will be no more suffering for you if you cooperate. Or, if you wish to be difficult with me, I can make you suffer unimaginably, and the choice is yours to make."

Annas returned to walking in circles again. Then he stopped in front of Jesus and looked him in the eyes. He wanted to appear to be a man of brutal power but as he caught the Rabbi's eyes in his own, the veneer of his power quickly melted away. The high priest asked Jesus, "Tell me about your disciples? Who are they? What are their names? I know about Judas. Did you know that he betrayed you for only thirty pieces of silver, the price of a slave who has been accidently killed?[1] If his loyalties to you were so thin, then what about the rest of your disciples! What would they do against you if they were made to appear here and compelled to testify against you? What would they do? What would they say? Think about it. What would they do

---

[1] Exodus 21:32

to try and save themselves from being accused right next to you in our court tonight? What if I had them arrested and tried for following an insurrectionist? They could be lifted-up right next to you."

Jesus remembered that he had prayed for his disciples so that they would be saved from that very thing. He did this because Satan had demanded of his Father that he be allowed to thrash and sift all of the disciples like wheat. Jesus knew that Judas had already made plans to betray him, that all of them would all fall away, and that Peter would deny him three times before the cock crowed twice. But he also knew that nothing worse would befall his disciples. He knew that they would, with the exception of the one, all turn back to faith in him again. Jesus knew that they would not become victims of this great injustice being done against him. He knew that Annas' words were nothing more than vain speculations. Jesus had prayed that they would not have to enter into his trial and his Father would answer his prayer, these things he knew.

Annas continued to badger him with questions one upon another, "What have you taught the people to mislead so many of them? Have you secretly raised an army? Do you have a fortress with a weapons hoard somewhere? Who are your military commanders? How much money have you accumulated in your treasury? What are your plans? Are you going to lead a revolt against the Romans? Do you want to be crowned our King?"

Jesus answered, "I have preached and taught from Galilee to Jerusalem and all my followers know my teachings. I have preached in fields and on mountains, on the shores of the Sea of Galilee and on the banks of the Jordan, in the synagogues and in the Temple. And you are asking me what have I taught? Why? Do you not understand the Law of Moses and the Prophets? They tell you that I cannot be forced to testify against myself and you are asking me so that you can use my words against me. But you must already know that even if I had committed a crime, my own admission would be worthless in your court. You must have two witnesses who testify and agree on all points. Any admission of my own cannot be used as the basis for a charge against me because our traditions forbid you from asking me for a confession."

Annas took insult at what the Rabbi told him and he backhanded Jesus' face with a swift and powerful thrashing of his arm. But Jesus merely took the blow and returned to looking Annas in the eyes. Then Annas shouted into his face spraying him with his spittle, "Do not speak so presumptuously to me, so as to think that you can teach me anything at all about the Law and the Prophets!" The high priest was fuming over the resistance he had come into. He was used to being a man who people respected and feared. He was well known for being able to intimidate others, but he was not able to overcome the resistance of Rabbi Jesus. He looked disappointed with himself because his powers had not compelled Jesus to answer any of his questions.

The officer there saw Annas' disappointment and his anger burned against the Rabbi. He immediately stepped forward and brutally hit Jesus in the face with a closed fist. He looked him in the eyes just as he had seen the high priest do and with his anger still burning hot he shouted, "This is the high priest that you are speaking to! You will not speak to him with such disrespect! You foolish man!"

Jesus bent over in pain and stepped back from the force of the blow. Then he defiantly stood up straight. He looked at the officer who was standing tall with a threatening posture. He boldly spoke to him, "If I have spoken incorrectly then instruct me about what that was. But don't you know that according to the Law you must testify to what I have done that was a crime so that I may be charged and only if I am found guilty may you punish me. But instead you hit me first. Moses prohibits that."

The officer motioned to slug Jesus again but Annas called out, "That is enough for now!" There was a pause and then he said, "Let's go to Caiaphas and meet with him, hum, shall we Rabbi?"

The officer resented being told that he could not strike his prisoner a second time. So as Annas moved to go outdoors the officer took his anger out on Jesus by jerking his chains hard to start him walking and then he jerked him again to get him moving faster.

Chapter Ten
Annas and Caiaphas

As Annas approached Caiaphas' palace the doors were immediately opened for him. He entered and along with him came his prisoner and the guards who held him in their custody.

Caiaphas issued an order to the guards, "Take him to the room where Judas was kept and have no less than three guards watching him the entire time." Then he turned to Annas and gestured with his hand for him to go ahead into his private office. Inside Annas presumed to sit at Caiaphas desk and though Caiaphas did not like this at all, he remained silent rather than protest the matter. Then he spoke to his father-in-law, "Well, what did he tell you, anything?"

Annas took control of the conversation away from him saying, "The officer reported that there was a fight during the arrest."

Caiaphas responded nonchalantly to him, "I heard. Malchus told me." He paused and then cheered up as he added, "It is an incredible story, isn't it? Two of his disciples drew their swords and one of them cut his ear off."

"That I had not heard."

"Oh yes. Malchus said that it was a tall disciple who was a very fearsome swordsman. But Jesus stopped them from fighting. He was very insistent. Then he picked up the severed ear, put it back where it had been, prayed and he was healed."

Annas laughed in disbelief, "Can you say that again?

"It was the strangest thing. Two disciples drew their swords and one cut Malchus' ear off. He said that after he

61

was cut the Rabbi himself stopped his disciples from fighting and then healed his ear."

"Healed his ear?"

Caiaphas asserted himself and he really enjoyed being right about it when it came to dealing with his father-in-law. "That is right, every word of it. He showed me. There isn't even a scab or a scar. Just some dried blood on his hair and clothes remained. It was hard to believe, but this servant would never lie to me, He is very loyal."

Annas nervously inquired, "What about the others? Were any others hurt?"

"Not a one. Can you believe it? It was the Rabbi who actually stopped the fight?"

"So you said." Annas wanted to make light of what he had just been told. He was more concerned with sizing up what kind of man this Rabbi was so he asked, "What sort of a man are we dealing with here?"

"You tell me. I don't really enjoy trying to unravel the secrets of troublemakers, but I know you do. Why are you asking me what sort of man he is? You questioned him?"

Annas was bitter as he answered, "You became the leader of our people when Rome deposed me from being high priest because they could not control me. You were appointed by our former Roman governor, Valerius Gratus. He thought you were better equipped to negotiate the continuing peace between us and them. But the truth is, you are just as cunning as I am and the governor just didn't know any better. That is why you need to size him up, so that he can be cut down."

"Ah yes, you want me to do your bidding for you. Is this why you gave me your daughter in marriage? So that you could keep me under your watchful eye and get me to do your will?"

Annas said, "How is my daughter?"

"She is asleep. Peacefully asleep and she wants nothing to do with the details of my responsibilities."

"No, she doesn't, but I do. That is why you suspect that she reports everything that she comes into knowledge of to me, don't you?"

Caiaphas mocked his father-in-law, "Suspect it? Why would I suspect her of it? She is my wife. It is well past suspicion, I know without a doubt that she does."

Annas laughed as he spoke, "Welcome to the family."

Caiaphas was now the bitter one. "Don't worry I won't hold it against you, we are family. But I do worry about how far your influence reaches to."

"Are you worried that you are more a puppet than a leader?"

Caiaphas nodded as he replied, "Something like that, yes."

"Then why don't you retire?"

"Retire? What then? We are all family. I imagine that then you would simply have one of your own sons replace me and then they would come to resent you as much as I do. And if I became a former high priest like you, I would still be drawn into whatever troubles are going on around here. Maybe then I would become more like you, working behind the scenes to get what I wanted. And I hate it when you do that. So, then what would I think of myself?"

Annas became sarcastic, "Oh, no, what could be worse? Then you would have the privilege of being able to get things done with none of the responsibility for it if it fails."

Caiaphas laughed, "It that how it works?"

Now there was an uneasy quiet between them that followed their candid exchange until Annas spoke up again, "You had asked me if the Rabbi said anything to me. He didn't say anything that I didn't already know. Nothing everyone doesn't already know. He even presumed to teach me about our Law and the traditions we follow in our criminal proceedings."

"Really? What was it that he said?"

Annas became irritated as he recalled the even. "He asked me if I understood Moses and told me that I cannot ask him to incriminate himself."

Caiaphas showed that he was humored by this. "This Rabbi is wise, and he knows Moses and the Prophets very well."

Annas nodded, "Right you are."

"I believe that he is also knowledgeable in the oral traditions of the Pharisees. It is among their beliefs that criminals cannot be compelled to testify against themselves."

"Yes, it is very likely that you are right about that too."

"I have worries about his trial."

"Relax Caiaphas. I think things are in our favor. It is seventy-one of us against one Galilean Rabbi." Annas paused as he spoke with a grave tone, "God help anyone who objects, they will need it, with the condemnation they will suffer from us if they do."

Caiaphas chuckled, "Yes, that is right, God help them."

There was a silence that lingered between the two of them. Annas was very confident and relaxed, but Caiaphas remained worried as ever because he was ultimately responsible for the proceedings and the outcome. He knew that Annas would only be held loosely accountable.

He nervously asked, "What about the witnesses? Has someone sent for them? Do we even know what they will say?"

"I have summoned them. And it doesn't really matter what they will say. We have already agreed that he must be condemned and put to death. The witnesses are only a formality. We are required to have some so we will have some."

Caiaphas felt like he had to stress his point, "But will they all agree! What if they don't?"

Annas assured him, "Do we really have to go through this again? The witnesses were prepared just a few days ago. You know this. They cannot do anything but agree."

He became even more tense as he blurted out, "What about that disciple we paid? Where is he? He can testify against the Nazarene. We will give him more silver if we have too."

Annas calmly spoke with a crooked smile, "He could be a problem. He is a potential liability. This whole thing could collapse on top of us if anyone finds out that we bribed this Judas to betray the Rabbi into our hands. Moses forbids such a thing. No one among us has seen him since the arrest. The captain of the guards reported to me that he was very frightened and ran off into the night during the arrest. He did not return with the guards and he has not passed through our gates. But I believe it would be best if he did not resurface until this is all over with anyway. Why don't you alert the guards and gatekeeper? If he reappears then we can take him safely into our custody until this all is finished."

"I will. But what bothers me is…, well, we cannot conduct a trial in the night."

"Our circumstances demand that we deal with this quickly, therefore we cannot afford to wait. So instead of it being a trial by the Greater Sanhedrin it will be an informal meeting of the Lesser Sanhedrin. A mere pretrial hearing, nothing more. And the rest of the requirements will all be taken care of first thing is the morning. Then we will reconvene with the full Sanhedrin to confirm his sentence in the Judgement Hall of Hewn Stones."

Caiaphas's worries never seemed to end as he nervously revealed more of his thoughts, "But something can still go wrong. We must consider all the possibilities!"

Annas revealed his one concern with caution in his voice, "The only worry I have is with this Pontius Pilate. He is not as easily manipulated as are the members of our Sanhedrin."

"This is the first opportunity we have had to take him into our custody. I know that we must act tonight before word of this can spread and bring us down in a riot of the people. Rabbi Jesus must be condemned and placed in the governor's hands as quickly as we can get it done. Then he must carry out the sentence of death for us. The salvation of our nation depends on his death alone."

"Relax, tonight he will be found guilty. He will be sentenced to die and we will do whatever is necessary to motivate this governor to carry out his sentence."

Caiaphas laughed as he spoke, "You make it sound so simple."

Annas did not respond right away and then he spoke with a shaming tone in his voice, "Have you forgotten all that we have already gone through with our members to get us to this night? We have all the support from them that we need to condemn him. It is a foredrawn conclusion that we have already come to in our past meetings. Now all that we need to do is see this thing through."

Annas stood to his feet, reached out and reassuringly patted Caiaphas on the shoulder, and gave him a reassuring look of full confidence. As he went to the door he turned back to say one more thing to him. "It is the nature of priests to keep the peace, that is our calling. Having a king to rule over us would bring a war, a war between us and Rome. Such is the nature of kings. We rule and we keep the peace. The history of our kings is all about their wars; it is their legacy. This Rabbi cannot be King over Judea. He is from Galilee. He does not submit himself to us. How then would he ever take orders from Rome or pay them taxes in tribute. If this Rabbi were to become our King, we would lose all our control over the people. You do know that, don't you?"

Caiaphas looked him in the eyes and didn't say a word. He only nodded and turned away to stare out the window as Annas left the room.

Chapter Eleven
Law Without the Law

Within an hour of the messengers being sent out to summon them, some members of their court began to arrive at Caiaphas' palace. Other members sent messages back to him saying that they would be there at sunup. For the proceeding to take place legally the official trial could not begin until after the first sacrifice of the day was made and it would take place at sunrise. That aside, the high priests only needed a minimum of twenty-three members of their supreme court to convene a trial. That would mean they were meeting as the Lesser Sanhedrin, which was their lower court, to try the case. The full court of seventy-one members was only convened to judge on matters of great weight. Their lower court had limited powers and, as such, they would not be able to legally convict the Galilean Rabbi of a capital crime. But that was not going to stop them from meeting anyway. At this point the high priests did not care about the requirements of the Law that they had to meet. They had set that aside as they would with many of their laws on this case. For now, the high priests and those acting with them cared only about steering the court members to their predetermined conclusion, which was to condemn the Rabbi to death.

As the court members began to gather, one of the chief priests asked Caiaphas, "However did you capture him at this late hour?"

Caiaphas looked worried, but he quickly responded with a lighthearted laugh, "Don't ask." His thoughts went back to the bribe that they paid out to Judas to betray him. That was illegal to do[2] and so was committing the

---

[2]Deuteronomy 16:19, 27:25

malicious act of arresting him without first having heard accusations against him in court[3]. And worse yet, it was illegal for the chief priests to be part of the arresting party as well. This disqualified them from sitting in judgement against the Rabbi in a court proceeding. The high priest hoped these would be the last of the miscarriages of justice that he would have to make but that was to become a short-lived hope of his.

A scribe spoke to Caiaphas, "I have to ask, are you convening a nighttime criminal trial? Or, for the sake of our Law, are you going to call this meeting something else?"

Their laws stated that from the time after the last sacrifice of the evening until after the first sacrifice of the morning, trials of any kind were not allowed. That was because the court members could not accurately reason the merits of a case when they were not properly rested and alert enough to hear testimony and ponder a verdict. Consistent with that point of the law it was also forbidden for them to reach a verdict during these night time hours as well.

Caiaphas gave the scribe his answer, "This is only a preliminary action that we are undertaking, and it is in accordance with our law. This is merely a gathering of the lower court members and it will not begin until the minimum number has been assembled as the law requires. So, the hour of our meeting is not really a factor in this."

Another scribe named Neriah, who was considered to be among the most expert of lawyers, took the high priest aside and quietly asked him, "Why are we meeting here at your residence for a criminal case before our law? We are supposed to hold all of our court proceedings at the

---

[3] Exodus 23:1

Judgement Hall of Hewn Stones that adjoins the Temple complex, aren't we?"

"Yes, I know we are supposed to. On the other hand, we don't want this to become known to all of Jerusalem, do we? We must to do this quietly otherwise the people will learn of it and they might rise-up and fight to have him released. Because of that, we are forgoing just that one point of the law. This is for the peace of our city."

Beyond the laws that they were already breaking, there were still more that would be broken, and they were all starting to add up. Trials were not allowed on festival days, which it was, it was Passover. As the high priests and other court members informally discussed these details their focus was changing. It went from the matters of procedure to the emotionally charged hatred they all bore against the Rabbi. With these sentiments they set aside their reservations and proceeded to convene their trail.

Chapter Twelve
The Lesser Court

As soon as the twenty-first member of the lower court arrived in meeting room at the palace, Caiaphas and Annas came in making their number twenty-three. Now there were enough members present to begin the preceding. Caiaphas hastily began the meeting by simply announcing, "Thank you all for coming at this hour. I know it is the middle of the night, but this urgent matter before us cannot wait. It must be addressed now. As you know this Rabbi Jesus has been captured by our guards and is in our custody, here, right now."

Among the members assembled there was a man who was a strong supporter of Rabbi Jesus, though until this time it was not known publicly. This was Joseph of Arimathea. He was from a very prominent clan in Judea and he was a man of great wealth and power. He was very influential in Jerusalem and in all of Judea. He was a member of the House of Elders which made up one of the three houses of the Sanhedrin. He stepped forward and spoke up, objecting to the proceeding, "Are you serious about beginning a trial at this hour High Priest Caiaphas? Our law forbids any nighttime trials."

Caiaphas looked directly at him and his eyes showed how much he despised hearing that comment. Yet he pasted on a friendly smile and spoke softly, "We have no choice about the hour Joseph. We cannot control when the sun falls. This crisis has presented itself to us at an inconvenient time, therefore we must begin at this hour of the night. The day is going to be too busy to address it later. But I will promise you this, after the first morning sacrifice the full court will assemble to continue what we have merely begun here. This meeting of the Lesser Sanhedrin is not an official one and we are not planning to take any formal action against the Rabbi. This is merely an informal pretrial meeting that we are conducting. If there is a reason for charges to be brought up, then we will carry that matter over for a formal morning meeting of our high court in the Judgment Hall."

Joseph was not pacified by that that answer, "High priest, I protest! Today is a Holy day, it is the Passover Festival. Tomorrow is the Sabbath. No one can be legally tried on a festival day or on a Sabbath day."[4]

Some of the members of the court listened attentively to Joseph and nodded in support of his point.

Then the high priest spoke again, "If we wait, it will be two days before we can hold his trial. That would be on Sunday and we are not going to wait until Sunday! The charges that I expect to be brought against him are too serious to wait until then. He has already caused great unrest among our people. If we delay, who knows what his followers may do to our city. They could rise up and riot. So, you see there are very good reasons for us to proceed and proceed we must. This must take precedence over all other concerns and so how can you or anyone possibly object to that?"

Most of the court members nodded and called out in support of the high priest and they refused to listen to Joseph as he continued to oppose holding the trial. Caiaphas called out, "Now if no one objects than we must continue with our proceedings. Is there anyone among us who still opposes this meeting at this hour?"

Joseph was growing tired of the opposition that he was facing and so he said to Caiaphas, "Me? No. No. I do not

[4] Leviticus 23:7

really have a problem with that, not at all high priest. But Moses has a problem with that! Do you have a problem with Moses? Our laws forbid nighttime trials. I fear that if you continue to trample your way forward with a nighttime trial that you will be tearing the very parchment that our laws are written on."

Caiaphas reacted to his assertive words with a stern and glaring look, "It may not seem to be proper at this time to you, I will grant you that, but it only seems that way. In the end you will fully understand why it must be this way, and now we must move forward." Caiaphas expected an answer from Joseph, but he received none at that time.

Joseph held back his protests for now. He had not changed his mind about anything he had already said and privately he remained skeptical of Caiaphas' assurances to him.

The high priest began to orchestrate what he was calling an informal action. He looked at the guards and ordered them, "Bring in the prisoner and let him stand before us." Then he looked at Chief Priest Rabsaris. He was the one who had spearheaded the effort to trick Rabbi in his words so that he would say something against Moses.

Caiaphas spoke again, "It is time for us to hear from our witnesses. Their testimony will accuse the Rabbi of the most serious of crimes. Crimes against Moses. Who will call for them?"

Rabsaris stepped forward, "I will call the first witness." Then he went to the door and waved in a night weary man. He shuffled in dragging his feet and then stood at the front of the room.

Rabsaris introduced him, "This man is Malluch, and he is a Herodian." The Herodians were Judeans who sided politically with Rome and supported their occupation of their country. Rabsaris asked him, "Can you share with us all that you heard Jesus the Nazarene say to you about the Roman tax?"

Malluch appeared droopy and was having trouble concentrating. He strained to listen to Rabsaris and struggled to keep his eyes open as he spoke, "I was in the Temple this week. I asked the Rabbi if it was permitted to pay the tax that the Romans demand of us."

Rabsaris encouraged him to continue, "Yes, tell us everything that he said to you."

Malluch shook his head hoping to shrug off his grogginess and recall the conversation, "I remember that he said that the money belonged to Caesar in the first place." He paused as he tried to recall more of the conversation, his hand rose as he scratched behind his ear. "He told me that I had to pay the Roman tax with Roman coin." Now he appeared puzzled by what he was able to remember, which was merely fragments of the conversation. He remembered that he had intended to embarrass the Rabbi but instead he had been terribly humiliated himself. He determined to keep that part to himself rather than share it and relive its plaguing memory. Finally, after a long pause he said, "The Rabbi said some of us must pay the tax because we used the Roman coins. I think he might have said that for those who did not use Roman coins that they would not have to pay the tax, maybe."

Rabsaris remembered the conversation Malluch had with the Rabbi very well and he knew that his witness had not accurately recalled all that Jesus had said. He worried that if he questioned him further that it might lead to more errors in what he would testify to. He was concerned that if he corrected him for his mistakes that his witness would lose credibility with the court. So, in order to reduce the chance of that disaster happening he said, "Thank you Malluch for your testimony." Then he dismissed his witness by motioning for Malluch to leave the chamber.

The chief priest did not lose any time as he called forward his next spy who had also been present for that conversation. His name was Reuel. Rabsaris had every intention of leading this sleepy-eyed witness into giving the incriminating testimony they needed for a conviction. In a not so subtle leading gesture, the chief priest looked directly at his witness as he shook his head 'yes' as he asked, "You were present when Malluch asked Jesus of Nazareth about the legality of paying the emperors tax, weren't you?"

Reuel strained to focus on what he was being asked but did not appear to fully grasp the question. In a sleepy daze as he noticed that the chief priest was nodding his head, so he did the same and then said, "Yes." He looked hopeful that he had answered correctly, and then smiled when Rabsaris approvingly smiled back at him.

"Now tell us what you heard the Nazarene say about paying taxes to the emperor."

Reuel listened carefully, but his blank expression reveled that he was not following very well. He simply replied, "Yes."

"And what was it that he said exactly?"

"Ah…" he paused, and he took time to consider the question and what was being asked of him. "I was standing very near to the man and I remember that I heard everything he spoke."

"Good." Rabsaris expected his witness to continue talking, but he said nothing more. He looked at him and again nodded 'yes' hoping to prompt his witness to say more. But his witness merely nodded back to him and smiled pleasantly.

Now Rabsaris did not want to offend his witness, but at the same time he needed his testimony so he concealed his frustration and asked again, "Could you tell me what you heard the Nazarene say?"

The witness now came around and spoke more freely, "Certainly. I was standing very near to Rabbi Jesus when he was asked by Malluch about paying the tax. He said that, ah... well he didn't exactly answer his questions. Instead the Rabbi asked him some questions. One question he asked was about where the coin was minted. And, hum, he asked if he had one of the coins with him which Malluch did. Then in the end, he said that it either was or wasn't forbidden to pay the tax." He nodded as he concluded his testimony.

Rabsaris' eyes grew large and being surprised by his uncertainty he turned to face his witness as he asked, "Which was it? That is was or was not forbidden to pay the Roman tax?"

Reuel was confused and simply said, "Well I'm not certain." The witness looked at the chief priest with hopefulness in his eyes as he both nodded and shook his head. It was as if he was hoping for a clue, a nod 'yes' or a shake 'no' from Rabsaris to guide him about what he should say.

The chief priest looked at his witness and with his back to the court members he gave the man a threatening look. Then he shook his head and repeated his question, "Did the Nazarene tell Malluch to pay the tax?" Again, he nodded his head ever so subtly.

"Yes, that's right, the man said the tax should never be paid."

The chief priest was pleased with his witness's answer. He smiled to show him his approval as he clarified, "And are you certain that he taught that no one should pay the tax?" Once again he nodded ever so slightly to lead his witness to where he wanted his answer to go.

Reuel nodded in unison with Rabsaris as he stated, "Oh, yes, that was very clear. I remember it so well because after he said that he said the most profound thing. He said that we must 'render to God the things that are God's.'"

The chief priest now looked at Rabbi Jesus and said, "Do you hear what these men are saying against you?"

Jesus looked at him but his face revealed nothing and he did not answer him.

Rabsaris, "Well, for a man who taught so boldly to the people you are strangely at a loss of words here tonight."

Rabsaris then called for another witness to come forward, "Baruch, come and tell us all that you told me earlier."

Baruch walked forward and stood facing the court members. "I overheard this man clearly say that 'our Temple could be destroyed in three days, but that he could build us a new one.'"

"Did he say that he would destroy our Temple?"

"I don't recall him saying that exactly."

Rabsaris' head dropped, and he looked at his witness out the of tops of his eyes. He had prepared this man to testify only days before. Everything had gone perfectly then. Now the words of his witness fell just short of what needed to be said and heard. So, he resolved to try and lead his witness where he needed him to go.

"Wasn't it said by the Rabbi who would bring down our Temple?"

"If he did I must not have caught that part of the conversation."

Then the chief priest dismissed that witness and called for another man named Kennan to come forward.

He was asked the same question and he responded, "Yes I heard him say that the Temple would be knocked down. But that he would build us a new one with his own hands in three days."

Rabsaris realized there was some inconsistency in what the two men said so he sought to clarify things as he asked, "But did he say how the Temple would be destroyed?"

Kennan responded, "I don't know."

"Did he say he would destroy it?"

"I don't know about that either."

"Did he say who would destroy the Temple?"

Kennan, "I don't know that either."

The chief priest had been expecting that his witnesses would state that the Rabbi told them he would destroy their Temple because that was what the Rabbi had actually said.

As before, the chief priest went to Rabbi Jesus and asked, "Do you hear how they accuse you? Have you anything to say about it in your defense?"

And as before Jesus offered him no answer.

Now the high priest was becoming upset over the testimony being offered because it was not getting them very far in their push to get the Rabbi condemn to death. He was furious that the Rabbi remained silent. It was part of his strategy to get the Rabbi to speak in his own defense then it could be exploited against him. Caiaphas rose to his feet and walked past Rabsaris and stood in front of Rabbi Jesus.

"Destroying the Holy Temple would be a very grave crime against our nation Rabbi. Any plan to do it, or even to speak of it as you have is certainly a crime against our nation. To destroy it would be a treasonous act!"

Joseph of Arimathea boldly stood forward and interrupted the high priest. "Listen here! There are inconsistencies in the testimony of these witnesses. None of it warrants charging Rabbi Jesus with a crime of any kind. Our Law requires the testimony of two and they must agree on all points.[5] Some of them were too drowsy from lack of sleep to offer reliable testimony; that is why nighttime trials are disallowed. And one of your witnesses smelled strongly of wine and he staggered as he walked."

"A moment, just a moment if you will Joseph." Caiaphas turned aside and spoke privately with Rabsaris, "Don't you have any other witnesses with all the efforts we have undertaken?"

"We could not find all of them at this late hour. These were the best we had. There are others outside, but I fear they will contradict each other too. If we bring those witnesses into the trial it may discredit our entire case. What can we do?"

Caiaphas' thoughts churned against his father-in-law who he felt had recklessly pushed this situation into being. Things were not falling into place as they had planned and rather than end in an acquittal he decided to take things into his own hands personally. There was no way he was going to let this Rabbi walk free if he could prevent it. "I will have to question the Nazarene myself in the hopes of provoking him into saying something that we can condemn him for."

"Is that allowed?"

"At this point I would say that it is absolutely necessary!" The high priest turned back to the members of

---

[5] Deuteronomy 19:15-20

their court and looked them over. Their faces showed deep concern. They been expecting the case to be more one-sided and that the testimony would have been much more condemning.

The members of the court looked back at their high priest in the expectation that he would be able to bring about a conviction so they could sentence the Rabbi to death. Many appeared dreary, others were disinterested in continuing if things were not going to go their way. They wondered if Caiaphas could make this work.

Caiaphas felt a great weight upon himself. He felt like he was losing credibility with the Sanhedrin in this crucial trial. He thought about his options and he knew there was really only one left to him. He needed to provoke the Rabbi into defending himself. Then by his own words the Rabbi would be found guilty and could be sentenced to die for his crimes.

The high priest stood near to the accused and asked, "You are Jesus of Nazareth and a Rabbi, are you not?"

But Jesus was silent before him.

"Have you made certain claims about yourself and among them is that you believe you are our Messiah, or at least that you are our King?"

Jesus gave him no answer.

The high priest stood close to the Rabbi and looked him directly in the face.

"Did you not hear the testimony given against you tonight? It did not speak well of you. Don't you want to say something to defend yourself?"

Jesus continued in silence which infuriated Caiaphas. He couldn't even get the Rabbi to simply admit to his own name. Jesus also knew what Moses wrote and the laws that governed court proceedings. He knew that he did not have say anything at all. So, he silently invoked Moses and remained silent even in the face of the high priest's persistence.

Caiaphas knew what the Rabbi was doing and he hated him for it. "Are you the Messiah?"

Jesus now replied, "If I tell you, you will not believe. And what if I was to ask you a question?"

Caiaphas steeped back in fear and his head shook. Other members of the court also gasped to imagine it. They all knew of the Rabbi's reputation for catching others in their own devices and exposing them in their own trickery this way. It was as though he knew the thoughts and secrets of men's hearts.

Now Caiaphas looked steadfastly at Jesus as he shouted angrily at him, "I command you under the Law! Tell me truthfully now! Do you believe that you are our Messiah the King and the Son of the Blessed One?"

In asking this question Caiaphas became an accuser who, depending on the answer, could then charge Jesus before the court members. However, in this one act he also disqualified himself from continuing on as a court member and sitting in judgement against him. He could not be an accuser and also judge his innocence or guilt.

Jesus calmly and clearly answered the high priest. He looked at him and at all the council gathered before him. "You say that I am. And the day will come when you will see the Son of Man seated at the right hand of the Almighty clothed in immense power and coming in all the glory of heaven."

At that very moment Caiaphas showed how shocked and outraged he was. He took hold of his high priestly robes, turned so that everyone could see him, and he tore his robe open. He cried out in an outrage, "What need do we now have for witnesses! We have become witnesses, we have heard him say it himself!" Then he took off his turban and threw it to the ground. He moved his hands dramatically for everyone to see and he acted as if he were picking up ashes with his fingers and throwing them into the air so that they would fall on to his head.

Though the court members were also upset about what Rabbi Jesus had said, they were also outraged over Caiaphas' actions. It was forbidden for the high priest to tear his robe.[6] But rather than objecting to Caiaphas' behavior, they projected their anger focusing it on the Rabbi. Then many of them shouted out, "Look at you! This is what you have made the high priest do because he is so outraged by your confession!" Now they all agreed saying with the high priest, "What further testimony do we need? We have heard it for ourselves from his own lips! We are all agreed that he has committed the worst blasphemy and he must die for this sin!"

Caiaphas was in his moment of glory. Against the odds he brought about the condemnation of his enemy. "We will have this pretender turned over to the governor for immediate execution." The court members in the room cheered, all but one. The meeting hall continued to be filled with riotous shouting.

As the noise subsided, Joseph of Arimathea stood forward to champion the Rabbi's defense. "We have heard no reliable witnesses here today! You have compelled the Rabbi to offer testimony to use against him! But this is against our laws and you all know it! And you, Caiaphas, our high priest, why do you tear your robes in this way? You know that this too is forbidden by Moses. So, you are condemning this man by the traditions of our laws and

---

[6] Leviticus 21:10

82

breaking them at the same time! You have no legal authority to condemn this Rabbi for anything."

Caiaphas spoke to him with a condescending and calm voice, "Joseph, you heard it yourself. He said he is the Son of the Blessed One."

Joseph said, "That is not blasphemy. Our law states that it is only blasphemy when the very name of our God is invoked and it wasn't. And he didn't say, 'the Son of the Blessed One'. You did! He referred to himself as 'the Son of Man.'"

Caiaphas protested his innocence, "When did I ever..."

Joseph knew what he was going to say and answered in kind. "Our members are not allowed to cross examine a prisoner in order to get him to incriminate himself. Even if he says something against himself, it cannot be used as testimony. The burden of the Law still requires two witnesses to confirm his uncorroborated confession. You accused him of being the Messiah in your question, but you are one of his judges, which prohibits you from being a witness or an accuser. You cannot charge him with anything, not even blasphemy. We all are limited to hearing the testimony of the witnesses on the case and then making our judgements. But there was no incriminating testimony given by your witnesses. Therefore, the witnesses cannot accuse him, and without an accusation, there can be no charges. If there are no charges, then there is nothing more that can be done against the Rabbi! The case against him is not proven and he must be released."

"Joseph," Caiaphas began, "that may be true in your own opinion, but we too have formed our own opinions. With this most serious of crimes, we have no choice. We all heard him make this claim and it cannot go unanswered for, therefore, he must be held accountable. We must act, and act we have. We have made our decision and the case is all but concluded."

Caiaphas and the rest of the court members fully expected that would put an end to the many objections the Elder made, but there was more to be said.

"There is no way that you can reach a capital punishment decision on the same day as the trial. Our laws only allow for a decision of an acquittal on the day of the trial. If you vote to convict and punish him by death, there must be, at a minimum, one full day between the day when testimony is offered and the vote to convict."

"Apparently you are the only one," Caiaphas chuckled, "who objects to the direction we are taking. I will tell you this, that it is because of the pressing nature of this case that we must push on and see this to its proper end. That is why we have moved to convict and condemn him today, so that he can be executed today. We cannot do it tomorrow, it is the Sabbath."

Joseph looked around the room and then at Rabsaris, "And who here was with the guards when he was arrested? You are also disqualified from sitting in the judgement seat against him."

At that comment Rabsaris and others with him looked away in embarrassment because they were there for the arrest.

"Already I can see that you have beaten him. Does Moses allow for this now too?"

"Joseph, listen to yourself and then listen to us. We are not objecting, and neither should you." Upon hearing these words from the high priest the entire council raised their voices against him. The high priest called for everyone in the room to calm themselves and then said, "Joseph, look around you. Do you see these many scribes? They are our greatest experts in the law. Do you hear them bringing up objections? No, you don't. These men do not find fault in how we have applied our laws here tonight. So then how can we give any consideration to you and your objections, a mere layman in these matters?"

"Sir, do not presume me to be a layman on these matters! I am very well educated and I understand these matters thoroughly. It is against Moses for you to interrogate him or to act as his accuser and then sit in judgement of him. And because you bear him so much animosity, you should be disqualified because you cannot be an impartial judge against him."

"We have already heard your objections once in this court and we will not hear them again. This estimable body is in agreement. He is guilty and condemned to die. He will be turned over to the governor for execution. And as to the finer points of the law, let me point out that we do need one person in our assembly to object in a capital case. Our laws require that so that we can impose the death penalty. A completely unanimous vote would have prevented his condemnation. So, as you can see, the burden of the law has been met thanks to you."

As the members of the court began to leave, Chief Priest Kallahadad approached Joseph of Arimathea. Strangely, he began a friendly conversation with him as they walked down a hallway toward the exit. Then he invited him into a private room. Inside was the captain of the palace guards and several of his men were with him. Joseph did not feel safe.

Kallahadad spoke very rudely to him, "Do you see now that despite your many objections and arguments that the Rabbi's fate has already been decided?"

"Does our Law condemn a man by the Law and at the same time break the Law to do it?"

"Do not quote the Law to me, you have no idea who, or what you are dealing with!" The chief priest was red faced. He stood blocking the doorway, "The full Sanhedrin will be meeting at sunrise. There the Rabbi's condemnation will be confirmed and everyone will be in agreement. I have assured the high priest of this. So, now things are set in place to bring about a high court condemnation of this man. You can join us and condemn him to die for his blasphemy if you want to. But we will see him condemned with, or without you."

"You must be out of your mind to think that I would ever do such a thing! He is innocent, and you and everyone out there knows it!"

"I thought you would say something like that. Now, I must ask you to wait here until the final proceedings are over."

"Not on your life will I ever do such a thing."

"No, not on my life, but on yours!" He stepped back into the hallway and gave an order to Jemel, "Keep this man locked in this room until I send you word that he may go free."

"You cannot hold me here! You have no legal right to do this!"

"Nevertheless, here you will stay so that the Rabbi may be put to death." Then he slammed the door shut.

Chapter Thirteen
The Judgement Hall of Hewn Stones

It was a longstanding part of their religious practices to start the morning sacrifices just as the sun rose up over the Mount of Olives. Once that first sacrifice was made, their courts could officially assemble and legally undertake matters of any concern, such as conducting a criminal trial. On this day, at mornings first light, High Priest Caiaphas and the former High Priest Annas arrived to be witnesses to the first lamb's death on that day. As soon as the first glimmer of direct sun light appeared over the mount they resolutely ordered the sacrifice to be made. Rather than staying for the entire ceremonial rite, as soon as the priest's knife touched the lamb's throat, the high priests promptly left the Temple. They proceeded directly to the adjoining building, the Judgement Hall of Hewn Stones. It was there that the official trial of Jesus of Nazareth would take place.

During the morning hour immediately preceding this, all the members of the Sanhedrin had made their way into their Judgment Hall. Many of them, especially those who had been awakened in the middle of the night for the first trial, were sleepy eyed and weary. Though all the court's members had been summoned in the middle of the night and were requested to come to the initial hearing, most declined. They knew that an actual nighttime trial was illegal and whatever might take place there in that hour would still have to be repeated in the morning.

Now this trial of the Rabbi had been anticipated for weeks and the details of it had been worked out earlier in that very week. It was a predetermined verdict that would be made official in this gathering. The real worry was not if Jesus would be found guilty, they would find him guilty, that was assured. The real worry was if the governor, Pontius Pilate, would carry out their sentence of death. The Sanhedrin was prohibited by Rome from carrying out a capital crime's punishment, which by their Law would be death by stoning.

In the empire, in all their provinces and territories, there was always a governor appointed by Rome who ruled supremely over the land. Commonly, as part of a power sharing agreement, Rome would sometimes also keep intact the indigenous monarchy's king or queen. But the Judean Province was different. Their local government was the Sanhedrin, which was normally made up of seventy members. This court had one extra member, Annas, the retired high priest, which brought their numbers to seventy-one. Included in the count was Annas' son-in-law, Joseph Caiaphas, the official high priest. Added to that were twenty-three chief priests who were mostly Sadducees. In addition to them, there were twenty-three scribal lawyers who were experts in their law. They were mostly Pharisees. Lastly, were the Ancients, or Elders, who were all religious laymen. Most of them were Sadducees. They were selected from the rich and influential families of the different tribes and clans of Judea that made up their nation.

Their laws did not allow for nighttime trials, but that did not stop them on this occasion. Also, their laws did not allow them to convict someone of a capital offence in a trial by the Lesser Sanhedrin, which only required a minimum of twenty-three members to be present. Again, that did not stop them. So, for appearance sake, so that jurisprudence would be fulfilled, they convened this second daytime trial. In the previous weeks the members of their court had meet several times to consider reports about Rabbi Jesus and all that he had been doing to unweave the fabric of their web of control over the people. The court members had been groomed in those weeks to do what was expected of them by their high priests, which was to condemn Rabbi Jesus to death.

Strangely absent this morning was the voice of Joseph of Arimathea, but no one made mention of it and many were glad for it. Even in the absence of one of their leading members, they gave no second thought to conducting the trial without him. Many knew he was missing, and a few of them knew that he had been placed in custody at the palace so that he could not bring up his objections at this trial.

As the final member of the court entered the hall and their numbers were complete, Caiaphas quickly called the meeting to order and began the proceedings. Though their trials were required to be open to the public, this one wasn't. The Temple guards were ordered to stand outside the doors and let no one else in. Now this second gathering was being conducted as a pretext, for the sake of appearances, as a formality, so that it would look as if they were meeting the requirements of their laws.

Caiaphas rose to his feet and looked his court members over. "Thank you all for coming so early in the morning and on such short notice. We are here over a matter of grave national security that has come to our attention during the night. Now we must all move swiftly forward on this and bring it to an end once and for all. Jesus of Nazareth was arrested last night and is in our custody. Now we are in a position to stop his trouble making among our people before he gathers any more followers. During the night our lower court heard from multiple witnesses. They gave their testimony and made accusations and charges were brought against this Rabbi. Many of our members standing here right alongside of you can attest to this very thing. But most importantly we heard the accused himself committing blasphemy in our very presence."

As Caiaphas first spoke many of the members had been staring with nearly blank and sleepy-eyed faces at him. It was questionable if they were awake enough to hear what was being said to them. However, when they heard the accusation of blasphemy they were quickly awakened and aroused to anger and began jeering Rabbi Jesus.

"All of you remember that this man has been claiming to be a Rabbi of the people. He has been in our temple teaching and undermining our authority here, as well as among our people everywhere."

At those words, the members of the high court reacted strongly. Reignited in them were the strong emotions of anger and hatred that had been sown in them from meetings over the previous weeks when they discussed the Rabbi. Their voices rose in a deep roar of dissention against Rabbi Jesus.

At that high point Caiaphas gave an order to his guards, "Bring in the prisoner so that he may be tried and condemned before us."

Two Temple guards brought Jesus into the forefront of the room and stood at his sides. He was bound hand and foot with shackles and chains. Most of the members hissed and jeered as he was walked passed them.

"This man before you now was carefully examined earlier today. Those among you who were there can all affirm for you what I am about to repeat to you now."

One of the lawyers, Abihuel, spoke out, "High Priest, do you plan on bringing any witnesses before us now so that we may hear their testimony? This is a requirement of our Law."

Caiaphas raised his hands and motioned up and down with them, "If you will bear with me on that point of the Law. Please, just bear with me for now."

Another lawyer spoke out, "This is hearsay that you are presenting! Do you expect us to rely on that?"

"As I have said, the Lesser Sanhedrin did hear the witnesses earlier. It was very incriminating testimony. Ask any of us who were there. Their voice is testimony enough to verify everything that I am about to say to you now. And let me remind everyone, all of you were summoned during the night to come at that hour and hear the witnesses. Those who bothered to come did hear the witnesses. You who stayed at home, well, if you wanted to hear the witnesses, then why didn't you come at that time? Hum? Thank you, now let me continue."

Still yet another lawyer spoke out, "Where are these witnesses you heard from? I would like to hear from them too."

"They were up very late and were tired so they were dismissed. Now please, you must let me continue. All that we are doing will be fully agreed to in the end, I assure you."

As he spoke these words Annas and three of the leading chief priests, Rabsaris, Elamadad and Kallahadad, rose and stood with him and nodded their heads heartily in full agreement.

Now Caiaphas moved to stand in front of Jesus, "So many of our people cling to the hope of the Messiah coming to deliver us from foreign rule and reestablish the throne of King David. There are rumors among our people wondering, some even believing and asserting that this Rabbi is going to try and do that very thing." He paused hoping that Jesus would say something in response to his leading. Jesus spoke nothing to him.

Caiaphas continued on, "Now, we are celebrating our Passover Festival today and all our people are enjoying the nostalgia of our heritage. Everyone is remembering how our ancestors were delivered by the mighty hand of God from bondage to Pharaoh. Of when they were led by Moses out of slavery in Egypt and into the Promised Land. But, this you know, don't you? Many of us worry, that you Rabbi, have made the claim to many of our people to be their promised Messiah. And worse, I suspect that you want to lead the people in an uprising against the Romans. But we have our nation working just the way we want it. We don't want you coming here from far away Galilee, Galilee of the Gentiles I might add, and stirring things up."

Many of the members again jeered against Jesus because he was not from among their own nation of Judea.

"We already know that you have been working to undermine our authority. So, my question to you is this; Have you presented yourself as someone who would be King over us?"

They all waited, hoping, that the Rabbi would say something, but he was silent.

Now Caiaphas again questioned him, "Well, why don't you tell us if you are the Messiah!? Or else deny it to us so we can release you and we can all go home?"

Jesus remained silent as he stood before them.

Now Caiaphas changed his questioning tactics. In an angered roar, he shouted directly into Jesus' face, "Tell me if you are our Blessed Messiah, the Son of God Almighty!!!" Caiaphas was certain that this would get the Rabbi to speak now as it had for him in the lower court.

Jesus was silent for the moment. Then after enough time had passed so that it would be clear that he was not reacting to Caiaphas' anger, he said in a clear voice, "If I tell you, you will not believe me."

Caiaphas laughed for a second because he now believed he was getting somewhere with his questioning. Then he quickly yelled even more vehemently, "TELL US!!!"

But this time Jesus gave him no response, so the high priest turned to walk away. Then Jesus clearly and calmly spoke, "If I tell everyone in this room who I Am, still who among you will believe in me? But so that you may know who I Am, I will tell you who I Am."

Caiaphas turned back toward the Rabbi and his face became reddened because Jesus used the words "I Am." Everyone there knew this to be one of the sacred names of God. This personal name was revealed to Moses in the desert. That was when God called him to go to his people and deliver them from bondage. Moses did not trust that the people would believe God had sent him to them. So, he asked God to give him his name to share with the people so they would believe. That was when God spoke to him giving Moses his name saying, "I Am that I Am" or simply, "I Am" for short.

"So, what is it to be Rabbi? You were bold before the sheepish masses, but here you are standing as a cowardly lamb before their leaders? Tell me what I want to know. You must tell me, are you the Messiah?"

Jesus turned his head so that his words would be well heard by all the Sanhedrin. "It is as you have yourself said of me. I am the Messiah and from now on when you look to heaven you will see with your own eyes that I am seated at the right-hand side of God my Father."

Caiaphas now turned blazing red in the face and he screamed, "There, he has condemned himself to die! He has committed blasphemy before us all!"

The members of the court all raised their voices and strongly affirmed what Caiaphas stated, and condemned the Rabbi as well. As the roar of their voices settled down, one of the lawyers asked again, "There has been no one here to accuse him and testify against him. Our Law requires this Caiaphas. Without it we cannot condemn this man of anything. Proper procedures must be followed."

Caiaphas stated, "Why? Witnesses! Testimony! Accusations and charges! What need do we have of any of them!? You have heard what this man said with your own ears." Caiaphas joyously laughed as he continued, "Do you need witnesses to repeat to you what you have just heard him say? No! There is no need here for witnesses any longer! Therefore, we can proceed to sentencing him for blasphemy."

Someone in the assembly called out, "For blasphemy he must die! Let us stone him to death!"

Caiaphas addressed the court members, "As you all know we aren't allowed to stone anyone, even in this terrible situation. The Romans would hear about it and then they would punish us. Also, remember this man's popularity with the masses? If we stone him ourselves, our people would hear about it and they will have vengeance on us. No, as we have planned all along, he must be turned over to the Romans for crucifixion. Then the people will not hold this against us alone and the flame of their anger will burn against the governor. We will deliver him over to Pontius Pilate for this sentence to be carried out. But now we must vote to complete his condemnation."

When Caiaphas called for the members to vote he prejudicially worded it saying, "Members of our Sanhedrin, I call upon you to convict his man of blasphemy and condemn him to death. What say you?"

Then all the high court members spoke in one voice and shouted out, "He is guilty of blasphemy. Let him be put to death."

Now Caiaphas raised his hands and called to his members, "Is there anyone among us who objects to this man being found guilty and condemned to die?" Their chamber was now dead silent, so much so that no one wanted to be heard breathing for fear that it might be mistaken as an objection.

Caiaphas spoke with a loud voice, "Jesus of Nazareth, you have been tried and condemned of the sin of blasphemy. Your sentence is death. You will be turned over to our governor for execution." He sighed deeply and reflected for a moment now that all they had worked so hard for was nearly accomplished. The many objections and obstacles he had faced were overcome. Only one difficulty remained, getting Pilate to put this man to death.

Annas and Caiaphas did not plan to approach Pontius Pilate on this case themselves. That would be too much. Their presence there would mean that it was a matter of the highest concern for their nation. And while it was just that in their minds, they did not want Pilate to know this. Not unless it was absolutely necessary. They were worried that if he rejected their request, it would also appear as though they had lost their power to rule over their own nation.

The two high priests met with several of the other leading chief priests to detail out their plans. Caiaphas assigned the task of turning the Rabbi over to the governor to Rabsaris. Then he told him, "Remember, you are my voice before Pilate. You must make him understand how serious this is and that nothing but his execution will be accepted." Caiaphas briefed those who would be accompanying them to the Praetorium saying, "Remember that Pilate has a mind of his own. He will not simply accept what we have done as the final word. You must all fully support Rabsaris and see this through to the very end."

Rabsaris questioned him, "Then what must we do to persuade the governor if he resists?"

"Whatever it takes and I mean just that. Do whatever it takes. You are my voice. You speak with my authority on this matter. Bring as many of the priests and Temple workers with you as you would like and see this through to the end."

Elamadad interjected, "Some of us are worried about his followers starting a riot to get him released. What should we do then?"

Caiaphas thought on this for a moment, then he thoughtfully spoke. "If a riot could get him released then, if need be, a riot might be needed to get him put to death. Regarding his disciples, they have most likely gone into hiding. I don't expect them to show their faces in public today or any time soon." Having given them his final instructions he left the Judgement Hall and went to the Temple where he resumed his duties as the high priest.

Then Rabsaris issued an order to the officer of the guards that they should prepare to march their captive to the Roman Praetorium.

Chapter Fourteen
Silver Regret

During the night Judas had become a restless spirit and a mere shadow of who he once was. He continued to follow all that was going on, but that was from a distance and in the darkness of the night. It was during the trial by the full court that he resurfaced when he ventured into the Hall of Hewn Stones. He tried to keep himself in low profile, but at that early hour of the day there simply were not many people moving about in the building for him to mingle in with. Though the trial was supposed to be open to the public, the doors to their courtroom had been closed and the Temple guards stood sternly in front of them. Judas eventually worked up his courage and ventured up to the guards and requested admission. "Is the trial of the Nazarene Rabbi going on inside?"

The guard did not even look his way as he inquired. He was silent for an uncomfortable period, until finally, he looked down at Judas. With a stone-cold face he said in response, "There is nothing going on inside that concerns you. Who are you, and why are you here? Why are you asking questions about a Rabbi?" His face now took on a brutal look and his posture changed as if he might take Judas into custody as he spoke, "Are you one of his disciples?"

Judas quickly stepped back, "Oh, no, certainly not." He did not want to be taken into custody, nor did he want to have to answer any of the guards imposing questions. He simply turned and walked away without delay. He came to stop at the main entrance and there he waited anxiously for the doors of the Judgement Hall to open. He hoped that then he would be able to find out what had become of Rabbi Jesus.

Before long the doors to the courtroom did burst open and out marched some of the scribes, elders and the chief priests. They were followed by Temple guards who held Rabbi Jesus in their custody.

Judas observed from a distance that Jesus was unable to stand up straight and he was weak and in pain. There were chains about his neck that connected to the shackles around his wrists and feet. The guards marched him at a brisk pace as they escorted him out the door. Judas was able to get a passing glimpse of Rabbi Jesus, but the Rabbi did not take notice of him. His former Master appeared to be very worn by the sleepless night that had passed. He could see that he had been beaten badly. His face was bloodied, and his eyes were swollen. His appearance was shocking to him, he never thought this would happen.

Judas saw the chief priest Jonas, who he first met when he conspired to betray Rabbi Jesus coming his way. He ran after him and asked, "What is going on? Where are you taking the Rabbi?"

Jonas did not slow his pace, but took one look at Judas and said, "The man has been found guilty of blasphemy and is condemned to die. He is being taken to the governor, Pontius Pilate, for his sentence to be carried out." Then Jonas quickened his pace and never looked at Judas again.

When Judas heard those words he came to a dead stop right where he was and then he staggered back and leaned against the wall. He was dizzy and he feared he would fall to the floor. He hung his head down low and was having trouble catching his breath. He was suddenly seized with terrible remorse and he put his hand to his face to hide his great shame. He could not believe what his ears had heard.

He didn't imagine that anything bad would happen to his former Rabbi. He had not given any thought to the consequences of his actions, other than that he would have thirty pieces of silver and he would be a rich man wearing the finest of clothing.

Now that he learned Jesus was found guilty of blasphemy and was condemned to die, his appearance aged years in only a moment. He looked terribly rough, like he had not slept in weeks. His clothes were wrinkled and dirty. His eyes had become bloodshot and were sunk back deep in their sockets. The wrinkles on his face multiplied and grew deep. His hands were trembling with palsy and his gait was unsteady. He felt completely exhausted and his back was bent. Now that the consequences of his action were made known to him he was sickened with nausea. He did not want to let himself even imagine that this was happening and yet he did know it was true. He had believed that he could live with himself for betraying the Rabbi, but now he found that he was overcome with immeasurable sorrow knowing that his betrayal was going to result in the Rabbi's death. He was certain that he must put an end to what he started. He believed that he could make things right and reverse the course that this had taken.

Though Judas was now feeling infirm, he summoned his strength and strove to go into the Judgment Hall's courtroom. As he studied the guard standing watch at the door he could see that he was very tired and his eyes were drooping with fatigue. He stood inconspicuously as though he was waiting for someone and then as the guard's eyes closed again he simply walked in. He saw the two high priests, Caiaphas and Annas, and rushed toward them until he stood ten feet from them. He spoke as boldly and as self-righteously as he could, telling them in no uncertain terms,

"I have grievously sinned by my treachery! I have wrongly betrayed innocent blood into your hands! I took your silver for a bribe! The Rabbi has done nothing wrong, nothing at all and you know it! He is innocent and you have falsely condemned him! He is innocent and still you sentenced him to die!"

The high priests did not move, not even to look at him. They froze in place, their necks and backs stiffened as they heard the dreaded remark about the bribe money. They had worried earlier about Judas appearing and the damage he could bring to their case against the Rabbi. Then they both looked around to see who might have overheard Judas. But no one had taken notice of his words or even his presence. Then Caiaphas slowly moved his head and looked at Annas who looked at him and the two men broke out in laughter. They knew that his presence there at that time was no longer of any consequence to their plans.

Now Caiaphas looked at Judas. He confidently smiled at him no longer feeling embarrassed or vulnerable. "Do you really think that matters to us now? What did you expect? That we wanted to capture him just to let him go? You got what you wanted and we got what we wanted. The exchange is complete!"

Judas just stood there in surreal shock as he heard the words of the high priest. He had set out to be so bold with him hoping it would force the outcome he now wanted. He wanted them to clear the Rabbi of any crimes and release him from their custody. He reasoned for himself that if it was in his power to betray the Rabbi into their hands, then equally true, it must be within his power to force them to release him. But it did not work that way at all. He grabbed for the bag of silver that he had in his sash, but his hand did not find it though he reached around for it several times. He looked down and searched behind his sash until he found the thirty pieces of silver and then he opened the bag. He poured some of it out into his hand and a few silver pieces fell to the floor and rang out in a melancholy, but muffled, "ting, ting." But Judas, he did not care about the silver or the sound it made anymore. The money that had meant so much to him before now took on a new meaning. One of shame and remorse without measure.

Judas shouted at them. His voice was shrill and raspy, and his emotions were so intense that their terrible affect was felt by the high priests. Sounding like a broken-hearted child he screeched, "I am giving you back your silver. Now release the Rabbi and let him go free!" In bitter remorse he threw the bag of silver at the high priests and they raised their arms to shield themselves from being hit by it. Some of the silver flew into the air, and it jingled as it spilled out from the bag as it landed at their feet.

Caiaphas and Annas looked at the silver that fell in front of them. They looked at each other and smiled to know they were getting their silver back. Then they looked at Judas and simultaneously burst out in hysterical laughter. They had worried about him becoming a liability if he came forward and spoke about what they had done. But now, here he was and there was no one else there who cared about what had been done.

Caiaphas spoke to Judas, "We don't want your silver. It is tainted because it was used as a bribe. And you cannot offer us a mere thirty pieces of silver to purchase his freedom now. No sum of money would be enough for that! His death means more to us than all the riches of this world, you foolish man! As far as we are concerned, you have served your part in our plans and we have no further use for you." Then his face grew stern and his voice harsh,

"Now get out of here or I will have the guards throw you into prison, you foul piece of trash!"

Judas' heart fell as he heard the finality of those words from the high priest. His bold and self–righteous veneer quickly melted away. His worn and aged state overcame his will to challenge them any further. He turned away and clumsily made his way out the Hall and into the streets of Jerusalem.

Caiaphas' eyes followed him out the door and then he summoned a Temple guard. "You and another guard go quickly and follow him! Keep him from telling anyone what has become of the Rabbi. If he goes to the governor, arrest him and bring back to us."

As he made his way out of the Judgement Hall Judas' eyes had a look of desperation in them. He wanted to unravel the madly twisted injustice that he set in motion by his greed. He walked to the Temple and there he broke down and wept bitterly. His last hope was gone and he could not get the Rabbi's conviction overturned by his appeal to the high priests. Now it was obvious to him that the religious authorities had no problem with breaking their own laws to get what they wanted. They both used it and broke it to convict Rabbi Jesus and condemn him to death. Judas had expected, at the very least, that he would have some sense of forgiveness and relief for his burden of guilt over his sin at this point. He had felt that way before when he worshipped in the Temple in the past when he offered a lamb for the forgiveness of his sins before a priest. This time relief was not found by him. Rather his sense of guilt overwhelmed him like a massive, crushing weight.

Chapter Fifteen
From One Courtroom to the Next

That morning when Pilate arrived at his headquarters the officer of the night watch gave him and the officer of the day a briefing of the night's activities. "Sir, the squad of soldiers you sent to the high priest's palace to assist them in an arrest returned here halfway through the third hour of the night. Their officer reported that they followed behind the Temple guards who, with their court officials, arrested a Rabbi in Gethsemane. During the arrest two of the men who were with the Rabbi drew their swords. Then the Rabbi stopped his men from fighting. He insisted that they not resist his arrest. After he was taken into custody, they returned to the high priest's palace where they were soon released from the mission. Their officer reported that while they waited outside the palace compound, many of Judea's governing leaders came and held a meeting at the palace. He wondered if they may have tried the Rabbi right then and there. Our soldiers were not called into action during their mission. Following the officers report to me, I dismissed him and the soldiers. I ordered them to return to their barracks and to sleep."

At that moment a soldier came and interrupted, "Sir, forgive me, but there is an urgent matter waiting for you at the gate. Some chief priests, elders, and others along with Temple guards are outside with a prisoner. They are demanding to speak with you."

Pilate shook his head and grumbled to himself, "Priests?" Then he addressed his officers, "Priests you say? No, they are not priests! I will tell you what they are. They are spoiled children who have no patience and even worse manners. I have already done enough for them today. Why should they have need of anything else from me?"

Pilate walked out of his headquarters into his courtyard and over to his gate. He looked at them and said, "This couldn't wait until later in the day or even until next week? First you disturbed my sleep in the early hours of the night, and now this? Shouldn't you be busy with your festival sacrificing lambs at your Temple and celebrating something?"

Rabsaris explained, "Others in our Order are doing that right now, but we need to speak with you."

"Well then, welcome. Won't you come in and sit?"

"No, it is a holy day and we cannot come in, you know our customs prohibit it."

"Yes, I do know. But I enjoy making the offer." What Pilate wasn't saying was that he wanted to offend them by making an offer he knew full well that they wouldn't and couldn't accept.

Chief Priest Rabsaris now stood boldly and very assertively expressed himself with flailing arms and great vocal fluctuations. "Pilate, this man," and he shoved Jesus forward, "who the people call Rabbi Jesus was arrested last night by our guards."

Pilate was neither amused or alarmed by the chief priest's display. He had long since grown cynical over all the religious leader's worries. They were dramatists and the pebbles under their feet were frequently made into national crises. "So, what do you accuse him of doing?"

"Governor, he is already a criminal We have convicted him in our own courts. This is why we are handing him over to you so that our sentence against him may be carried out."

Pilate saw their statement as an evasion of the truth. Being trained as a lawyer and serving as a judge before them now, he wondered what they were they keeping back from him. His mind was busily occupied with thoughts about what it was that they didn't want him to know. "Have you judge him by your own Law, already, this early in the morning? Well, if you have found him guilty of crimes under your laws then you can punish him according to your own laws too. Good day to you." He turned away and began to walk back to his headquarters hoping that gesture would send them on their way.

Rabsaris pled their case to him assertively, "Governor, we have already done this. That is why we are turning him over to you."

Pilate looked back at the chief priest and said, "Is that right?"

"Yes, Governor."

He turned to face him again, "Then why have you brought him to me? As I said, punish him yourselves and leave me out of your troubles."

"We are not permitted to put him to death."

"Death? Why this must be a very notorious criminal that you are bringing to me, one who needs to be put to death. Tell me, what accusations do you make against him?"

"We have convicted him of misguiding our nation and leading our people astray from our laws. He has publicly forbidden paying the Roman tax. Worst of all, he is destroying the peaceful order of our nation. We fear that his followers may riot and he has made the claim that he is our Messiah!"

Pilate was unfamiliar with the title, "Your Messiah?"

"Yes, our Messiah. A King specially called and anointed by God to reign over us."

"What is wrong with that? I thought all kings were chosen by the peoples' gods."

Pilate turned to Jesus and said to him, "Don't you hear these many serious accusations they are making against you? What do you have to say in your defense?"

Jesus remained calm and said nothing at all. This amazed Pilate greatly. It was at this point that the shouting matches typically broke out between the accusers and the defendants. Never before had a man who was already convicted, even a minor offender who would only suffer a small punishment, not spoken up and either protested his innocence or pleaded for mercy in an admission of guilt.

The other chief priests joined in and accused him relentlessly before the governor too.

Then Rabsaris spoke out about the Rabbi's silence. "He is acting like an innocent man with his sheepish ways here now. But before the people he is very bold. Do not let his silence dissuade you of the guilt that is laid upon him."

Pilate grew tired of the many accusations he was hearing from the chief priests. Their presence was making him feel nauseous. He did not want to hear anything more from them. He turned and walked away and waved them off as they continued to badger away at him. From a distance Pilate shouted, "Very well, I will inquire of him about his claim to be your King." Pilate ordered his officer to open the gate and take the Rabbi into custody. Then he walked into his headquarters where he sat and pondered all that Rabsaris and the others had said.

The Province of Judea that he ruled over was unique from all the others in the empire. They had no local political leader like a monarch or a sovereign to led them.

Rather, they were led by their religious leaders beginning with the high priest and his judicial court. Pilate wasn't as alarmed as they were about a man making a claim to be their King. There were many such minor kings and rulers throughout the empire that were officially recognized. Rome found that it was sometimes easier to rule over the people and keep the peace by putting a ruler from the local population on a throne. These kings would work under their governors. The truth was that these local rulers had very limited power and autonomy. They were for the most part figureheads and underlings who still had to submit to the oversight of a local governor put there by Caesar or the Roman Senate. Provincial governors were the ultimate local authority and they ruled with a very powerful strong arm and were backed up by the Roman soldiers they commanded.

Pilate gave a moment to imagine what it would be like to work with a local king instead of the seventy-one members of their local government. It even humored him to think about working with one. That might prove to be easier than putting up with Caiaphas and the badgering of his chief priests. He wondered if it was out of jealousy that they had turned this Rabbi over to him. The governor's spies and informants had already told him how this man had worked hard to uproot financial corruption in the Temple. Pilate knew that their large local ruling body did not want to enter into a power sharing arrangement with a local king. That would be too disruptive to their way of running things.

Chapter Sixteen
Pilate's Courtroom

Having taken time to shrug off the obnoxious feeling he was left with from his encounter with Chief Priest Rabsaris, Pilate called to his officer and asked him to have the prisoner Jesus brought to him. When he was brought in, the governor dismissed the soldier who was standing guard over him. Though the chief priests held the Rabbi in disregard, Pilate had no reason to do so. He wondered, perhaps this man was born into a royal line. If so then he could truly be a King. He was himself an appointed government official and easily disposed of. But a king, born of royal lineage, that was different. The entire empire recognized that a king was selected by the gods to be a ruler over the people and was there to support a civil and prosperous society among them.

Nonchalantly Pilate asked, "So, Rabbi Jesus. You are supposed to be some sort of a King, a Messiah-King. I've heard reports about you. I've been told that you are a prophet and a healer of the sick. Now I've been told you have made a claim to be a political monarch. That could explain why you made such a grand entrance into the city on Sunday."

Jesus was silent, just as he had been silent at the gate. He did not even beat an eyelash or give any indication that he had been spoken to.

Pilate said, "I am a foreigner living in your land. I do not know all that I should about your customs, or your religion. So, what do I know about your nation's Messiah? If you are their Ruler, then why have they turned you over to me? They should have embraced you as their King, shouldn't they have? They tell me that your followers may riot and fight for your release. But my own people told me that when two of your followers did rise-up to fight, you promptly stopped them."

The governor paused, casually looked away and waited for the Rabbi to speak for himself. He waited patiently, but the wait became embarrassingly long for Pilate to have not received an answer. He was accustomed to having his questions answered promptly, he was the governor. He turned and looked to see if there was a detectable reason for Jesus' silence. He stuck out his head and turned it slightly to the side as he bent an ear in his direction.

Jesus said nothing at all to him.

Now Pilate cleared his throat and in a very friendly voice asked, "Is there something I am missing here?"

The silence continued.

He apologetically explained, "I am not a Jew. I don't know anything about you. These are members of the government of your own nation. They are the chief priests from the governing body that rules under my authority. Them I know, you I don't know. They brought you to me and I am wondering what you have done to upset them so much?'

Pilate got up from his chair and paced himself casually as he walked about the room at random. "We are an empire of laws, just as yours is a nation of laws. Did you know that Rome and Judea have much in common between our two systems of law? Your laws and courts are administered by your chief priests and the others with them, the elders and the scribes. A long time ago, that's how it was with Rome. Just as in your nation now our laws were originally kept by the priests of our Roman state religion. We had a high priest back then, just as your nation has this Caiaphas for its high priest now. Later, your nation had a king, King David, who governed over your people once, and I am told he was very powerful. Are you a descendant of this king?"

After hearing nothing he continued his one-man dialogue, "But now the role of a king has been eliminated here in your land. The role of your local government has been taken over entirely by your religious leaders. They administer your laws and courts. In Rome things went the other direction. The practice of law was taken out of the priest's hands and given to our king, who we call the emperor.

Both of our law codes state that you cannot be compelled to incriminate yourself. So, I understand some of the reasons for your silence, or so I presume anyway. Both our laws say that there must be witnesses to testify against you and their testimony then becomes the basis for the charges that are brought. If that happens, then you can be convicted of a crime. So far, in the case they have brought against you that has not happened. The burden of proof has not been met to my satisfaction."

Still Jesus did not speak with him.

"So those who judged you in their own court now want to become witnesses against you here in my court. That creates an interesting legal question for me to ponder. You see, anyone who sits in judgement against you cannot cross that legal line of becoming a witness and giving testimony against you. Simply put, they cannot bring charges against the same person they have been a judge of. If there is an exception to that, if there is one, it could possibly be when they do it in two different court systems. They were your judges in their Judean Court and here they want to be witnesses against you in my Imperial Court. And I am undecided if I will let them be witnesses against you."

Jesus stood in silence and did not show any signs that he was liking or disliking what he was hearing. Pilate stopped periodically as he spoke, hoping that Jesus would open up to him.

"So, yourself, you are a man of the people, aren't you? My own informants have told me about how very popular you are with the masses. The question I have rolling around in my head is how can you be so beloved by the people and so hated by their leaders? Do you claim to be their King? Is that why they hate you so? I imagine they don't want to share their governing powers with a ruling monarch. And I am sure they do not want to share the great wealth in their treasury with one either. I will allow you to speak in your own defense against their charges."

Jesus was, as always, silent before him.

"Do you know that I believe they have turned you over to me because they are jealous of your influence over your people? I think they are worried because they might be forced by Rome to share their power with you as their Messiah-King. Suppose that Rome did grant you a crown and a scepter and you ruled here too. Then the priests would have to finance your reign with their precious Temple treasury and they are very jealous of their money. But you know that also."

Pilate pondered his legal options. He gave a passing thought about sending a letter to Rome, proposing Jesus of Nazareth be appointed as their King. That way the priests would have to enter into a power sharing arrangement with him. But that would take months, if not years to happen, even if Rome was to agree to it at all.

"I have not heard you say that you are a King as they claim you have said. Do you deny it?" Pilate waved his hand to show Rabbi Jesus that it was his time to speak, but he said nothing. Pilate shrugged his shoulders as he asked, "Do you admit to it?" Again, the Rabbi said nothing so Pilate threw up his hands in frustration, "Do you have anything to say for yourself?"

Jesus remained silent before him.

Pilate looked at his prisoner and questioned him again with a more serious and concerning tone. "The leaders of your own nation, these many chief priests, scribes and elders, have handed you over to me. I know them, they would have sooner stoned you to death than hand you over to me, if only they were allowed to put you to death. But fortunate for you, Rome reserves capital punishment for itself. You might say that the laws that I enforce have saved your life." He paused hoping Jesus would talk. He had hopes that by putting Rabbi Jesus' fate before him in this way, that he would motivate him to say something on his own behalf.

"Now I may not be very fond of those men who handed you over to me, but you must understand that I am forced to work with them. I don't believe I have ever seen them so upset over anyone or anything before. What is it that you did to upset them so much?" Pilate chuckled to himself and saw some humor in the situation. "I have to admit, I like upsetting them a little bit every once in a while, but that is just for sport." Pilate liked knowing that these chief priests were being upset by someone other than himself.

But Jesus remained silent before him.

Eagerly he asked, "Was it your grand entrance on Sunday? The people made quite show of your ride into Jerusalem on that day. Oh, yes, I know all about that. I did not see it, but it was reported to me. That was the kind of grand entrance a King would make. All except for the donkey of course."

And the silence continued.

As Pilate continued in his private examination of Jesus he disclosed more of his own secrets, "You know personally, I might prefer to deal with you as their King rather than these chief priests, their scribes, and elders. That might make my job easier. Then again, it could make it much more difficult for me too. I wonder what it would be like working with you as their King, Rabbi Jesus. How would we get along?"

But Jesus did not look at him as he spoke and he did not answer him when he was questioned this entire time. Neither did he act frightened as many accused do, nor was he defiant as a few with courage have acted. Jesus' composure was uniquely his own and Pilate took note of that.

"So, here I have been doing all the talking. Did you want to say anything for yourself?"

Pilate saw that his leveling with the Rabbi in a more casual style was accomplishing nothing, so he switched to a more direct approach, "You must tell me truthfully, I insist, are you actually their King?"

"Yes, as you have said, I am their King. I was born a King, and this is why I came into this world. I came here to testify to the truth, and those who are of the truth hear my voice and live by my words."

Pilate pondered what Jesus said. It was cleaver how he chose his words. Pilate felt as though he had been setup to confess that Jesus was a King rather than merely asking the question if he was a King. He wondered if Jesus was silent that whole time, just waiting for him to ask that certain question with just the right words, in the right order, so he could answer him the way he did.

113

Pilate continued his questioning, "So, you are their King. Are you this special type of King, a Messiah-King?"

"This is why I was born, to be their King and their Messiah."

"And your followers, the subjects of your Kingdom, are they going to rise-up and fight for your release?"

"If my Kingdom was an earthly kingdom, my followers would have already risen up and fought to keep them from handing me over to you. But my Kingdom is not from this world, it is from heaven above."

Pilate stepped back as he heard these words. He was at first relieved that there would be no uprising according to the Rabbi. Then from the floor beneath him, he felt a strange cascading vibration. Not much unlike the beginnings of an earthquake. He looked down and around but did not see anything shaking as he expected. The feeling rose and swept over his mind and invaded his thoughts leaving him feeling a bit dizzy and momentarily confused. He did not fear it though. He almost enjoyed this new sensation. He felt like it was some kind of celestial phenomenon that was aligning on him. He felt like there was a strong feeling of familiarity to it, but he could not understand exactly what it all was.

Pilate knew that the Rabbi had given him honest answers to his questions. He wondered if Rabbi Jesus was, in fact, their King and Messiah. He also wondered if he was divine, but not like past emperors who were declared divine. He wondered in truth if Jesus was divine just as they believe their God Yahweh was the only true God. This was but a fleeting thought and he dismissed it as quickly as it had come to him.

He restated what they had just discussed, "There, you are a King, their King, and their Messiah. And your followers will not revolt. Good."

Pilate couldn't have felt a greater sense of relief. He detested rioters and the fights that they started. He said, "There are many throughout the empire that can make that claim about themselves in their own homelands you know. They have kept the genealogies of their royal lines that are needed to prove it. By the way, are you a descendant of your great King David? Anyway, some of their claims are true, to a degree. It is not against the law to claim that you are of royal blood. How could it be? It is only when someone tries to independently establish their own government that it is a crime. But if they wish for their claim to be recognized so they can share in governing or merely be a figurehead among the people, they must apply to Rome. If they are approved, then they can rule under the jurisdiction of the Roman governor of their province. Is that what you want? To become a monarch? Then I would have to petition Rome for you. Under them, you would not be their Sovereign King though, you would only be a petty king ruling under my authority."

Jesus listened to his every word and then he spoke to correct the governor, "It is not as you think. My Kingdom in not of this world." He paused for a moment as he considered how well Pilate was grasping the idea that his Kingdom was not of this world, and that he was the Messiah, and not like earthly kings. Then he spoke, "You are searching for the facts in all this so that your verdict may be truthful."

"Yes, I am. That is exactly what I am doing. I have heard the words of those chief priests and their many supporters. Now I have heard from you. I am wrestling with that question, what is the truth?"

The governor concluded for himself that there was no basis for a case against the Rabbi. Yet, he dreaded going outside to meet with those religious leaders again to tell them his verdict but there was nothing else left to do. He invited Jesus to accompany him and they went to the gate to address them all. As they arrived, the chief priests were impatiently waiting for word on what Pilate was going to do about carrying out their sentence of death against Rabbi Jesus.

When they arrived Rabsaris confidently spoke first, "So, Pilate, has he confessed his crimes to you? Will you now send him to his death?"

"Listen." He said to the priests quietly. Then he rather nonchalantly turned his eyes to Jesus, "Are you their King?"

Jesus looked at him and simply answered, "It is as you have said. Yes, I am their King."

Rabsaris quickly shouted out, "There, you have his admission, he is guilty!"

Pilate simply shrugged his shoulders and looked at the whole company of religious leaders and softly said, "But to make that claim alone isn't a crime under Roman law. For it to be a crime he would first have to try and set up a kingdom without the endorsement of Rome. He hasn't done that."

"We have suspicions that he may have a hidden cache of weapons and armed his supporters who will fight for him."

"And you have proof of this do you?"

"No. But he spoke about such things."

"Your suspicions are not supported then. You have no proof which in legal terms is called speculation and it is not allowed to be considered with the same weight as the facts."

"So what! He is already condemned to die."

"So what, you say? There is a difference between claiming to be a king and committing sedition or treason. This man has not committed sedition nor treason."

Rabsaris reacted demonstratively by throwing his arms high up into the air and saying a prayer. But before he began to address the governor again he was interrupted.

Pilate told him, "You brought me this man, Rabbi Jesus, and accused him of many crimes but you had no witnesses to testify against him. If their testimony was incriminating, then charges could be made against him. This is necessary for you to do, to fulfill the burden of proof before the law, yours and mine. You are trained in the law and you have lawyers here with you. How is it that you do not act accordingly? Therefore, I have to conclude that you have not proven your case. In fact, I have spoken with the Rabbi and I find that you have no case against him on any crimes, none whatsoever."

Rabsaris shook in anger as he listened to all that was said to him. He stomped his foot and shook his arm with a fist. His voice demanded that Pilate listen to him rather than release the Rabbi, "From as far north as Galilee, and all the way here to Jerusalem he has been stirring up all of our people. He teaches them to act disrespectfully to us and condemns our leaders publicly saying that we are corrupt!"

Pilate grinned and lightly chuckled before taking the moment to poke at their self-righteous pride, "Are you corrupt?"

The chief priest did not take kindly to that comment. And to his credit he did not digress on to that subject either. That was because Elamadad took hold of his arm to caution him. Instead, he pressed their case forward, "We have convicted him in our highest court and condemned him to die. We expect you to confirm our sentence and execute him accordingly."

"From what my informants have told me, he is not a troublemaker among your people. But I have heard that he is uprooting corruption among your own priestly ranks."

Rabsaris' face turned beet red, but he did not respond directly to Pilate on that point. Again, that was because Elamadad warned him not to by clearing his throat.

The governor spoke sharply, "You should know better than to make demands on the empire like this one. Do not ever forget what I remind you of now; you may find someone guilty in your courts, you may sentence him, and you may punish him according to your Law, save one count. You do not have the power to put anyone to death. And I am not obligated to carry out your sentence of death."

The governor continued to mull over in his thoughts what they had said. He smiled widely and felt a wonderful sense of relief to have heard that the Rabbi was from Galilee. This gave him an out, one that he would take full advantage of. Employing this would free him from having to deal with them any longer on this matter. He addressed the chief priests with a tone of stern indignation and shaming them as he said, "What do you mean Galilee? Is this man from Galilee?"

"Yes, he is also known as Jesus of Nazareth. But why should that matter? His crimes have been committed here in your jurisdiction."

Pilate walked closer to them and spoke again with a shaming tone, "You have brought me a man who is from Herod's jurisdiction! Surely you must know that he is in residence here for your festival! Why then didn't you bring this man to him, who you say is Herod's subject and first created trouble in his jurisdiction!? Do you intend to cause me troubles with Herod!? Is that what this is all about!? Is it Rabsaris!? Answer me now!"

The chief priest coward with embarrassment and with a shallow, outward show of respect he offered an apology, "No, certainly not governor, of course not. Did you not hear us when we said that he has made trouble here in your jurisdiction, in Judea? Therefore, we brought him to you, as your loyal subjects."

Pilate could hardly believe his ears when he heard them say that they were his loyal subjects. That made him want to laugh, but he held it back. He gave them a smug and disbelieving stare though. He knew better, they were no more loyal to him than they were to the emperor. They obeyed the rule of Roman law because they did not want to incur Rome's wrath.

"So, you high and mighty leaders of the people. How they must suffer from your incompetence. You didn't have enough sense to bring him to Herod, so I will send him to Herod myself. Other than that, we are done here and I am dismissing you." Then he did a military style about-face and marched away.

Pilate did not care to become ensnared in the middle the empire's regional conflicts. This was especially true when it involved another Roman governor, most of all Herod Antipas. The two of them were not just on bad terms with each other, they hated each other, and Pilate certainly did not want to make that worse. So, upon hearing that the

Rabbi was from Herod's province he was glad to pass this problem off to him for his consideration. Perhaps he could even use this opportunity to foster some good will with Herod and repair their relationship.

Back in his headquarters, the governor issued an order to his officer to prepare to march Rabbi Jesus to Herod's residence. He sat at his desk and after a moment of thought he crafted a letter in his own hand to Herod that would accompany the Galilean Rabbi. He hoped his choice of words would mend their enmity. He handed this letter to his officer and dispatched a squad of his soldiers in full battle dress with their officer to bring Jesus to him. Then, as a last-minute thought he told them, "And bring five crates of those grapes that just arrived to him with my complements."

Chapter Seventeen
High Priestly Garments

Having disposed earlier of the Galilean Rabbi by sending him to Pilate for execution, it was time for Caiaphas to don his high priestly festival robes. That morning at the ninth hour in the day, he strolled to the Praetorium to meet with Pilate. It was the governor who held in trust the special garments that he, as the high priest, would wear on this festival day. This set of robes were the ones he wore when he sacrificed the national Passover Lamb. It was Rome who no longer allowed these robes to be kept at the Temple or at the palace. This was a safeguard that they insisted on to help keep the peace in Judea. Rome knew that these high priestly garments were a powerful symbol of his divine appointment to serve the people. When the high priest wore them, he was acting with the greatest authority, their God's authority. The worry was that when he wore them and spoke to the people, he would be able to move the people to do whatever he commanded them to do, including rising up and fighting against the Romans. That put too much power in any one man's hands for Rome to live comfortably with. The empire feared that if the high priest would wear his festival robes to do something like that, if he was to call on the people to revolt against them, that it would bring a massive uprising in Judea and Galilee as well. This action would cause every man to gladly pick up arms and viciously fight to the death against them. So, as a peace keeping measure, the garments were kept at the Praetorium under Pilate's careful watch. He allowed the high priest access to them only on festival days.

Inside his office Pilate was alone, somberly sitting at his desk and enjoying the feeling of relief he got from sending the Rabbi's case to Herod. Before long a soldier entered and spoke, "Sir, Caiaphas's servant has arrived at the gate just now. He states that his master will be here shortly for his robes that are in your keeping. He requests that we be ready for his arrival and that we should not keep his master waiting."

Pilate did not react to what he said, he just stared at the wall before him as if he were daydreaming.

The servant spoke again, "Sir?"

A moment passed and then Pilate turned his head, nodded and said, "That is rather arrogant of him don't you think?"

"Sir?"

"You must have an opinion about his actions. This high priest who sends his servant ahead of his arrival and urges me to be prepared, doesn't he sound arrogant to you?"

"Yes sir. You are the governor. You rule with Rome's authority. He is your subject."

"Well, we best get going. Come with me and we will dig them out of storage." Pilate took his time getting up from his chair. Then he looked at the soldier and said, "Lead the way."

The soldier stood there for a moment and wondered about what he was told. It was not military protocol for a soldier of lesser rank to lead the way like this, but he did not question his commander's instructions. He knew that he had heard him correctly. He turned and entered a back room that was used to store records, correspondence, books of law and other important items.

It was in that back room where two chests were stored. They both had a set of the high priest's garments in them.

One set was made of simple pure white, finely woven linen. This robe was woven of one piece and without any seams. The garment was worn only once a year on Yom Kippur, which is the Judean's Day of Atonement. That was when the high priest entered the most sacred room in their Temple, the Holy of Holies. He went in there to sprinkle blood on the Ark of the Covenant. It was reported that on any other day of the year, if anyone including the high priest was to enter this most revered holy place and see what was in there, they would die instantly. That was because it housed the very presence of God on earth. If you went in there, then God would see you, and if he saw you, then he would see your sins. If he saw your sins, he would have to do something about them. Death was the result because all sins require the death of the offender.

There was also a second chest which contained the high priest's gold trimmed garments that were worn by him on all the other high holy days such as the Passover Festival. In there was a gold embroidered turban for him to wear on his head. It was similar to a king's crown. The entire set of clothes included: a pair of linen pants, a tunic of the finest and purest linen woven of one piece and without any seams, a sash of fine linen that was embroidered in blue, purple, and scarlet threads, a vest, a breast plate with twelve gems on it, each one representing one of the twelve tribes of their nation, and the elaborately decorated high priestly robe.

As the soldier saw the chest he said to Pilate, "I will get another soldier to help me move it."

Pilate motioned with his hand stopping him and whispered, "Don't bother, I will help you carry it."

The soldier was quietly surprised by his commander's willingness to do this menial task. It was one that would normally be given to a soldier to carry out. So, the two of them carried the chest out to the gate where Caiaphas and several of his servants were impatiently waiting.

As they were setting it down in front of the closed gate Caiaphas objected, "I prefer to not have it set down on the pavement. It holds very expensive garments you know and they are sacred to the people."

Pilate looked at him as if he was ignorant of that fact. Then he stood up and put his foot on the top of it. Caiaphas and his servants were aghast.

The Roman governor looked directly at the high priest and spoke flippantly, "So, it was a busy night for you and the Sanhedrin over at your palace."

Caiaphas now wondered if Pilate knew that he held a night time trial, but he showed no reaction to the comment.

Pilate spoke on, "I was surprised that you, or at least Annas, did not accompany Rabbi Jesus to my Praetorium here after your night...tim...". Pilate stopped himself mid-word and corrected what he was saying, "Your ah, very early daytime trial." Then he stared at Caiaphas. He wanted the high priest to know that he knew more than he had been told by the religious authorities who delivered the prisoner to him.

Caiaphas stepped back and was now certain that Pilate knew his dirty secret. He opened his mouth to speak but stumbled on his words as he was still formulating what he would say. "What? Ah, well, hum, I handed those responsibilities over to very competent men who are high ranking chief priests. I gave them authority to act on my behalf, and in my name, so that I could attend to the preparations for the festival."

At that moment Caiaphas realized that none of them were there to be seen at the gate and so he speculated to say, "I don't see any of my chief priests here attending to his case. Have you sent him for execution already?"

"Caiaphas, you rendered a verdict of death to him on the same day of his trial? Don't your laws prohibit that?"

"We normally don't allow it, no. But on holy days and festivals there are modifications that ha, our, ah, we must make allowances for. It is at times such as this, which is one of the finer points of how we apply jurisprudence and practice law, where we must make it fit the circumstances. The scribal lawyers can best explain it."

"I am certain they can. Did you know that Herod is in residence here for the festival?"

"Of course, and we are honored to have him among us."

"That is not what I was driving at. I learned that this Rabbi Jesus is from Galilee. That makes him Herod's subject. I sent the prisoner to be examined by him, jurisprudence and the application of Rome's laws and all, you know." Pilate was silent for a minute, which made Caiaphas uncomfortable, but that was exactly what the governor wanted.

Caiaphas was tired. He had lost a night of sleep because of the trial he conducted and he was not at his best. Finally, he spoke, "I was up all night preparing for the case against the Rabbi."

"Preparing 'the case against the Rabbi?' You make it sound like you were on the side of the accusers rather than an impartial judge."

Caiaphas realized his choice of words had betrayed him, and he stood there frozen in the moment.

Pilate wanted to let the high priest feel some of the political pressure he had himself created. "And then you sent him and your subordinates to me so that they would do your dirty work for you."

Caiaphas was on the defensive now, a position he did not care for at all, "I could not come myself at that hour, you know that. I have had to hastily make my preparations for today's festival because of that criminal stealing my precious time from me."

Pilate had made his point to the high priest, so he returned to the matter directly at hand. "So, under the peace accord we have with your nation you are allowed to wear these garments for this festival day. You must return them to me as soon as you are done with them. When will you be making your sacrifice?"

"It will happen at three o'clock this afternoon."

"Fine, I will expect them to be returned to me no later than, what, four?"

"Agreed."

Caiaphas did not like being given orders, nor did he like the restrictions that were being placed on him according to their treaty. Just as Pilate had pressed his authority on the high priest, now the high priest tried to exercise his, "These garments are not yours to do with as you please. They belong to the people of our nation, and to the Temple, and to me. They are mine alone to wear. If I do not wear them, the sacrifice cannot be made, and the people will wonder why. They will not stand for that and it could lead to rioting in the streets."

Pilate, whose foot remained on the chest, turned his head away and with the wave of his hand he invited Caiaphas to look at his many soldiers that had been brought into the city for the festival. The Praetorium was overcrowded with them. "I have brought extra soldiers into the city for the festival. So far, they have already put down one revolt this week. They captured the leader, someone called Bar-Abbas. He has been tried in my court and found guilty. I have sentenced him to die. And what did he rebel over? Was it because I forced you to use money from your Temple treasury to build an aqueduct for your own people!? It was not as though you don't have a huge surplus of money that you don't know what to do with. And what did this little uprising accomplish? Nothing! It was all for nothing." Then his voice took on a harsher tone, "We are crucifying Bar-Abbas today and now you find it necessary to make threats to me of more rioting? I don't think it is a very wise move. My soldiers are well trained and proven in combat. If history is any use in predicting the future, I suggest you do what you can to keep your people from rioting rather than suggesting that they may riot again."

Caiaphas and his servant stood there wide eyed and speechless. The governor's shaming of them had made its full effect.

Pilate looked the high priest directly in the eyes and said in no uncertain terms, "The treaty will be upheld by me, of that you should have no doubts. Will you uphold your part of the accord Caiaphas? Will you abide by the laws that govern us? Will you uphold both your laws and the laws of the Empire? This is what I am asking you."

Caiaphas felt like a child being scolded. He felt ashamed and stared at the ground, then he simply nodded.

Pilate told him, "The Pax Romana will be upheld! There will be peace in Jerusalem. If I find that you have done anything to disrupt it, I will have you deposed. Understood?"

Again, the high priest nodded.

Now Caiaphas looked at the chest with his priestly garments in it. Then he spoke in obedience to him, "Yes, of course the treaty will be honored and all of its requirements. This chest and all the garments in it will be returned to you at that hour. You have my promise on it, governor."

"Then I will hold you to your promise." So, he removed his foot from the top of the chest and stepped back.

Pilate's soldiers opened the gate and carried the chest outside. They attempted to hand it directly to Caiaphas' servants, but they stood back and pointed to the ground to indicated they wanted them to put it down. This was so they did not accidently touch a Gentile during the holy festival.

Caiaphas spoke, "Rome will be glad to know that you are so good at putting down riots once they have started. But wouldn't it be something if you could somehow treat us so well that you could prevent them in the first place?"

Pilate knew a vailed threat when he heard one. "I always keep that in mind in all my affairs with your people, of course."

They both nodded in agreement and found it possible to even smile as they did. They both wanted peace in the land. With that accomplished, Pilate turned and swiftly walked back to his office.

Caiaphas and his servants left quickly too, and as they did the high priest spoke just under his breath, "May God curse that man and rid us of him."

Chapter Eighteen
Death on the Desert Tree

Having wept in deepest bitterness at the footsteps to the Temple, Judas suddenly felt self-conscious as he realized he was in a public place and people were taking notice of him. He looked up and saw people busy with their day. Some of them glanced his way but hoped not to be noticed by him. There he was putting on such an unlikely display of downcast emotions. He realized how out of step with the day he was. It was early in the morning, the sun was up, and most of all it was a grand festival day. The people on the street were all so very happy, but there he was, this one man, weeping like a wailing woman, as though someone had just died. He tried to compose himself and gather in his sorrows, but they were a consuming fire, deep in his belly and he could no longer sit still.

Suddenly, like a crazed madman, he got up and ran widely into the city streets. He was overcome with guilt and his sorrow was without measure. He had not slept at all that night and he was not in his right mind. The brightness of the sun was nearly blinding his eyes, and as he turned away from it he saw the Temple's highly polished white marble walls brightly reflecting the sunlight back into his eyes again. He screamed in horror and threw up his arms in fright as he called out in fear as he tried to block his eyes from its brilliance. He was emotionally overwrought over how Jesus' arrest had now led to his condemnation and the sentence of death. His eyes twitched wildly about, and his face quivered nearly nonstop. As he ran, he pulled the hood of his robe over his face to shield his eyes from the sun and cloak his identity. Never had it come into his mind that Rabbi Jesus would be found guilty and sentenced to death.

Now his mind was filled with irrational thoughts. He felt the absolute fool for having tried in vain to secure his release by returning the money. He did not know and could not imagine what he should do now.

Still running in the streets without a destination to arrive at he eventually came to a fountain. There he tried to splash water on his face in the hopes of finding some relief for the torture that he was undergoing. He lowered his hood and took off his hat, but it slipped through his fingers and fell to the ground. Then as he looked at the fountain's still waters he screamed out as he saw his reflection. This was more than he could bear as he hardly recognized his radically aged appearance. In his panic, he left his hat behind, which he had worn as a symbol of his submission to God behind and returned to running through the city streets. He thought that he heard barking dogs behind him, and then reached out with his hands to shoo them away, but as he looked about he could not see any animals. He worried that the people in the streets were getting in his way, so he tried to dodge about trying to avoid them. He realized that he was behaving crazy and he laughed loudly. He thought that if he made light of it and simply tried to act normal, that he would return to his right mind.

He stopped his running and took a few slow steps, but that did not last. Though he was tired, he could not stop himself from running. Again, he felt as if dogs were chasing him and now they were biting at his ankles. He tried to shoo them with his hands and kick at them too, but as he looked about, he saw none. His ankles were so sore though and it felt to him as if he had been bitten many times. He looked about and saw that the streets were getting very busy with large crowds of people preparing to celebrate the festival. He called out to them for help, but he did not immediately hear his voice as he shouted. It was delayed. It was a moment or two later that he heard himself shouting, "Help me!" It was as though there was a strange echo in that place. Then as he shouted again, he did not recognize his words or even his own voice when they resounded back to him. He called out again, but this time he did not hear his own voice, it was the voice of a stranger shouting painfully in his ears, "There is no help for you! No one can help you now!" He looked in desperation for someone who might help him, but they turned aside and hurried away. He tried again to call for help, but it was like a bad dream when you try to call out and are speechless. He could hear some of the people speaking to him, but he could not make sense of their words.

He came near to a marketplace and he could smell the wonderful aroma of fresh bread. He realized that he was famished, but as he came near to them and saw the food, it made him almost violently nauseous. He returned to running and while he experienced this great hunger, he also was terribly sickened, not just by the smell of it, but by the mere thought of it. He tried to hold onto his belly because the gnawing pain was too great to bear. That only worsened his nausea and now he began to gag. From the depth of his belly there shot up a fiery acid. It came up and burned away in his throat and made it hard for him to breathe and impossible for him to speak. It even burned up into the back of his nasal passages and the smell of it was vile. He jumped up and down like a nervous little child because he could not imagine how to find relief for himself.

The city's noise and the busy people hurrying about continued to inflame his mind. He ran. He had to get out of there. He felt as if everyone was staring at him, as if they all knew what he had done and hated him intensely. He ran wildly about, not remembering how to get to one of the city's gates until he, by chance, found one which he rushed through. The soldiers there stood and stared at him, wondering what was going on with him. His untypical behavior was suspicious to them, like he might be a thief running away from his pursuers. They called to him because they wanted to question him. But he continued to run as fast as he could, away from the people, away from the roads, and into the barren countryside. He imagined that because this was all happening to him in the city that he must leave it to find relief.

The Temple guards who were dispatched to follow him were still close behind. They had seen people acting irrationally before, but never had they seen anyone behaving this wildly. They kept their distance so they would not be noticed by him. And because of Judas' strange behavior, they reached for the handles of their concealed weapons, both clubs and swords, to ensure that they were handy if they needed them.

When he betrayed Jesus, Judas knew he was giving up his life as a disciple. He wanted to fulfill his dream of becoming a rich man instead. He knew he was giving that dream up when he returned the thirty pieces of silver. Then he found out that he could not bring about the Rabbi's release. He recognized the futility of his life and all that he had lost. His distress over it all was too much for him to hold in. His emotions, in unison with his stomach and all the way down to the bottom of his bowels, were also bringing him great distress over it. He was in such severe anguish that he could not see a future for himself. He only knew about the urgency of his pains: the gnawing in his abdomen, the nausea, the burning acid in his throat, and the imagined dog bites on his ankles. He was certain in his own mind that if he stopped running, those dogs would tear away at his flesh. So, he continued to run relentlessly about madly as if he was in an invisible maze, and he worried about what he could do to save himself. He was in torment and his mind leapt from one devastating thought to another. Every thought was unbearable to him because it always led to the same condemnation that was his.

He dodged about trying to avoid the imagined dogs at his heels. He thought that if he was just fast enough he could catch one of the dogs and break its neck. If he could do that the other dogs might be frighten enough to stop chasing him and that would bring an end to his torture. But as he looked about, as before, there were no dogs. In his mind he could not reconcile why he thought there were dogs chasing him. He saw no evidence of it, but he did feel the proof of it.

Now his mind was suffering from one endless vivid recollection of all that he done. The memories that flashed before his eyes were becoming more real to him than his actual surroundings and he started to believe that he was slipping away into complete madness. He looked heavenward thinking he would plead to God for mercy, but as he did he was blinded again by the sun that shone brightly down at him. He fell to the ground, and as he opened his mouth, he had no words that he could pray, not thoughts to draw from, and then the shock of it hit him in waves of endless torture. He had no God to plead to.

He wished his life could return to the way it was, not as a disciple though, but he wished he could return to his life as a child when things were so much simpler. Then he reached down as if he was searching for something, desperately patting the ground and running his fingers through the sand. He did not know why he was compelled to do this, or what he was looking for. Whatever it was, it was not to be found, because it did not exist. He shook his head wildly hoping to not think about what he had done, trying to shake those memories out of his mind. But in his growing madness, that was all that remained for him. His head suddenly fell forward and dropped, the weight of it was more than he could hold up. He reached up with both of his hands and covered his face, trying to hide his shame. Then he grabbed hold of his head by the ears and twisted it about, as if to remove it from his body and throw it away. He began to pick away at his scalp, scratching it until it was bleeding. He was hoping that he could remove the thoughts out of his head. He was also pulling his hair out, just hoping that his tormenting thoughts would stop, even if only for a moment.

He was increasingly nauseated, and with that came dizziness, but he reasoned that if he acted normal, then things would return to being normal for him again. So, he stood to his feet and brushed the desert sand off his robe. As he did, his arms and legs, his entire body was pushed and pulled in all directions. He was overcome with tremors and spastic muscle movements that he could not control. He jerked about in uncoordinated movements even though he tried to fight against it. He could not understand what was happening to him, but it was all for one simple reason. His body was doing as his mind commanded it to, and his mind was twisted and increasingly filled with the imaginings of a madman.

His distress and the uncertainty of what was overcoming him lead him to hyperventilate. He tried to slow his breathing and relax by walking around slowly. But his stomach was churning and even his bowels had expanded causing his entire abdomen to bloat outwardly.

He felt as if he might vomit and he tried to hold it in by putting his hands to his mouth. But he vomited and gastric acid spewed out his mouth and nose, and it was very fowl. It burned his throat, his mouth and nostrils, making it still harder for him to breathe. It had gotten on his hands and face and they too burned. He looked about for a pool of water to wash in, but the desert wasteland did not have that to offer him. He reached down and ran his fingers through the sand and tried to wipe his hands clean. He threw sand in his face and tried to wash the burning vomit off with it.

As he reacted in rage to what had become of his life, he could feel his emotions stirring from the bottom of his belly. He felt such deep agony, more than he ever imagined possible. It was then that he remembered what the Rabbi had taught him, "What comes out your mouth comes from the fullness of your heart. This is what defiles a person, from the heart comes evil intentions, wickedness, murder, greed, pride, theft, lying, folly and worse."[7] He whimpered in pain and continued to look about for a pool of water to drink from and to wash in, but there was none. He looked at the distance and thought he saw water, so he ran toward it, but it was a mirage of water vapor on the horizon. He ran but he never arrived there, and the water was always the same distance away from him.

Now he screamed in fear and trembled as he saw a dog appearing out of nowhere and racing towards him. He stood to his feet and as he looked again he thought he saw three of them, but he couldn't be sure. He raced as fast as he could to escape from them, but being exhausted, his arms simply flailed senselessly about as he scurried away. The dogs lunged at him and bit his ankles hard, and when he reached down to grab one or push them away, they simple

---

[7] Matthew 15:11, 18-20, Mark 7:15-22.

moved away from him. He changed direction and tried to run harder, but the dogs continued to attack him relentlessly.

He struggled in what was left of his rational mind to complete a thought and make sense of what he was going through. It was then that he realized he was losing touch with reality and madness was going to soon overtake him completely. He looked about and saw an old dead tree in the distance and ran directly to it. The dogs raced after him, but he escaped from them as he jumped up and grabbed the lowest branch. It was a broken stump with sharp ragged edges that stuck out just about a foot. It was all he could do to pull himself up so that he could stand on it.

He breathed hard trying to catch his breath, but it was a laborious effort and his lungs burned. He looked about and the dogs he had seen were now gone. He tried to think about his condition with what reason remained for him. He was terribly hot. He felt such pressure in his head it was like ropes were wrapped around it in circles and they were being pulled so hard that they were near the point of snapping. He feared that he would soon be lost to the world and condemned to living in hell on earth. He struggled to think, hitting the palm of his hand to his forehead and trying to complete a thought. But the powers of his mind were failing to serve him. All that was left for him were fragments, thoughts that all ended in the dreaded horror that he was being overtaken by endless tortures to his body and his mind.

Even though it was a cool spring day he was terribly hot, so he dropped his robe to the ground below. Then he tore open his tunic from the neck down to belly and opening it up he hoped to cool himself down. He untied his sash and wrapped it over his shoulders and he feared for his life, but he did not know why. No one threatened him and yet he was sure he would be murdered by someone taking revenge on him for what he had done.

He feared that with his failing strength he would not be able to hold himself up in the tree for much longer. He took his long sash and tied it to the branch just above him and then he began to tie the other end around himself so that it would keep him from falling to the ground. As he did this he began to weep uncontrollably. He reasoned that his only escape would be to take his own life. He worried that if he waited too much longer, he would no longer possess a state of mind that could do anything of reason anymore. If he was to live on, he would be left in endless torment, raving mad until the day a natural death came to him.

He continued to wrap the end of his sash, but no longer around his body to keep himself from falling to the ground below. He tied it around his own neck and securely made a knot that would hold him until death came to him. Standing on the broken tree branch he dove out and away from the tree. Then falling downward his body swung back toward the tree. The fall did not snap his neck bringing him to an instant death as he had thought it would. When he reached the end of his sash his body was jerked turning him so that he was facing the tree. Then he swung back toward the tree and crashed into it. His belly struck hard against the stump from the broken branch. It cut him open, leaving him with a large gaping wound across his abdomen. His bowels that had been so torturous to him in the last hour now fell out of his abdomen and spilled out onto the tree and to the ground beneath him. His face became deep red from the strangle hold of his sash that now choked him. He spun around slowly as he hung there looking down at himself. The lower parts of his bowels were scattered on the broken stump, down the tree and laying on the desert ground below, contaminating everything they touched. His lavish dream of being wealthy and wearing the finest of clothing was now replaced with the dire straits he had brought upon himself. He languished there in excruciating pain in the moments before his death, alone and forsaken by God.

Chapter Nineteen
Before Herod

When in Jerusalem, Herod stayed at the Hasmonean Palace. It was luxurious and it suited his tastes very well. This Roman governor who ruled over Galilee was not a morning person. He liked to stay up late, very late. That was because he found it hard to fall asleep and so the two went hand in hand. He enjoyed his lavish lifestyle, so he frequently entertained his friends late into the night as well. He loved fine wine and fine food, and lots of it. He was a large man because of this, and behind his back he was called the *fat-man*, but he simply told others he was thick skinned.

So, when Pilate's soldiers arrived at his door shortly after the ninth hour of the morning he was still asleep. His attendant spoke quietly to him, "Sir, there is an urgent matter that is presenting itself at court." But Herod did not stir. He was hard to wake up and when he was awoken he took it rudely.

Again, his attendant spoke to him. Louder this time and he poked his shoulder, then he quickly backed away to avoid getting hit, "Sir, Pilates soldiers are here with a prisoner."

Herod was half awake at this time and all he heard was, 'Pilate's soldiers' and the word 'prisoner' which didn't please him. He thrashed about and tried to hit his slave.

"What!? Pilate, that bastard isn't going to be taking me as his prisoner, he has no cause! Rome will hear of this!"

His attendant spoke forcefully, "No, my lord, no. Pilate's soldiers have brought you a prisoner. It's the Rabbi known as Jesus of Nazareth. And he sent over five crates of these grapes as a gift to you with his complements." His attendant hoped to sooth his temper as he held up a platter with bunches of the fresh purple grapes for him to see. "Here, wouldn't you like to try them? I believe they are very fresh and tasteful."

Herod calmed down and thought to himself for the moment. He put his hand to his forehead and rubbed his head to try to ease his headache, the result of being short on sleep and still drunk on the wine from the night before. He spoke in a murmur to himself to calm his paranoid worries that he was going to be taken prisoner by Pilate. He struggled to sit upright on the side of his bed. He rubbed his eyes and tried to focus. Then he delighted himself with the sight of the grapes and took hold of them as he tried a few. "These are good. How nice of Pilate to send them to me. But he must be up to something, I wonder what he has on his mind."

Herod got up and his attendant helped him dress as he told him, "A squad of soldiers brought the prisoner over along with a letter from Pilate explaining the situation. There's also a number of chief priests and other religious authorities who came along with them. They are very adamant about speaking with you about this prisoner."

Herod did not care to have to deal with those people any more than Pilate They typically made many demands upon him. "Great, now I know why Pilate sent me the prisoner. He doesn't care for dealing with those religious sorts any more than I do."

Herod slowly made his way down to his meeting hall to speak with Pilate's officer about the prisoner. He dreaded having to address the chief priests and the rest of their company. He ordered that the prisoner be brought in to stand before him. There he finished the cluster of grapes he had in his hands and then told his servant to bring him

140

more. He had heard some extraordinary stories about this Rabbi and was giddy to meet him.

He made his way over to his couch where he reclined as was his custom. Then he ordered the prisoner to be brought to him. Pilate's soldiers entered the room and brought Jesus before him. Jesus did not bow before Herod, so the soldiers kicked him in the back of the knees and shoved him so that he fell to the floor before the governor. Then Jesus slowly rose to his feet and stood quietly without making eye contact with anyone. Herod dismissed Pilate's soldiers and then his own soldiers now stood by the Rabbi.

Herod stood to his feet and looked at the rabbi to size him up. "I've been hearing about you for many months now. I even ordered your arrest some time ago, but you escaped from my jurisdiction before you could be found. I was worried that you were John the Baptist raised from the dead, but clearly you are not him. Do you know, I used to enjoy listening to John? So, what do you have to say now that I am prepared to listen to you?"

But Jesus did not speak for himself, he simple stood there without making eye contact with anyone.

Herod was surprised that the Rabbi said nothing to him, "I have heard that you are very eloquent with words. Might I hear something from you today? Perhaps one of your sermons or a lesson about our religion?"

The Rabbi did not respond, nor did he move so much as an inch.

"You are said to have the power to work wonders and perform signs. So, … go ahead Rabbi, show me your powers, do something, a little sign for me to see, would you?" Herod waited but Jesus did nothing. "If the power of God is at work in you, then perform a sign to prove it to me so that I can believe that this is true about you."

But again, Jesus did not move or say anything.

Herod was disappointed. He wanted to see something that would amuse his self-serving interests. "What's this? No sign or wonder? I would have thought that a man with your reputation would be glad to show me some small sign at the very least. How much trouble can that be for a man with your reputed powers? I am giving you the opportunity to impress me here. Don't you know that if I am pleased with what you say, or do, that I could set you free? You're from Galilee, you're my subject, I am your ruler. Now go ahead, why don't you?"

Still Jesus did nothing. A moment passed, and Herod spoke to him again, "No? You're not impressing me, not at all. Don't you care that this is upsetting to me? John I threw into prison because of what he said. Shall I have you thrown into prison for saying nothing?"

More time passed and Herod popped more grapes one by one into his mouth. His boredom led to impatience, "They told me you could give the power of speech to the mute, is that true? Perhaps you need to use these supernatural powers on yourself Rabbi Jesus."

Jesus continued to maintain his silence and he made eye contact with no one all this time.

Herod spoke again trying a new approach, "Here, I have been doing all the talking. You are my guest, please say something. You must have something to say for yourself? Would you like some of these grapes? They are very good."

There was a long pause before Herod got up. He walked in a circle around the Rabbi so that he could look him over closely, from head to toe, and front to back. He was disappointed with the Rabbi over his silence so he circled around behind him and spoke, "You are nothing much to look at Rabbi. Isn't there something you would like to say for yourself though? You do understand that I have the power to release you from custody and have the charges against you cleared, don't you?" Herod returned to his couch and said to Jesus, "Do you know how our justice system works? There is testimony offered against you. This becomes a statement of the charges. Then I inquire into the charges and issue a verdict. Your fate is in my hands and I can do anything that I like with you. Don't you care?"

Herod had not addressed the chief priests, nor had he even looked at them up until now. "You there, priest, step forward. What is your name, and what are the charges that you are reporting to me about this man?

The chief priest stood forward and vehemently accused Jesus. "I am the Chief Priest Rabsaris, governor. This man deserves to die for his crimes. He has taken a stand against you and your rule. He has created dissent from Galilee all the way to Jerusalem among our people. His followers want him to ascend to the throne of David and they hope that he will overthrow Roman order."

Herod was giving more attention to the grapes that he was eating than he was to listening to the chief priest.

Rabsaris went on, "He has worked among the people by enticing them with lies and making promises no man could keep. He is much like the Baptist that you had put to death. He has even threated to destroy the Temple that your father built. Your father would never have let things go on with him like this, He would have had him put to death long ago." Rabsaris was very pleased with himself as he made the accusations against him and how he tied in the charges to the Temple and Herod's father. He was sure that would infuriate the governor. The others with him smiled and told him what an excellent argument he made against the Rabbi.

Herod looked at the Rabbi and said, "Do you hear the many things they accuse you of? Have you nothing to say about them? No? Well, here is a letter addressed to me from Governor Pontius Pilate. Let's hear what he has to say about your case." Herod nodded to his scribe who had the letter in hand and the scribe read it aloud:

TO HIS MOST MAJESTIC MAJESTY
THE IMPERIAL GOVERNOR HEROD ANTIPAS
TETRARCH OF THE PROVENCE OF GALILEE AND PEREA

YOUR EXCELLENCY,
I AM TURNING OVER TO YOU A MAN FROM YOUR JURISDICTION. HE IS A RABBI CALLED JESUS OF NAZARETH. SOME OF THE CHIEF PRIESTS HANDED HIM OVER TO ME. THEY STATED THAT HE HAS BEEN JUDGED THIS VERY MORNING ACCORDING TO THEIR LAWS, FOUND GUILTY, AND IS DESERVING OF DEATH. THE CHARGES THEY HAVE MADE AGAINST HIM INCLUDE;

PERVERTING THEIR NATION.
FORBIDDING TAX PAYMENTS TO THE EMPEROR.
CLAIMING TO BE THE MESSIAH, WHICH IS SOME SPECIAL KIND OF KING
THAT HE IS WIDELY TRAVELLED, AND THAT HIS TEACHINGS HAVE SOWN DISCORD
EVERYWHERE FROM GALILEE TO JUDEA.
THAT HE PERVERTS THEIR PEOPLE AND TURNS THEIR HEARTS AGAINST THEIR
LEADERSHIP AND LOCAL GOVERNMENT.

THEY HAVE ASKED THAT I CONFIRM HIS SENTENCE AND EXECUTE HIM. I WAS FULLY PREPARED TO HEAR THEIR CASE. HOWEVER, WHEN I LEARNED THAT HE WAS FROM YOUR PROVINCE, I DETERMINED THAT HIS CASE SHOULD RIGHTLY BE HEARD BY YOU, MY COLLEAGUE. ADDITIONALLY, YOU ARE MORE FAMILIAR WITH THEIR RELIGIOUS TRADITIONS AND UNDERSTAND WHAT HIS CLAIM TO BE A MESSIAH MEANS.

IN CORDIAL REGARDS,
PONTIUS PILATE
IMPERIAL GOVERNOR OF THE PROVENCE OF JUDEA

Herod had listened with great interest in the letter and then commented, "There, that makes it plain enough, doesn't it?"

Rabsaris spoke again, "He is a false messiah who believes he can conquer the Romans and restore the Kingdom of David to Israel. And he is so high and mightily minded that he is calling it the Kingdom of God."

In all this Jesus remained silent. He showed no reaction to anything that was said against him.

Herod spoke to the chief priests, "Hum, look at him. He must know the Law, he is saying nothing." He looked at Jesus and said, "So, Messiah, you must know that in legal matters, both under Moses and Roman law, it is the right of everyone being accused of a crime to not self-incriminate themselves. Of course, you may also speak in your own defense if you so choose."

The chief priest asserted himself, "Governor, we have tried him in our high court! He was found guilty of blasphemy, I heard it myself. He is guilty and must be put to death, that is his condemnation."

The other priests tried to stir things up by shouting accusations at Jesus also.

Their screaming worked against their case as Herod's patience grew thin with them. He stood up and shouted, "Silence!" At that word, Herod's guards clenched their weapons and stood sharply to attention. The voices of the chief priests quickly fell silent for fear of reprisals. "I know the law and it is not complicated. You cannot accuse him, you were his judges when he was tried." Herod paused and looked at all the religious authorities. "Did you bring any witnesses who can confirm what you are accusing him of?" The room remained dead silent. "I though as much." Herod waited to see if the authorities had anything else to say before concluding, "So be it. No witnesses, then you cannot charge him with any crimes."

Even though there was no judgement brought against Rabbi Jesus, Herod was not happy about Jesus' silence and inaction, so he took some time to treat him with contempt. "Rabbi, in person you don't resemble at all what the many people describe you as. Why ever did I think that you were somehow John the Baptist raised from the dead? You are not like him, are you? John wasn't afraid to speak up, in fact he couldn't help himself. That's what got him killed. He said he wrong things about the wrong people. You are very different than him. You won't speak. Is it because you are afraid to? Are you silent because if you speak it will be used it against you? If you would have shown me one sign, one out of the ordinary thing such as a miracle, then I would have believed you have the power of God working in you. But no, you won't do so much as that for me. And now that we have met I don't even have the pleasure of hearing your voice, do I? You have been a waste of my time."

Herod looked at the chief priests and loudly spoke out to them, "And the Sanhedrin has condemned this man. But for what? He is as harmless as a little lamb."

Herod looked at Jesus and said, "Well Rabbi, I had hoped that you would have been more entertaining to be with. But you weren't. You were a disappointment. So, let us see what fun we can have with you now. You supposedly have made claims to be a King over the people, not only my people, but Pilates people too, I presume. But you don't act like a king. You don't talk like a king. You don't talk at all and you are certainly not dressed like a king, are you? Here, let me talk to you as one ruler to another. But for that to happen my friend, you need to at least keep up appearances or your followers may begin to wonder if your claims are true. I am worried about you. Let me give you something more fitting to wear so that your boast may have some resemblance of being true. Bring in one of my robes, a truly nice one, so that he may wear it like the King that he is. And be quick about it!"

One of the court attendants left the room and returned with an elegant robe and it was put on Jesus.

Herod sized him up and said, "There, now with this fine robe perhaps you will convince someone regarding your royal claims, and based on my experience, you need all the help you can get. Not that it is going to help you, but let me indulge myself here, won't you. Now, all of you, what do you say to the new King?" Herod looked at his soldiers and waved them over to his side, "Say whatever you want to the King, entertain me, ha, ha, you know what I mean."

One soldier said, "So King, I serve Herod, what would you offer me if I leave his service and declared my allegiances to your Kingdom?"

147

And the next one said, "So King, are you going to be paying me my wages? Let me see your royal treasury? Does it have enough gold and silver in it to support your army?"

Herod took his turn too in mocking Rabbi Jesus, "Hail King of no one. Your dominion over the land is so small that I can't even see it and now I am wondering if it even exists. A king has an army. Where is yours? Why aren't your subjects mounting a campaign to rescue you?" Then Herod told the soldiers that they must bow down and praise him, which the men did with mocking remarks of their own. Finally, Herod told him, "Well, Rabbi, you didn't do my bidding and so I am not going to do anything for you either. You're the sorriest example of a king that I have ever known. I am not going to sentence you, punish you, or release you. From Pilate you came to me and to Pilate I am returning you." Then Herod called for his scribe and composed a letter to send to Pilate regarding his findings. He gave his orders, "Return this man, along with my letter to Pilate. And send him some of my reserve stock of wine as a gift to thank him for his consideration in sending the Rabbi to me."

Chapter Twenty
A New Trial Granted

Pilate was in his headquarters when Jesus of Nazareth was returned by Herod. Along with him came the same group of chief priests and their supporters, all lead by Rabsaris. These men had long since determined not to let the matter rest until they had exactly what they wanted, which was the death of the Rabbi. Pilate had hoped that Herod would have seen the case to its end and dealt with the Rabbi accordingly, rather than return him to his custody. The officer in charge of Herod's soldiers reported directly to the governor and handed him a letter from Herod. Along with him were two soldiers who brought in a large case of Herod's finest reserve stock wine. Pilate ordered that the Rabbi be held in chains in his prison yard for now.

Then he filled his chalice with the wine and he sat down to consider the letter, which he read most anxiously.

TO THE IMPERIAL GOVERNOR OF THE PROVENCE OF JUDEA
PONTIUS PILATE

YOUR MOST EXCELLENT GOVERNOR,

I THANK YOU GREATLY FOR ALLOWING ME THE OPPORTUNITY TO EXAMINE JESUS OF NAZARETH, WHO IS A SUBJECT OF MY JURISDICTION. I HAVE HEARD OF THIS MAN BEFORE WHO YOU HAVE POLITELY SENT TO ME. I HAVE FOR SOME TIME DESIRED TO MEET HIM BECAUSE HE HAS THE REPUTATION OF BEING AN INFLUENTIAL RABBI, A PROPHET, AND THE POWER TO HEAL THE SICK.

IF I MAY, I WILL PRESUME TO OFFER YOU SOME ADVICE REGARDING HIS CLAIM TO BEING SOME KIND OF A KING. HE TRUTHFULLY MAY HAVE SOME CLAIM TO BEING A MEMBER OF THE ROYAL LINEAGE OF THE HOUSEHOLD OF DAVID. HOWEVER, I HAVE LEARNED THAT THERE ARE MANY WHO ARE ABLE TO MAKE THIS CLAIM. I WOULD NOT TAKE HIM TOO SERIOUSLY IN THAT REGARDS. AS YOU KNOW THEIR LOCAL GOVERNMENT, AS ALLOWED BY THE SENATE, CONSISTS ONLY OF THE SANHEDRIN. THERE WAS NEVER A POWER SHARING AGREEMENT TO REINSTATE THEIR FORMER MONARCHY. FURTHERMORE, I DO NOT BELIEVE IT WOULD BE WISE TO GIVE CONSIDERATION TO THE REESTABLISHMENT OF THEIR MONARCHY. THAT WOULD REQUIRE EITHER THE DISMISSAL OF THEIR SANHEDRIN, OR AT LEAST SEVERELY LIMITING THEIR GOVERNING POWERS. IT COULD ALSO REQUIRE A POWER SHARING AGREEMENT WITH THEM, A MONARCH, AND ROME. THE MEMBERS OF THEIR ROYAL LINE WERE A VERY WAR LIKE PEOPLE, AND THEY COULD ONLY CAUSE GREATER CHALLENGES TO YOU, OVER YOUR RULE.

THERE IS A RELIGIOUS SUPERSTITION AMONG THEM ABOUT THEIR ARISING A SPECIAL KING, WHO IS CALLED THEIR MESSIAH. THIS MYTHOLOGICAL FIGURE IS SUPPOSED TO BE SOMETHING OF A PROPHET, WHO KNOWS ALL, INCLUDING THE FUTURE. I WOULD GIVE THIS CLAIM NO CREDENCE WHAT SO EVER.

LASTLY, I HAVE EXAMINED HIM AND FIND NO BASES FOR THE CHARGES THAT HAVE BEEN BROUGHT AGAINST HIM. HAD HE BEEN BROUGHT TO ME DIRECTLY BY THE CHIEF PRIESTS I WOULD HAVE RELEASED HIM FROM CUSTODY BECAUSE THEIR CHIEF PRIESTS WERE NOT ABLE TO MAKE A CASE AGAINST HIM. HOWEVER, AS YOU HAVE TURNED HIM OVER TO ME, I AM THEREFORE RETURNING HIM TO YOU.

WITH CORDIAL REGARDS,
HEROD ANTIPAS THE TETRARCH
IMPERIAL GOVERNOR OF THE PROVENCE OF GALILEE AND PEREA

Pilate held off tasting the wine because he wanted to get through the letter quickly, so he could see what Herod had written him. Pilate was very pleased about the content of the letter. In the past, he and Herod had behaved like enemies towards each other. Now he believed this situation created a good foundation for them to build a friendship upon. This new beginning gave him as sense of optimism and he sat back and tried a small taste of the wine, which he found exceedingly fine. He reread the letter slowly and was happy for Herod's advice to him. Being in no hurry to be treated abrasively by the chief priests again, he decided to sit back, kick back and enjoy the wine. He hoped that it would shield him from the coarse nature of those religious authorities waiting for him at the gates.

Having finished his wine, which he drank down to the last drop, he walked out to the gate and spoke with Jesus' accusers. Chief Priest Rabsaris tried to speak first, but the governor made a point of clearing his throat loudly and kept this up for the entire time Rabsaris carried on. The chief priest finally got the message when the governor stoutly looked him in the face. "I have examined the Rabbi and Herod has examined the Rabbi. Neither of us find any reason for him to be charged with a crime. Therefore, I will release him and be done with the matter."

Reacting to this, hotheaded Rabsaris, the more sensible Elamadad, and the somewhat reserved Kallahadad took turns rotating through and trying to wear Pilate down with their quick and insistent demands.

Rabsaris went first, "He is a criminal according to our Law! If he was not, we would not have brought him to you!"

"So, if he is a criminal according to your Law, I will have him punished according to your Law. He will be thrashed, and then I will be releasing him."

Elamadad asserted strongly, "We have a Law and according to our Law he must be punished more severely than that."

"You have the option of taking him back and punishing him yourselves, so long as you do not put him to death."

Kallahadad reminded the governor, "He deserves nothing less than death. This is why we have brought him to you, so that you may carry out his execution."

"If you want him punished then give him a lesser punishment than execution."

Rabsaris took his turn to speak, "We cannot do that! Our Law is very clear about it. Our Law does not provide a lesser punishment for his crimes. It demands the offender's death."

"He has done nothing deserving death and I have no reason to hold him any longer. I will release him."

All the chief priests and their growing number of supporters arriving from the Temple stood at his gate and objected to him being released. They were all protesting against the governor's plans by insisting that the case be further pursued. Now, none of them were Roman citizens, and so they had no guaranteed right to appeal to a higher Roman court to hear their case in the hopes of getting a conviction and a death sentence. So, they persisted with Pilate because they were determined to not let him drop the charges so easily.

Rabsaris lead off, "Governor, sir. I do not understand your reasons for acquitting this criminal." The truth was Rabsaris knew exactly why Pilate was prepared to release him. He knew full well that they had not presented a properly prepared case. But he was not going to let that stop him, so he resorted to playing ignorant and taking up a position of presupposing that it was Pilate who was without the insight that he possessed. "We have presented our case, which is a sound case and is undiminished even though you had not seen fit to carry out his condemnation. We are calling on you for this final step, which you have reserved for yourself."

Pilate was not about to act like a mindless fool because of Rabsaris' manipulation. "We have been through all this before! I will not simply carry out your wishes here. He has already been tried under Roman law. I have already ruled on it. You have not made your case against him and I cleared him of the charges."

Elamadad reasserted their position, "Governor, we still have a case to be made and we won't leave here until you hear all of it up to the final word. As we have said once before, I say again, if he wasn't guilty we would not have brought him to you."

Pilate wisely questioned what he was hearing. This twice made reference, 'If he wasn't guilty we would not have brought him to you just did not sit well with him the first time he heard. Now, it concerned him even more. He saw it as an evasion of the truth, one that was meant to mislead him, and he took that took personally. He wondered what it was that they didn't want him to uncover? He wondered if they had an ulterior motive for bringing this man to his courtroom. And he believed this because things simply did not add up correctly in his mind.

Pilate toyed with them projecting an eagerness that he did not actually possess. "Fine, fine. My court is open. You may present your case."

The chief priests smiled brightly showing their new optimism about the governor's willingness to continue the case. But this willingness to proceed was part of the governor's tactic against them. He had no intention of letting himself be forced into condemning a man who was innocent.

"Let's begin immediately so that we can be done with this as soon as possible. What are you charging him with?"

Rabsaris stepped up and stood tall as he loudly proclaimed, "Jesus of Nazareth is charged with forbidding tax payments to the emperor and claiming to be our Messiah. That he is widely travelled and his teachings have sown discord everywhere. He perverts our people and turns their hearts against our leadership and our government."

Pilate chuckled over that last charge and countered what the chief priest said, "And don't forget that he has done this all the way from Galilee to Judea."

Elamadad, who was working as Rabsaris' second in presenting the case added, "I am adding the charge that he resisted arrest. When he was taken into custody, his followers drew swords and fought with our guards."

"Yes, I heard about that."

Rabsaris cheerfully added, "Yes, and if it hadn't been for our guard's quick response, a battle would have surely broken out. We even suspect that his followers are now gathering in secret to fight for his release."

Pilate responded to him, "What I heard was that the Rabbi did not resist and that he stopped the fight immediately."

Rabsaris retorted, "Not from our people you didn't hear that. We were right there. We know what happened."

"My people were right there too. They know what happened. They told me the truth and they have no reason to lie to me, Rabsaris."

Rabsaris cowered and his face grew red with embarrassment. He quietly worried that he had just injured his reputation by his little lie.

Pilate directed the hearing to the original charges that had been brought. "As you know I must judiciously review all cases that you bring to me, retrying them according to Roman law and using our procedures. This is especially true when you are asking for the death penalty to be administered. So, let us begin with charges you first made against him. You said you had convicted him of forbidding tax payments to the emperor. But, let me ask you this. Does your nation actually have a law that states your people must pay the emperor's tax? I thought that it was Rome's law that enforced the tax."

Elamadad spoke out, "Just a moment governor, let me confer with the others." Now he crowded together with the other chief priests and scribes who were experts in the Law. After they finished their discussion he paused to compose in his head what he would say as he turned and faced the governor, "No, we actually don't have a law such as this. We felt, however, that it was prudent for us to charge him with this crime to preserve the good will between our nation and the empire."

Pilate unenthusiastically responded, "Ah ha, you did, did you? You actually felt that way, all of you? I will rule on this count. You don't have a law like that, so you cannot convict him of breaking it. Secondly, you are not a judicial body of the empire, so you cannot convict him of breaking our laws. Next, you have accused him of perverting your nation, that he claimed to be your Messiah, and that he turns the hearts of your people against your leadership."

Rabsaris, Elamadad and Kallahadad all stood to attention and responded in unison, "That is correct governor."

"So, next, let me hear from your first witness who will substantiate these charges."

Abihuel, a scribal lawyer, stepped forward, "I will speak as a witness to what I heard directly myself. Today I heard from several witnesses who testified against him saying things against our Temple which has turned the hearts of our people against us."

The governor took offense at this secondhand report, but he did not want to show it. Instead he wanted to mock that lawyer by it. "So, let me get this right. You heard a man say these things yourself?"

"Yes."

"What was his name?"

"His name?"

"Yes, his name?"

"Well, I did not actually meet him I just heard him testify."

"And you heard him firsthand."

"I did."

"Which means you are giving me a secondhand report."

"Well, yes. But it is an accurate report."

"So, your law actually allows for the admission of secondhand reports in trials were the death penalty is being considered?"

"Why no, not at all. We require that there be two witnesses that must agree on all points."

"Yeah, and Roman law does not allow for secondhand witnesses either. Do you have among your growing numbers out there any witnesses who can give me a firsthand report?"

Abihuel responded, "Just one moment governor."

The lawyer and the three chief priests conferred together.

Rabsaris stood forward and addressed the governor, "Abihuel is not merely giving you testimony. He is offering testimony that has already stood up in our court and been accepted."

"Let me ask you this. How do you define hearsay?"

Abihuel was still standing in the forefront of their delegation and quickly spoke, "It is a secondhand report."

"Yes, it is and that is all that you have offered me here today. Let me hear from your witnesses, the ones who actually heard him say these things or witnessed him doing something criminal. Preferably the same ones who accused the Rabbi in the trial you held. The ones who heard him with their own ears, you know, that sort of thing."

Bacchus, another lawyer asserted, "This Rabbi...", he was using a sarcastic voice indicating he did not think much of Jesus, "he has also ...."

Pilate stopped him immediately because he questioned in his mind if this man, being a lawyer, was an actual witness or not. "Excuse me. Are you one of those who sat in judgement against Rabbi Jesus? Or, are you an actual witness to one of his supposed crimes?"

Bacchus was not a witness, but in his arrogance he was not going to let that stop him from speaking. "I am not a witness, but I can faithfully recount what I have heard from those who offered testimony and made accusations."

"We have been through this once already. Do you really expect me to allow the introduction of hearsay and secondhand reports into my proceedings?" The chief priests and lawyers were silent. Pilate assertively spoke, "No, you don't allow it, and I don't allow it. Do you understand that this is the time of his trial? Do you have any witnesses here, right now, among yourselves, who can testify about what they actually heard the Rabbi say?"

Rabsaris though usually very outspoken was silent. For him to admit to such a thing, of not having a single witness, was not something he could easily admit to.

Finally, after a long pause, Elamadad answered Pilate, "They were dismissed."

Pilate explained, "What!? You had witnesses here who could have testified against the Rabbi and you dismissed them?"

Bacchus gladly told him, "We had witnesses, but they were dismissed after the trial we had. We did not feel it was necessary that they be held over and brought to this trial. But, we are able to produce witnesses that will give testimony to these things."

"That is not what I asked lawyer." Pilate used the same kind of sarcastic tone Bacchus used just a moment ago. "Just simply answer my question. Do you have any witnesses here, right now?"

Reluctantly he answered. "No. They are not here at this time. They were up all night. They were very tired so they were dismissed."

"Great! In your trial you used witnesses who were deprived of their sleep and overly tired, and in a capital case no less. How very professional of you all. Apparently, I have higher standards when it comes to applying the law in my courtroom than you do in yours. That being so, it is best that I do not simply carry out your sentence against him."

Many of the priests and the rest of their company too were terribly embarrassed by this. They looked down and around when they heard it, as if it did not bother them or were ignorant of its implications.

"Gentleman, this trial is underway right now! And at your insistence no less. Apparently, many of you were up all night preparing for this case so that you could get this conviction and sentence him to die. But despite the great lengths and many measures you have taken to be here today, you just happened to forget that you needed witnesses. What a sorry bunch of fools you are!"

That touched a raw nerve for Rabsaris. He felt like Pilate was shaming him as if he were a child, which he was. He protested and tried to push the case forward, "We are witnesses to what we heard him say."

"Okay, let me get this right. You were his judges who presided over the case, right? How in the name of Mars did you think you could be both judges then and witness against him now? If you wish to be a witness now, I rule that you must first overturn the sentence of death that you made against him earlier because you were his judges then. And if you were to do that, then you will not be able to bring him to me as a convicted man, will you?"

As Pilate took time to ponder this case, there was something they said that did not sit right with him, so he paused and thought about it before addressing them again. "You said the witnesses were up all night. Why would they have needed to be up all night? Was there a nighttime trial? You did not try him at night against your own laws, did you?"

Bacchus, who had not presented himself very well so far quickly spoke up, "He was tried after the sun came up."

"Ah, ha. Am I missing something here, or are you just not telling me? What occurred during the night?"

"It was merely pretrial activities."

"Of course. But then is it wise for any judicial authority to short themselves on their sleep before a trial, especially when it is a capital case?"

Rabsaris was not going to let their earlier trials be criticized, or their current one be derailed. And, both he and the Temple leaders were getting very worked up, "He must be punished properly for his crimes. We insist on no less than that. It would be too great of an injustice for us to allow this case to be dismissed. We must see it through to the end. He must be put to death."

Bacchus spoke up in defense of their case too, "We have sent messengers to bring our witness here at once."

"Some of you are lawyers, are you not? You do understand how things work here, don't you? Our laws, and court procedures are very similar. Under Roman law, as well as your own, you must first produce witnesses who testify and make accusations against him. These are used to bring charges against him. But you would like to skip having witnesses and their testimony, have me confirm the charges anyway, and go straight to the punishment. Now, after the witnesses and statement of charges, there is what we call in Latin, the Cognitio. This is where I make my inquiry into the charges to see if they are true or not. If the charges are true then I find him guilty and determine the fitting punishment. If it is determined by me that you have not made your case against him, the charges are dismissed. Or, I may even go so far as to decide that he is not guilty, or one step further and find him innocent. In either of these three finding, I release the accused from custody. But this you should know already. Or, do I need to instruct you further in the law, yours or Rome's? And so I am left wondering how it is that you have come to me, with a capital case, that is so poorly prepared. This is very unlike all of you."

The religious authorities ranted and carried on, shouting to Pilate, "He is guilty and must die! Crucify him, crucify, crucify, crucify him."

Pilate stood before them, unshaken by their up roaring, and he raised his hand calling for their silence. "Also, you should know that the report my spies brought to me is that he did endorse paying the emperors taxes. His words were something to the effect of, 'Give unto Caesar, that which is Caesars.' So, on that charge you brought against him, you have lost much of your credibility before me."

Rabsaris was about to rebuke Pilate severely by giving him a piece of his mind, but Elamadad stepped in front of him and quietly insisted that he needed to get his anger in check and let his own calmer disposition handle it with diplomacy. "Rumors abound governor, but truth and consistency among them does not."

Rabsaris, still steaming over Pilate's rebuttal of him, boldly tried to rebuff him, "Let me give you a little bit of free advice governor. Don't take his claims to be our Messiah lightly. We are suspicious that he may have been raising an army and building a fortress tower. He spoke publicly of both in his parables. That is a direct threat to your government and to Rome."

"His parables were taught as allegories. He used figures of speech to get his message across. There is a limit to how much they translate into real life. You cannot use them to prove treason or sedition."

Pilate's face showed that he did not take the chief priests choice of words or tone well, so Elamadad moved the discussion forward to keep it from being weighed down by their prejudices against each other. "What we are trying to establish here is that the Rabbi is guilty of sedition and treason because he wants to establish himself as a ruler over us, and in opposition to you and Rome!"

Pilate, "So you say. But I have already examined him privately on that count and from what he himself said to me, he is not guilty of sedition, treason, or any other crimes for that matter."

Rabsaris insisted, "We have a case against him and we will see our case through so that he is put to death, governor."

"Yes, I understand that you believe that. And now I will rule on this case right now. Your witnesses should have been here before we got started, not arriving during the trial, or after things have concluded. You have no case against him. One Roman governor has already found that there was no basis for the charges you brought against him. But, since you are demanding a verdict from me, I find him not guilty of all charges. Gentleman, we are done here." And with that said, Pilate turned smartly away from them and with all the glory of Rome in his strides, he marched into his headquarters.

Chapter Twenty-One
Jesus of Nazareth or Jesus Bar-Abbas

At any given hour, of any given day, people would gather at the Praetorium's gate to make requests of the governor. It could be for justice over matters of crimes against them that went unpunished, to report abuse by his soldiers, or for the release of a loved one from prison. When Pilate had the time and the patience for it, he went to the gate to hear some of these requests. When it was reasonable, he would grant a few of the people what they wanted. This was not an uncommon practice among all rulers in the empire. These mercies that he would show went a long way to pacify the anger of the conquered people, and Pilate did it for the purpose of promoting goodwill among them. In Judea, it was well known that on their high religious days he was more likely to be generous about these requests.

It was about halfway past the tenth hour that there gathered a crowd of people at Pilate's gate. They came in the hopes that the Roman governor would grant them their requests for mercy. He came out from his headquarters to meet with them and the people cheered as he waved to them. Not that they held him in high regard, they were just going through the motions of honoring him in order to win his favor. Pilate knew this was true of them, but he did enjoy the attention as well as the favor they showed him, even if it was superficial. He waved to them again and the people cheered. He smiled brightly as he approached the gate. After they quieted down, he spoke to them, "People of Jerusalem, it is good to see so many of you here today and to hear your voices cheering. My hopes are that you are enjoying the celebration of your festival. As I have done in the past, I will again forgive the sentence of one of my prisoners, grant him clemency and release him from my custody."

The people cheered on and a few of them called out the names of those that they wished to have the governor release, but there was no consensus among them. Some called out for a man named Peresh. A woman cried out for the release of her only son and claimed that she was a widow. But there was no majority among them. And another group called out for Bar-Abbas.

Now Bar-Abbas, whose sir name means *son of the father*, had led a popular revolt against Pilate. It was all because the governor, rather than using money from his Roman tax, had compelled the Temple's leaders to pay from their treasury for one of his civic improvements. It was an aqueduct to increase the fresh water supply coming into their city. Now the Judeans had no national treasury, but their equivalent to having a central bank was their Temple treasury. The vaults there were overflowing with an abundance of funds and it was no burden to anyone for the Temple's money to be used in this way. No one objected to the aqueduct, but the Temple leaders were upset about how it was financed. Their anger over this was also taken up by the people who became enraged over how it was paid for.

The Temple leadership strongly protested this use of their money. Even though they would take months to get there, they even sent letters of protest to the Senate in Rome and the emperor as well. They knew that their objecting this way would probably not do them any good. Rome was not in the habit of reimbursing their provinces for their own civic improvements. But at the very least, they wanted to smear Pilate's name before the people that he had to answer to for his actions. This would, they hoped, make Pilate less daring with them in the future.

In the end of this local power struggle over the aqueduct's financing, Pilate demanded the money of them and he compelled them to give it to him. So, for the religious leaders, it became a sacred matter for them and their dislike of the man was cemented into place. Now, as Pilate considered who he might set free from his prison, these leaders used this opportunity as a means of rubbing Pilate's face in that mess. It was Bar-Abbas, who was the only man to lead an armed uprising over the aqueduct, so they strongly supported him being released.

Now, when Bar-Abbas rioted, his fighters attacked Roman soldiers out in the countryside and in the city. However, they were no match for the professional fighting skills of the Romans. Even still one of Pilate's soldiers was murdered by Bar-Abbas himself. Though the people were glad for the trouble they caused the Romans, they kept that to themselves for fear of reprisals. This insurrectionist was, in the eyes of the Romans, a notorious criminal, but many of the people saw him as a local folk hero. Pilate was proud of what he had accomplished by building his aqueduct, but he was very grieved over the death of one of his soldiers. He took it personally when there was an uprising over it, and he came to vehemently hate this Bar-Abbas.

At the gate the people continued to call out many different names in the desperate hope that they could get their loved ones released. Pilate said, "Is there no agreement among you? Not even a simple majority that can be agreed to?"

As the people continued to call out he heard someone say Bar-Abbas' name again. Only this time they called him Jesus Bar-Abbas. That got his quick attention and it sent his

165

thoughts in another direction. He eagerly nodded his head, hoping to persuade the people into asking for the release of a different Jesus, Jesus of Nazareth. He raised his hands to them and waved for them to quiet down, "I have in my prison right now, the man called Jesus of Nazareth who is a Rabbi. Many of you know who he is. Do you wish for me to release him to you?" He said this because the priests had been after him since shortly after sun up to execute him. He hoped that the people would take up his suggestion and demand his release because this Rabbi was incredibly popular among them. Then he would be obligated to release him and his problem would be solved. He expected that the power of the people's popular sentiment would surpass the Sanhedrin's condemnation of the Rabbi. Then he would not have to answer to the chief priests over releasing the Rabbi. The people's choice would be honored by him. That, however, would not turn out to be the case and it was all about to backfire on Pilate.

Many of the chief priests and scribes, and even workers from the Temple were present as they followed their case against the Rabbi. They did not like the fact that Pilate was using his public position to influence their own people. Now the chief priests knew about Jesus Bar-Abbas. After all, it was him who had, without their endorsement, championed their cause against Pilate regarding their treasury's money. They knew how much Pilate hated this Bar-Abbas for what he had done. The man was Pilate's most hated prisoner and he wanted this murdering insurrectionist crucified. So Rabsaris took this unexpected opportunity to manipulated things their way. Jesus of Nazareth was Rabsaris' most hated prisoner. He wanted him put to death above all else. So, he and the other chief priests all called out for the release of Jesus Bar-Abbas.

They shouted nonstop, "Not Jesus of Nazareth, but Jesus Bar-Abbas."

They also encouraged the people to join in with them. In their positions as religious leaders, they were considered trustworthy and they held great sway with the people. They told them about the crimes they had convicted Jesus of, and they especially played up their claim that Jesus had threatened to destroy their Temple, which angered them greatly. Then the people readily condemned Rabbi Jesus and called for Jesus Bar-Abbas to be released.

But Pilate said to them, "Bar-Abbas is to be crucified for insurrection and murder!"

The people shouted, "We don't care! We want him released and no other!" And they all became very agitated as they shouted out for his release.

Pilate called out to the people in disgust, "Now I am releasing one prisoner for you, for I am honor bound to do it! But know this, I would sooner kill him with my own sword in front of you then release him. He murdered one of my soldiers! He deserves to die a completely miserable death on a cross!"

The crowd persisted in making their demands, and Pilate offered to release Jesus of Nazareth one more time. The crowd rejected that offer and again insisted on the release of Jesus Bar-Abbas, and Pilate asked them, "Then what should I do with Rabbi Jesus?"

The religious leaders stirred up the people and they called out, "Crucify him!"

Pilate saw that his words did not influence the people as he had expected. They did not care that Bar-Abbas had murdered one of Rome's soldiers. It was that Jesus, the one who rose up against the empire that they hated being occupied and oppressed by, that they wanted released. Now their protests grew stronger and Pilate feared that they might riot. They were crowding against the gate and shaking it. Some were raising their fists up and down in the air, and others were picking up stones to throw. At the same time, Pilate's soldiers were alerted to the situation and many prepared themselves should they have a fight on their hands.

For Pilate, he sulked over this irony, that he was being forced to release a murderer who had led riots in order to prevent another riot from breaking out. And by exchanging one for the other, he would be sending Jesus of Nazareth, an innocent man, to the cross that had been meant for Jesus Bar-Abbas. And he thought to himself, that in the end, he would be committing murder himself.

In this short time that past the people continued to become more and more agitated, even though he had agreed to this demand of theirs. Others were also coming to the gate to see what was going on and joined in their protesting. Pilate looked down at his own sword and he knew that if he drew it, the people would riot. He knew that if he struck down Bar-Abbas there would be a massive riot. So, he looked at one of his officers and gave him his order, "Go to the prison and have Jesus Bar-Abbas released and let him go free." Then the people cheered for Pilate, as if he was somehow their hero.

Now there were three criminals who were in the prison yard that were scheduled to be crucified that morning. Due to the chief priests pressing their case against Rabbi Jesus so strongly, Pilate had delayed giving the final order for them to be taken for execution. Two were thieves. The third one, Jesus Bar-Abbas, was the most dangerous of them. He knew he was to be crucified and so he acted very unpredictably and dangerously toward the soldiers. For that reason, he was bound in leg irons, his wrists were cuffed, and he was chained to a tall wooden post that was used to thrash prisoners on.

As the soldiers approached Bar-Abbas he tried to charge them and made sounds like a wild animal. He knew he had nothing to lose and did not fear them. He faced the soldiers with a cruel smile and acted like he was ready to fight them. The soldiers were none too fond of the man because they had been among the ones who chased him down and captured him when he was trying to lead a bloody uprising. Bar-Abbas thought that since he was going to die, he would not go willingly, not without a fight anyway. These soldiers did not speak Aramaic, and Bar-Abbas did not understand their Latin. A nearby officer came over and spoke in Aramaic to him telling him he was being set free. He was completely surprised by this and wondered at first if it was a trick. So, the officer explained to him what Pilate had agreed to. To please the chief priests and the others at his gate he ordered his release. Bar-Abbas was in shock and still unbelieving of what he ears heard. This good news he was given, that his sentence of death for his crimes had been forgiven him and he was to be set free was incredible. He laughed, as if it was a joke, then he laughed in joy. In his mind, his thoughts wavered back and forth, suspicious it was a cruel trick, or that it was really true that he would soon be freed.

The soldiers moved in close to Bar-Abbas and unfettered their prisoner, removing the shackles and chains from his hands and feet. Their prisoner then became very jubilant as he walked out of that hellish prison. Now they simply escorted him to the gate and he walked out a free man.   There he was quickly joined by his family and friends who were waiting there in the desperate hope of some incredible miracle happening, just like this one. Now they embraced a euphoric Bar-Abbas with joy and hurriedly left the Praetorium.

Chapter Twenty-Two
Preponderance of the Evidence

Now the chief priests continued in their vigilant presence at the gate and they pressed their case against the governor again. They called out to him saying, "You must now crucify the Rabbi and send him to the cross."

Pilate was fuming mad over the way they had just tried to manipulated him. He shook his head in disbelief over what they had accomplished. They had used his tactic of using the popular demands of the people to achieve a goal against him. They used their powerful control that they held as religious leaders over the people. Jesus Bar-Abbas, a man who the chief priests cared nothing for, was released as a free man and cleared of all the charges because of them. It was irony at its worse. The man who lead a terrible uprising, who committed murder, who was to be lifted-up on a cross that very same day, walked out a free man. This other prisoner of Pilate's, Jesus of Nazareth, whom he believed was not guilty of all the charges railed against him, was condemned to die by the Judean court. Now they expected him to confirm their verdict against him and crucify him. Even though the Temple officials were there expecting to reengage him, he simply turned a deaf ear to them and walked into his headquarters. It was there that he would brood over the release of Bar-Abbas and ruminate over the case against the Rabbi.

Once he was out of sight and there was no audience before him, his exterior of fearlessness and the all-wise ruler quickly faded. The morning was only half over with, but already he felt as if he had not slept in days. His body ached and his mind struggled. He removed his helmet and set it and his sword down on his desk. Then he removed his

171

restrictive body armor. His head was spinning from going round and round with those chief priests. He understood that for this case that he was presiding over, he needed to employ all his learning and experience. He needed to reconsider it legally as well as politically and militarily, giving thought to what all the possible outcomes could be. Pilate was well educated according to Roman standards, which made him most knowledgeable. He was also a man with much political experience which made him a wise man, or so he wanted to believe. He was a man devoted to much thought, and now he would consider all the possibilities to their final ends.

As a military commander he was highly disciplined and was well trained as a tactician and strategist. Strategy was, of course, the general plan for battle, and tactics were the minute to minute modifications and adaptations to the plan that were needed as that fight unfolded. Victory was always the goal. These principles he applied to his interactions frequently and most often in his encounters with the religious authorities. That was not what he wanted though. His first choice was to use his training and success as a government administrator which had earned him the high honor and title of Perfect. He believed that if he just employed the powers of his mind and reason that he would find a favorable outcome to this. He formulated his plan. He reasoned that with the law on his side and upheld by the strength of his militia, that he could navigate through this and bring about a solution that everyone could live with.

As he took stock of what had already played out, he reminded himself of the hope that Herod would have disposed of this case and how that did not play out for him. He had also hoped that he could have used the sway of popular demand and that the people might have called for the release of the Rabbi. This not only failed, it failed miserably because a murderer walked free.

He looked about the room searching for something, searching both his mind and the room for something to guide him. There were many law books, but in those he was already more than well studied. There were many letters of correspondence from Rome that instructed him in how to rule over this people. There were his commissioning papers, the order appointing him as governor over the small province. These he once held proudly in his hand, now he was not sure if he should have accepted this appointment. All these documents he knew full well, he could even recite many of them verbatim. He was to collect the Roman tax, maintain a civil and productive society, provide law and order, suppress rebellion and punish lawbreakers, provide civic improvements to such things as the roads and bridges, provide clean water, and promote agriculture. Still, none of these documents offered him any of the guidance he desperately needed on how to close out this case that was brought to him.

He looked at two shrines in his office. One was of the divine god, Augustus Caesar, and the other was of the goddess Iustitia. He was not religious though. It was his wife who was the devout one, though she was not someone who accepted all that the pagan world offered to her. He had little faith in the gods, but he did claim to believe in Mars and a few of the other gods from the imperial cult. Yet in his life, he had no experiences that tied his infrequent prayers to the outcome of anything going in his favor. Therefore, he did not believe that the god's heard or answered his prayers, and he wondered if they could. What he believed in was politics and the great things that could be accomplished by it. It was through politics that he had furthered his career so well. He feared very little in his life but among those few things, he feared the thing he believed most in. He feared the political influences that worked against him. These could bring him down and even take his life.

This case had not brought him to his wits end yet, not at all. But he did believe that he needed to consider something beyond his normal routine. Mars was the Roman god of war and he was victorious and ruled over a vast and far reaching empire. But he was also a god of agriculture and it was time for the harvest of the first fruits of the spring wheat. This meant that Mars was strong at that time of year. On the other hand, the God of these people was considered by them to be the God of everything. He was invisible and everywhere all of the time. Therefore, in this conflict, he wondered who would prevail. Would it be the Roman god or their God, if they even would have anything to do with it?

He saw the need to consider something from beyond his typical sphere of influences as he weighed the merits of the case and pondered the charges that had been brought against the Rabbi. There was in his office a shrine of Caesar Augustus. He had it brought into his office because Augustus was a great politician and emperor. He admired the man and it was important to Pilate to remember him and follow in his ways. Now, while Augustus still lived, it had been proposed that he be declared to be a divine god. Augustus strongly opposed this suggestion and so it never did happen. However, after his death he could not object to this and so it was officially declared that he was divine, and he was made into a god. Pilate did not see it that way though, but for political reasons he kept his opinion to himself. True, the man was great among great men, but he was mortal, and his death was the final word on that point, having proved it beyond a reasonable doubt. So, after he died, Pilate believed it to be very contradictory to make the claim that he was a god, all of whom are immortal. Pilate believed that what was a popular rumor while he lived, that Augustus was divine, was proven to be impossible by his death.

As the governor turned to his shrine and admired the memory of the man, he began to imagine what it would have like to have an audience with him while he still lived. What would he say to him? Could he ask him for advice and legal counsel on this case that he was trying? Would the emperor agree to hear the points of law in the case? If he agreed, how would he begin? What would he say first? Pilate began to think of himself as arguing the case before him, acting in the defense of the Rabbi. He let his thoughts run and he pretended in his mind to be using the most eloquent voice he could muster. He considered how he would use the technical and exacting legal phrases of Latin to counter the Rabbis' accusers. He would create doubt over the legality of the trial they held, telling of his suspicions that it was a nighttime trial, showing that it was illegally conducted in the first place. He would neutralize their testimony because they were presenting hearsay instead of producing witnesses. He imagined what Caesar would ask in the trial and how the two of them would enjoy great professional rapport. He visualized how facing the chief priests in the highest court of the empire would be the greatest legal battle of his life. Their cunning ways and their devotion to practicing the law would challenge him in new ways that he could not even foretell. And in the end, it would be clear beyond a doubt that this Rabbi Jesus was innocent of all charges railed against him. He could almost hear the verdict being declared, 'not guilty.' That would end it all because Caesar had ruled. He would have saved an innocent man's life, won his case, and proven himself to possess one of the greatest legal minds in his day.

This exercise, though only imagined in his own mind, was a great relief to Pilate. He could see it so clearly now and he trusted that his thoughts had faithfully enacted Caesar Augustus resulting in a true verdict. *'It was helpful to do this,'* he thought to himself. "Hah," he laughed aloud and then quickly looked around the room to see if anyone was watching. The room was empty, other than himself.

Pilate believed that he had found that something that he needed to aid his skills and resources. It was a vivid imagination that was led by free thought. In his newfound experience, he looked around this office and took notice of things there that he hadn't had the time to pay much attention to in the past. There was a new shrine that had been given to him. She was called Iustitia. She stood high and mighty on a pedestal and was more than head and shoulders above everyone, including the shrine of Caesar. Pilate had no time for her even if Caesar Tiberius declared her to be the very image and god of virtue and justice. Women were not educated, and they were most certainly not trained in the law. When they tried to extend their influence into politics it was dangerous. Too often they upset the delicate balance of power. Women, the Roman cult claimed, gave birth to the gods, and though he hated to admit it, they were sometimes gods themselves.

Now what she looked like caught Pilate's interest. She was a beautiful woman, but she was blindfolded. That he chuckled about thinking, *'Yes, frequently women have no idea what in the world is going on around them.'* He continued to study the symbolism of this god. She held a

176

set of scales in her left hand, which he had been told was the unbiased measuring of the strength and merits of a legal case; both those matters in support of and in opposition to a verdict of innocence or guilt. In her right hand she held a sword because she defended these matters with her life and upheld them against all enemies of the truth. He told himself she cannot wield a sword of that weight and size to save her own life, let alone defend justice. However, he was impressed with her holding the set of scales. Then he reconsidered her blindfold and came to believe that she could offer an unbiased verdict. Still, he had his reservations about her because she was holding the scales in her left hand. It was a widely held superstition, held to by some with religious devotion, that left-handed people were by nature sinister. Therefore, anything done by the left hand alone was by its very nature evil. That gave him an ominous feeling about putting his trust in her.

Pilate now tried something out of the ordinary again as he approached her. As he had done with Augustus he would imagine conversing with her. For fear of being over heard, he began by keeping his conversation with her in his head alone. *'What say you, goddess Iustitia? I have pending before me a most difficult case and so I call on you for your wise council.'* Pilate's mind did not produce for him a conversation such as the one he had just had with Caesar. Perhaps that was because of his attitude toward women in politics and matters of the law. Perhaps it was his general disbelief in what the gods were supposed to be capable of. He looked upward to her as though she was real and this time he said aloud, "What say you, Iustitia? Did you not hear me? Did you not rule over my case just now before our Emperor, the great Augustus?" Because of her silence to him he smirked, "I thought as much would happen before you." Now it could be called a coincidence, or it could be called an answer, but Pilate could not deny what happened next. A gentle breeze must have passed overhead and dislodged a cluster of dust from the shrine. The currents of air brought it down in a slow moving, swooping spiral, round and round as it made its way down, until it slowed and landed at his feet. Pilate first took offense at this. Not at the goddess though, but at his housekeeper who was trained to keep things more than immaculate in his office. Then he thought it to be laughable, that it should happen at that exact moment. He called out to her, "What answer is this my lady? It is not a verdict but a riddle that you have given to me this day. Are you more oracle than goddess?"

At the sound of his voice his attendant came into the room to see what the governor needed. It was rather surprising to him to see his commander standing before the shrine and talking to it. He had never been known to do this in the past. Upon seeing him there he bowed his head in embarrassment and turned to leave the room, but Pilate asked him to stay. He felt he owed his servant an explanation and said, "A cluster of dust has drifted down from our lady of justice here." Now he wondered, why did he ever bother with offering an explanation to a lowly servant? He felt he needed to redeem himself from such an action, lest he leave the lowly man with the wrong impression, that he mattered that much to the governor. "Could you inform the housekeeper that he needs to attend to my office more thoroughly, both high and low. I do not care to have these trivial distractions diverting my attention away from the weightier matters of governing these people." His servant answered him, "Yes, my lord." And Pilate dismissed him.

He took another look upward and reflected again over her blindfold and he thought, *'Not only is she blind, but she is deaf to my prayers and a mute who cannot answer me anyway.'* As he walked away he realized that he had used the word prayer to describe his imagined conversation with Iustitia. This was so unlike him. He sat to think about his case. *'I have never spoken to the gods about such an important matter before.'* As his thoughts continued to pour out he fretted, *'I have a hard-enough case to decide here. Why did I invoke the gods? If they were to have heard me and taken an interest in this case, who could help me then? I have no patron god who would rally to my cause. I fear that by calling on them, even mocking Iustitia, that they will come into his world, involve themselves in this case, and make matters all the worse for me with their meddling, and one of them is a woman!'*

He laughed to himself thinking that now the man who did not take much stock in the gods should worry this much about them. They were the inventions of the priests who claimed to serve them. Those priests used them to control the people's superstitions and their lives. Now, here, his time with these two gods was somehow so very real to him, more than ever before, but still he gave them very little credit for being able to accomplish anything. Paradoxically, though he didn't know it as such, he had spoken with the Son of God and was remiss to not have asked him what he wanted done with his case.

Now he wondered why the chief priests took such a great chance when they gave the Rabbi the one sentence they could not carry out themselves? They knew that it was not assured that he would confirm and carry out their capital punishment sentence. They knew if they sentenced him in their own court to a lessor punishment, that they could have at least carried that out unhindered.

As he began to draw his conclusions, he determined to find a way through this. By the powers of his mind and reason, he assured himself that he would bring it all to a rightful ending. He determined that his concession in this courtroom battle would not be to send the Rabbi to his death. Instead, even though he was not guilty by Roman standards of law, he would forego that, and he would offer to thrash him according to the Law of Moses. He felt that if he conceded on this count and used their Law, it would give him the upper hand that would lead to a final victory. He hoped that by making this offer the priests would have no choice but to agree to it and leave. This way he could also avoid having the order carried out and he could quietly release the man. If they stayed, he would issue the order, have him thrashed, and that would be the end of it.

His only other worry was another uprising. He had initially worried Jesus' followers would rise-up and fight. But, as Jesus had told him, his Kingdom was not of this world and they would not be rising up to fight for his release. However, he knew that Jesus had also told him that his followers would not rise-up to keep him from being turned over to him. What if he was to send the Rabbi to his death? Would his followers rise-up then? That aside, he was now worried about the religious leaders who were stirring up their people at his gate. If they became agitated enough they might riot. And he had just released Bar-Abbas without punishing him whatsoever. What if he was to rise-up again, or simply send his followers to join in with the chief priests? This could lead to a terrible riot. The people in the city were celebrating their deliverance from Pharaoh and bondage in Egypt. With those memories aroused among the people, with the population of the city being at a high point for the festival, it could become a widespread riot. But if that were to happen he was already prepared with a contingency plan. He had brought thousands of soldiers into the city and stationed them everywhere. He had stationed more just outside the city for that very possibility. His Cohort in his headquarters alone was nearly 800 soldiers strong.

As he came to the end of his review of the case, he reminded himself that he had the authority and the means to do whatever he needed to do. He was the governor, clothed in great power, and with the might of his soldiers, his decision would be final, and it would be carried out. He had considered his many options, which were fewer in number than he was comfortable with. But armed with these, he took confidence in himself, believing that he would resolve the situation. As he prepared to go out and announce his decision, he redonned his armor, put on his sword and held the hilt of its handle firmly in hand. Then he tucked his helmet with its high standing red plume of feathers under his left arm. Standing tall he faced the doorway and marched out to meet again with Rabsaris and the rest of his company.

Chapter Twenty-Three
The High Priest's Garments

The number of people following and believing in Jesus had grown monumentally in the past few weeks. This began with the rapidly spreading news of how Jesus raised Lazarus back to life after he was four days dead and in his tomb. The Rabbi's fame became widely know because so many pilgrims who were traveling to Jerusalem for the festival passed through Bethany where Lazarus lived with his sisters. The people of that village were glad to tell them all what had happened there and the pilgrims gladly carried the miraculous news into the Holy City and they shared it with everyone they met.

In those days, Jesus came to the Temple to instruct the people every day. Their numbers grew and they were very devoted to his every word. Rabbi Jesus brought them hope for their futures and he spoke with authority, explaining the mysteries of the Scriptures in ways that everyone could understand. The Rabbi made practical what the religious leaders made obscure and burdensome.

On the day of the Passover the largest crowd ever had gathered to hear him, but he was nowhere to be found. Many of the people there had just arrived in the Holy City and had never seen him before, so they sought him out diligently, but to no avail. Though many looked for him that day, they did not find him, nor would they.

It was during that time that Caiaphas put on his high priestly garments. As he donned the robes Levites serving in the Temple helped him and chief priests stood nearby and looked on. They all marveled at the garments because they were of the very highest quality possible. They were made of pure linen, finely spun and perfectly tailored to fit him. Together they all flattered Caiaphas with praises about how wonderful he appeared.

Also, with him was his father-in-law, who stood nearby. Annas spoke to him in his cunning way, words of truth mixed with a little sarcasm and cynicism. "There now, you look the part. The people will have no idea about your doubts and worries. Your heart can also rest assured that soon this imposter supposing to be our Messiah will be crucified shortly, I'm sure of it. Then all your fears will cease, or so I hope. And what the people don't know, they don't need to know. They will admire you and show you high reverence when they see you wearing your finest robes with these elaborate gold trimming. They will love you when they see you with the lamb today. They will not know your inner thoughts or the secrets of your heart. So, smile when you are out there among them. Let the confidence you must project become a sense of security for them."

Caiaphas spouted back, "You're right. Every word you spoke, is true. But somehow, they do not ring true in my heart and mind. I hear a condescending spirit in your voice. At the same time you are telling me to do for the people what they need from me, I hear you speaking down to me."

"Funny how that works, isn't it?"

"No, not really. I have grown tired of your jabs, so why don't stop making them?

"Why should I stop? I like doing this to you too much."

"You ask why? You need to stop because if you don't, I will do something about it. Something that you won't like."

This was a first between the two. Caiaphas had been subservient to him ever sense he entered the priesthood. When they first met, Annas was the high priest and he was only a novice priest. Now, he was fed up with his father-in-law and the way he always took jabs at him. So he used this opportunity to rise to the occasion and put him in his place.

"Look old man, your day has passed. I don't care for your meddling in my responsibilities. I never have. If I need your help, or if I need your advice, I will ask for it. Until then just keep it to yourself."

Annas did not react to him the way he expected which was to become subservient to him. No, Annas had been anticipating this action from Caiaphas for some time.

So, Caiaphas demanded an answer from him. "Did you hear me old man?"

Annas simply looked at him and nodded in agreement. He did not mean it though and he would not abide by it. That was his nature, being passive-aggressive to get what he wanted.

Chapter Twenty-Four
The Thrashing

Pilate wanted to release Jesus and for more reasons than one. He wanted to free him because he was not guilty of the charges made against him by the chief priests. Herod had examined the Rabbi and found no reason to convict him of any crimes. If he convicted him, it could look like Herod had missed something when he heard his case and he did not want to put his colleague in that light. Neither did he want to look like he was incompetent in hearing the case. When he first heard the case he found there was no basis for the charges, and if he convicted him at this time, it would look like he ruled incorrectly in the first trial.

Now it was only at the unyielding insistence of the chief priests and scribes that the matter was further pursued. Then Pilate became convinced beyond the point of any doubt that the Rabbi was not guilty. More than that, he issued a stronger verdict in the Rabbi's favor, finding him not guilty of all the charges leveled against him. Jesus was not a troublemaker as far as the governor was concerned. On a personal level, he was glad to know that releasing Jesus would upset the chief priests, a lot. Though that was not a legal, or political matter, it was personal for him. One that Pilate took up against them but spoke to no one about. It was his personal vendetta against them for all the trouble they created in his life. However, up to this point in the ordeal, the religious authorities had not been willing to accept anything that Pilate had said or offered to do for them. Now, he hoped to satisfy them by acting in accordance with their Law, by punishing Jesus with a thrashing. He calculated that this halfway measure would pacify the religious leaders from the Temple. It was a compromise he was willing to make and he hoped the priests would settle for it as well.

Pilate knew that Moses had written in his final book of the Law that they were allowed to whip a person no more than forty lashes[8]. In practice it was their custom, that as a precaution to not accidentally go over that number, to whip a person no more than thirty-nine times. Less lashes could be given for lesser crimes, but for the greatest of offenses they delivered this modified maximum count, forty-save-one. It was out of respect for their local laws that the governor observed this practice. The belief behind this number was that forty lashes o more would definitely kill the person. So, thirty-nine lashes brought a person into the very shadow of death, but still not kill them. But, the truth be told, many died from much less than the thirty-nine lashes.

To have a man thrashed was also to humiliate him beyond description. It physically incapacitated him. It left him with deep gaping wounds, through the skin, down through the muscles, right down to the bones. At times the thrashing would slash open veins and arteries and they would bleed to death before it was complete or shorty there afterword. Those surviving the thrashing frequently suffered a massive infection and died. Those who survived were left with hideous scars to the back of their head, necks, backs, and down to their legs. Frequently, the wounds would not fully heal, leaving the person with painful and weeping wounds for the rest of their life. In every case, the person was left crippled, unable to stand up straight, and in constant pain. Emotionally, the traumatic experience of being so severely thrashed left the victim with unrelenting and frightful memories and nightmares.

---

[8] Deuteronomy 25:1-3

They were so crippled by it that they were unable to be employed or useful in anyway and dependent on others to care for their needs.

Pilate never did secure an agreement with the chief priest over his compromise. That did not stop him though, he simply went ahead with it. He was their ruler and he simply expected them, like it or not, to accept it. He hoped that once it was done he could parade the Rabbi out for them to see and that the butchery of it would be enough to get them to abandon their demands for his death, and then they would leave. At the gate with all of them there to witness it he issued the order to his officer, "Have the prisoner thrashed to the fullest measure!" He believed that by doing this he had done the right thing and saved this man from going to his death. He had a little smug smile on his face and he bounced as he strode back inside his headquarters to await word from his soldiers who would tell him that they had carried out his order.

Many of the soldiers in the Praetorium were witnesses to the drama that was playing out that morning between the religious authorities and their commander. They followed the manipulations being acted out. Still, they did not fully understand the weightier matters of law and politics, or of faith and the will of God. However, they did see the great emotions that were in play during his trial. They saw the sheer and unwavering determination of those who accused Jesus and the strength of mind and character of their commander, Pontius Pilate. These soldiers were not trained as diplomats or as administrators of the law, but as fighting men. They understood that when push came to shove they were the ones who stepped in and provided the shove, and they were the world's greatest professional soldiers.

187

The Rabbi had simply been held in custody by a couple of soldiers further back in the open courtyard this whole time because Pilate expected to be releasing him at any moment. However, now Jesus was moved into the prison's courtyard where thrashings were carried out. Pilate had his agenda for thrashing Jesus and the officer in charge of the prison had his. This man had to deal directly with the discipline of his soldiers who bore much anger over being stationed in Judea. They despised the people, they hated their food and their restrictive customs that they unwaveringly devoted themselves to. They detested their God, the one they claimed was the only True God and they hated being told their many gods were no gods at all. The soldiers did not have any respect for the religious authorities who ruled over the people. They despised having to accommodate this people's religious observances. Though the people feared the soldiers they also looked down upon them as if they were animals. The soldiers had their pride, they were the ones who had conquered the Mediterranean world. They were revered, feared and envied everywhere in all the world, everywhere except just not in Judea. This sense of exclusivity, of the Romans and their sense of eminence, and the Judeans and their sense of prominence, all multiplied and compounded each other's sense of animosity against the other. This gave birth to a hatred in the hearts of the soldiers against them. This was then focused at any authority of the Judean people and even more harshly at their prisoners who had broken Roman law. This was particularly true regarding Bar-Abbas, who Pilate had just released. That brought their own blood to a boil, that this murdering insurrectionist should escape his own punishment and go out as a free man.

These soldiers were the ones who, at Pilate's order, had fought at sword point to put down a riot and captured Bar-Abbas. He and his rioters had injured some of them and they resented him bitterly for it. They wanted to see him crucified for his crimes, it was personal to them. They simmered in their anger wanting their justice against him and now it was denied to them. They were very worked up that the chief priests had stirred up their people to ask for his release forcing their commander to simply let him walk free. Some of them had been tempted to throw a spear into Bar-Abbas' side as he walked out. They didn't though, because they knew they would be severely disciplined for it. But in their minds justice would have been better served that way. Pilate's men knew that Rabbi Jesus was accused of stirring up the people, which was what their prisoner Bar-Abbas had done. They had learned that he was accused by the chief priests of having followers who would rise-up and fight. To them, that was a close enough exchange for them and so they turned their hatred of Bar-Abbas and heartlessly focused it on the Rabbi. Now, all their anger was about to unraveled at the point of the whip.

The soldiers had seen how the Temple authorities scapegoated and mocked Rabbi Jesus as they accused him before Pilate. This only served to embolden them in their ill treatment of the Rabbi. As Jesus was taken to be thrashed, many of the soldiers gathered around to witness it. Three of these were quietly talking in a tight circle. They were conspiring to make the thrashing as brutal as it could be for their own sadistic purposes. They were coarsely jesting and in mocking laughter making their own plans to heap their wrath on this man who was accused of making himself out to be the King of the Judea.

The officer in charge of the prison gave the order for Jesus to be bound to a thrashing post. A couple of the soldiers grabbed Jesus. One of them took hold of his robe and took it from him, another removed his tunic. Then he was led to a blood-stained wooden beam that stood nearby. They tied his wrists to the top of it and stepped away. Another soldier readily emerged from among the rest with a whip coiled in his hand. He walked over to the post and faced Rabbi Jesus. He let him see the whip, then he let it unroll in front of him and he moved it about like a slithering snake that was about to strike. He stepped up to the Rabbi and whispered in his ear, "In the late summer farmers planted their seeds of wheat you know. Their crops grew well this season and now it is the spring harvest time of the first fruits. So, I'm going to thrash you like the wheat they are reaping in the fields."

Soon the resentment of all the soldiers would be unleashed on him and the officer called out, "Forty lashes less one. Broken, but not dead, shredded, but still alive."

Then Jesus reached up and took hold of the straps and gripped them tightly.

Now the soldier stepped behind Jesus and reached back with the whip in his hand. He took a deep breath and lunged forward with great force, throwing his hand forward with immense speed, and sending the tail of the whip flying onto Jesus' back. Metal shards that had been tied to its end sliced deeply into his skin. As the soldier retracted the whip back it tore portions of his flesh away with it. Now, this soldier was given to a sadistic personality, and he took a very twisted sense of pleasure in what he was doing.

One of the soldiers called out in Latin, "Unus!"

Jesus rose up to the top of his feet and then retracted in withering pain as he screamed out, "Ahhh...!" Then he fell suddenly silent.

The torturing soldier closed his eyes and prepared to do it again. He took in a deep breath and swung the whip back, then with a galloping start he swung it forward with lightning speed. It cracked loudly as it lashed forward and struck squarely across Jesus' back and wrapped itself over his shoulder and struck him in the cheek.

And the soldier called out, "Duo!"

As the torture continued nonstop, sometimes only the very tip of the whip struck his back and when it did, it left a deep wound that dripped blood. Other times the length of the whip ripped along his back and wrapped itself around his torso. It cut his skin open and when there was no longer any skin to cut open, it sank in deep and sliced away at his muscles.

Jesus cried out loudly each time he was struck. The shards of metal always dug in deeply, embedding themselves into his body, and causing great damage. The soldier now snapped back his hand forcefully retracting the whip so that it caused as much pain and damage being removed from his flesh as when it first struck. At times a portion of his flesh remained on the end of the whip as it was flung back and flew free. Sometimes the whip struck high, wounding his head and neck, and even wrapping around to injure his face. Before long Jesus wept constantly as he endured the unimaginable. Yet, as he had set his face to go to Jerusalem to be rejected by the chief priests, scribes and elders, so also now, he had set his face to suffer through this, as it was according to his Father's will for him to surrender, suffer and die.

At the beginning, Jesus had stood on his feet with his arms stretched overhead. He had tightly gripped the straps that held him to the post. Before long he no longer had the strength to stand up, or to grip the straps. Now he hung like a child's ragdoll from the beam and swayed from side to side. At the strike of each whip he retracted in pain, but then fell again in complete exhaustion. Most men, even the strongest of them, would typically pass into unconsciousness from the pain. However, even as his strength waned, he was fully awake the entire time.

All the criminals who undergo this terrible punishment react by swearing at the soldiers, cursing them, cursing one of the gods, and threatening reprisals. Many wept in self-pity and pleading for mercy saying they cannot take it anymore. A few even ask to be put to death rather than endure it further.

Rabbi Jesus was not like any of the others who had been whipped. He accepted the punishment without showing contempt towards the soldiers. When at first the soldiers punished him, they also mocked him and had fully expected Jesus to insult them back, but he never did. In the hardness of their hearts they never came to wonder why Jesus did not hate them for what they were doing. None of the soldiers took notice of Jesus' facial expressions. However, Jesus appeared to be sorrowful for the soldiers and for what they were ordered to do. Because Jesus failed to react the way they wanted him to they continued to mock and insult him all the more, hoping to get a reaction out of the Rabbi.

So great was the strain of the work of the soldier in thrashing Jesus that at about the halfway point another soldier was ordered to replace him. When the punishment was first underway, many of the soldiers took a personal interest in seeing the Rabbi tortured. It was an outlet for their pent-up anger over so many things. Jesus was the perfect person for them to vent it on, being the King of Judea.

As his injuries grew, he began to bleed more and his blood dripped down his back and legs slowly. Before long the blood dripped down to the ground and in a short time the blood flowed in a slow but steady line until it formed a small puddle at his feet beneath him. And Jesus cried out with each lashing with inexpressible cries of pain that were too terrible to describe.

The thrashing continued nonstop until the full measure of his punishment was brought to bear. As the end came, the soldier who was finishing this terrible job slowed, the final count was being given out loudly, "Trīgintā septem, trīgintā octō, trīgintā novem. Ah, eatis est!" which means it is enough. Then the soldier who did this was exhausted. He staggered over to a table and sat in a chair there and then he refreshed himself as he gulped down a jar of water.

Jesus now hung in silence, not moving as if he was a dead man. He looked like a slain lamb hung up to be bleed out. Soon the flow of blood that had been running down his back stopped. But so much of his flesh had been torn away that some of his bones could now be seen.

A moment passed before they untied him from the post and let him fall to the ground. Many soldiers had taken a strong interest in him and they gathered around him. They hated him and all that he represented to them. Having physically abused him, they now wanted to emotionally and mentally torture him for their own personal gratification. He had claimed to be the King, so they used that to taunt him with. They stood him up on his feet and began to enact their own drama. One of them brought out a

Roman robe and carried it to him as if it was a fine luxurious garment. When he neared the Rabbi, he bowed low and let his knee touch the ground as he looked down. Then he acted like a fool and jumped into the air and landed on his feet, dancing in a clownish act of mockery. In a comical voice he said to the Rabbi, "Your royal robe my King! It has been fitted for your use and is ready for you to wear." Then he stepped forward and stood nose to nose with Jesus and exhaled heavily upon him so that his foul breath could offend the Rabbi. Another joined in with him, placing this robe on Jesus' shoulders and tied it on him as they imitated the fan fair sound of trumpets. Then as their mocking music came to an end, one grotesquely let loose a roar from the rear of his shorts, and everyone there howled out in laughter.

There were other soldiers who sadistically grinned as this took place. One in that bunch elbowed the one next to him as he pointed to a large pile of dried out branches. These were used as kindling to start warming fires in their braziers with. He broke away from the others, walked over there and carefully picked up some of the prickly barbed, thorny branches. He fashioned them into what at first looked like a victor's laurel wreath, the kind a victorious military commander or Olympic athlete might wear. Then he pulled the leaves off it and the wreath no longer looked like a crown of high honor. It was frightening, and it looked torturous. He laughed as he walked over to Jesus and he called out in a comical voice, "Hail to thee, oh mighty ruling King. Let me offer you this crown so that you may begin your Kingdom's rule. May it never come to an end." He bowed as he drew near and then lifted the wreath of thorns high over Jesus' head before placing it softly on his head. Then, suddenly, he burst into sadistic laughter as he pushed it down hard, jamming its sharp thorns into his flesh. Jesus fell on his knees in pain. The soldier wiggled the mock crown still further downward tearing long jagged cuts into his flesh. The soldier turned it from side to side so that it fit snuggly, down low on his forehead, and down to the tips of his ears. The terrible thorns bent like tiny springs and held it firmly in place.

Jesus accepted what the soldiers were doing to him, so much so that they marveled. However, in his receiving the crown he was not without great excruciating pain. At first, he gasped for breath. Then he summoned his strength and held still. His face contorted in agony, and in his mind, he worked to resist the wrenched pressure put upon his skull that was working to distort his very thoughts. His eyes could not hide his pain as they rolled back and then darted left and right repeatedly. He looked downward and as his head shook in pain, his expression looked as if he was saying, 'Why do you want to hurt me so? I have loved you all as no other could. Why are you hurting me?' Truly, Jesus was beside himself as he strained to endure the torture. His scalp burned with great intensity as his blood dripped out and it ran down upon his face and dripped onto his shoulders. It was at that point that he grit his teeth together and clenched tight his jaw. Then he cried out, "Ahhh..."

As the soldiers marveled at Jesus' resilience to their tortures they shouted out loudly for all to hear, "Look! This man is not fighting us off. He wants to be crowned a King. Hail, all hail the King of the Jews!"

Another said, "Arise, O Great Ruler and be recognized!" Many of the others joined in with him. One soldier standing their held a long rod used to strike prisoners with. He came up to Jesus and struck him on the arms and shoulders. Then he repeatedly struck the crown of thorns causing Jesus' head to jerk in pain.

Jesus stumbled as he tried to continue standing in place. A soldier mocked him saying, "What is the matter here? It the weight of your new crown too much for you to bear? So much that you cannot stand up straight and tall for yourself?" Then he grabbed the tail of the robe they had put on him and began to swing Jesus around himself in circles saying, "Where are you going King of the Jews? Are you trying to view the vastness of your kingdom, or are you looking for a way to escape?"

Others circled around Jesus and they forcefully snapped their arms into a Roman salute, striking him in the face and saying, "Hail, O Great King, hail!" and spraying him with the foulness of their spittle.

Another called out, "Now, here is truly a King. He is wearing a robe of the empire and a local crown. Truly he is a King sanctioned by the empire."

Now the soldier who held the long rod stood before him again and struck Jesus on the fingers until his hands shook in pain. Then he placed the reed into his hand and told him, "Here is your royal scepter to rule over your Kingdom with!"

Then their officer sent one of his soldiers to Pilate to tell him that Jesus had been thrashed.

Chapter Twenty-Five
Behold the Man

With his head held high, Pilate swaggered out to the chief priests with his helmet on. Its tall red feathered plume bobbed up and down as he moved. Though he was already wearied by their nagging, he walked slowly wanting to disguise his fatigue with a noble appearance. He spoke to the priests, "As I have said I would, I have had your man thrashed and so I will be releasing him."

Rabsaris nastily snapped back at him, "And as you know, we never asked you to thrash him. We could have done that to him ourselves if it would have fit his crimes. This punishment you have administered to him has not changed anything. As we have said, we want him put to death, and we will not be satisfied until you have done nothing less than just that."

Pilate sneered at them, "As I already said, I will release him."

"We want him crucified."

"My soldiers have shredded him. He is but the shadow of what he once was."

"We want him less than a shadow. We want him dead."

"Don't you understand? He is as good as dead. And, he may very well die from his thrashing. He is a broken man. He has been reduced to a tattered heap of flesh that is laying in a puddle of his own sweat and blood just inside the bars of my prison's courtyard. I am sure he will be of no more trouble to you. In fact, the only trouble he will ever be is to the nursemaid who will have to care for him. He is an invalid. I will have him brought out for you to see what he has become." Pilate waved to his officer to have Jesus brought out. As they waited the governor shuffled his

197

feet about. It was an awkward moment as they waited in silence.

His officer hurried to the prison compound and ordered for Jesus to be brought out immediately. The soldiers scrambled to follow his order. They did not even take the time to remove the crown of thorns, his Roman robe, or to take away the scepter they had put into his hands. When the officer saw the way they had dressed him up, he also mocked him, bowing and nicely saying, "The governor requests your presence, your Majesty." Then he and several soldiers marched Jesus out the prison gate and into the main courtyard.

As Rabbi Jesus first appeared from the gate, Pilate majestically raised both his arms as if he was welcoming someone with great honor, magnanimously announcing, "Behold, here is the man!" He wanted to show these religious authorities that the Rabbi was clearly no longer a threat them. As Jesus drew nearer, Pilate saw how his soldiers had taken the liberty to dress him up with a robe, as if he was a King and placed the crown on his head. He chuckled and reflected that it could not have been more fitting, that the man who claimed to be their King was now coronated.

The soldiers who brought Jesus out remained at his sides. Though they were there to guard him as their prisoner for all outward appearances, they looked like the personal escort and bodyguards of a government official. There they all stood. Pilate, his officer, and the soldiers next to Jesus. The chief priests were enraged by what they thought they were seeing. But as they looked closer, they saw that Jesus was not wearing an official crown, but one of thorns.

Rabbi Jesus was in terrible pain and bloodied from head to toe. He looked at the Temple authorities, but they remained as steadfast as ever, stout and without compassion for him. Pilate hoped that the authorities would be sickened by the sight of him, and that they would know that he was utterly crushed and disgraced. He hoped this would satisfy them and they would give up their demands that he be crucified.

It was just after the eleventh hour when he spoke to the chief priests saying, "Be certain of this, I have examined him very thoroughly, and I find that there are no grounds for him to be put to death. The case is clear and let no doubt remain in your minds, he is not guilty. Therefore, I am going to have this King of yours released."

Rabsaris was very calm as he reiterated their demands, "We have a law and by it he must be put to death, Pilate."

He laughed and told them, "Fine, crucify him yourselves." But this was his way of mocking them and showing them how powerless they were. They could not crucify the Rabbi themselves. It would take his order and his soldiers for that to happen and he wasn't about to issue that order for them. The governor was losing interest in arguing any further with them and he shifted the weight on his feet back and forth and wondering if he should just quit talking to these men and walk away.

They seemed to sense that Pilate was about to disengage from their case. Rabsaris then stepped up and leveled a new charge against the Rabbi. "We have a Law, a supreme Law, and he has broken it. There will be no compromising on this! He must be put to death."

The reference to a supreme Law had not come up before and so Pilate wondered what they were talking about, and he listened attentively.

Now the Chief Priests Rabsaris, Elamadad, and Kallahadad called out in one voice, "He committed blasphemy. He has claimed to be the Son of God, our God, and for that reason he must die. It is our Law!"

As he heard the charge, Pilate felt cascading waves flowing in his head and over his thoughts. Their reverberations were as though a deep revelation had come to him, and it was tearing at every thread that held the fabric of his mind together. Now he knew the answer to the question he posed to the Rabbi earlier. This is what made them so extremely mad. He recognized that this was quite a claim, to be the Son of God in this Provence, given the peoples religious devotion. In his reaction he angerly exclaimed back, "What is this!? First you made a false statement that he had forbidden paying the tax. Then you made one against him for claiming to be your King and Messiah. And you have withheld this charge against him from me until now! What do you mean that you are charging him because he claims to be the Son of God? What all did you actually charge him with in your own court?

Elamadad calmly recited back, "With all these crimes governor, with all of these crimes."

Pilate said, "You have brought him to me and told me half truths about his case and withheld this charge against him until now. What else haven't you told me?"

Now, in Pilate's world, the Roman world, a man, or even a woman for that matter could be a god or the offspring of one. He was told this happens from time to time, though he was inclined to not believe it. In his experience he found that occasionally it was a local egotist who thought so very highly of himself that he made this grandiose claim. At other times, it was someone claiming that one of the gods was their father or mother. Sometimes it was a person who had an underlying belief that they were a child of entitlement and wanted to be richly provided for by others. He remembered Alexander the Great, who was said to be a son of Zeus, or Helene of Troy, she was believed to be a daughter of Zeus. Even a few emperors were declared gods as had been his wife's grandfather, Augustus. But among the people of Judea this kind of claim was entirely unheard of and he did not find it difficult to believe that it was against their Law. In the rest of the Roman world it was no crime to make this claim. The empire was very tolerant of the many religious cults throughout their vast domain. For a Galilean Rabbi to make this claim, that was very much out of the ordinary.

Having given it a brief thought, Pilate addressed the growing crowd of religious authorities, and their many supporters who continued to arrive and follow the case. "I am surprised that someone from among your own people would make this claim. It does seem a bit out of the ordinary given your religious devotion. However, while you are offended by it, this claim is not a crime in the Roman Empire, let alone a capital offense."

Led by these three chief priests, Rabsaris, Elamadad, and Kallahadad, all the protesters who stood against the Rabbi turned their eyes on Pilate and in one voice vehemently shouted, "We don't care! He has made himself out to be the Son of God, our God. We have a Law to put this to an end. It is a high Law and by our Law he has been sentenced to die."

Pilate echoed their harshness back to them, "I am not concerned with your verdict."

The priests shouted back, "We don't care!"

In silence Pilate threw his hands up and showed them that he was offended with them. He felt it was impossible talking to the chief priests. If it wasn't one thing, then they brought up another issue, and he wondered what it would be next. Now, rather than debating any further with them he ordered his officer to bring Jesus with him and then he stormed into his office. He wanted to go the source of this supposed claim, the Rabbi himself, so that he could question him further in private.

In his office he paced the floor wondering what to do. Then as Jesus was brought in he put on a more casual appearance. He was almost laughing as he spoke to Jesus, "So this is what you did to upset the chief priests so severely? Now I understand why they hate you so much."

As in the past, Jesus was silent before him.

Pilate took off his helmet as an act of respect wondering if Rabbi Jesus might have a higher ranking in life than what he had assumed. "Well, don't worry, your claim to be the Son of their God is not a crime against Rome." He found relief in saying that and now he took a serious look at Jesus. He worried a little because this King of theirs, who the chief priests accused him of claiming to be the Son of God, was treated very disrespectfully by his soldiers.

Pilate opened his mouth to speak but his words were slow to follow, and then he found the courage to venture asking, "Rabbi Jesus, where are you from?" He was bit afraid to ask this and now he was even more fearful to hear what the answer might be. The scene was almost dreamlike to him.

Jesus was silent before him.

Then he spoke more assertively, "Rabbi, I was told you were from Nazareth in Galilee. Is that true or are you from somewhere else?"

But Jesus did not answer him, he did not even blink. Pilate felt like Jesus was ignoring him as before. His worries over the case gave way to anger and he erupted, demanding an answer with an intimidating voice, "You are refusing to speak to me? I am the emperor's appointed ruler standing here before you! I have been given immense power by him!" He raised his clenched fist up for Jesus to see, "You need to know that I alone have been granted the power to set you free and the power to send you to your death!"

Jesus looked at him nonchalantly, examining him from head to toe. He lightly chuckled and he clarified the limits of his power, "So it would seem. You think your power comes from Rome. You have soldiers who take your orders and carry them out even if it means their death. You also think you have power because of the strength of your mind. Don't you realize yet that the only power you have over me was granted to you from God, who is my Father in heaven."

Instantly, Pilate knew in his heart that this was true and he had a knee jerk reaction to this revelation. Jesus' words rang out like a great ah-ha moment for him. He wondered if all this was a divinely guided drama orchestrated by some of the gods who he had prayed to. Maybe this was why things were fitting together in front of him the way they were. Up until now he felt that his gods had not involved themselves in his life. Now he strongly wondered if they were, and if they were putting him in the middle of their affairs, which he hated them for.

Then Jesus spoke again, "But, regarding what you have ordered your soldiers to do to me today and for what you are considering doing to me now, know this; The ones who brought me to you have the greater sins and it will be held against them all."

The governor swallowed hard and he worried about what the gods would do to punish him for his involvement in all of this. It was no comfort to him that the chief priests were greater sinners than him. He feared that if the chief priests were right in their claims to there being only one true God, then this might very well be the Son of the one True God.

Pilate left Jesus in his office and returned to the chief priests telling them, "Just like you, I am very shocked to hear that Rabbi Jesus made the claim to be the Son of God. But I am sure we have very different reasons for feeling this way. His claim to be your King and this new claim to be the Son of God, whether he truly is or not, neither of these are crimes in the Empire. Therefore, I will be releasing him from my custody without any further punishment."

Rabsaris made a counter point to Pilate's conclusion, one that was very unexpected. Now in matters of law, a Roman citizen could appeal to the Emperor and have their case tried before him. But that option was not available to the chief priests. Still, there was another way they could appeal to Caesar. It was not a counter point of law though, it was one of politics. So, in the most serious way he made eye contact with the governor telling him in no uncertain terms, "Pilate, if you release this man, you are no longer a friend to the emperor!"

The governor felt like he had just been slapped in the face. Rabsaris had completely sidestepped the points of law being argued and changed the nature of their sparing entirely. The emperor was Caesar Tiberius, his wife's uncle. As an in-law, how could he possibly live this indictment down. By their accusations, they were making it look like he was betraying not only the emperor, but also his own family if he were to allow Jesus to go free.

This struck at a raw nerve. Just as Rabsaris changed the nature of their confrontation from the courtroom to the political arena, so he was ready to change it from political to physical. Pilate angerly kicked the dirt and a cloud of dust rose up. Then he kicked his foot up hard as if he were striking an enemy and he wanted to believe that this was still a fight he could win. But the truth be told, he was feeling more and more boxed in. He believed he had won in the courtroom, not just because he had found Jesus not guilty, but because the priests no longer argued the legal points of the case. Now, they had pushed it into the political arena and this frightened him. It seemed to Pilate that there was no way around it and it worried him that he might lose the fight because of the politics. Still, he was a brilliant tactician in war, in politics, and in law, and he was not going to simply give in. He loved a good challenge, a good test of the will, and a good fight as well. But this new level of the battle was a dangerous one for him.

From the moment he showed the chief priests his potential for an actual fight, when he kicked the dirt up and raised his boot to them, they were highly offended by it. All those with Rabsaris were enraged over this terrible breach in social manners. They shouted and shook angry fists at him and told him, "If you release this man you are no longer a friend to Caesar!"

This sudden inflammation of the situation was very worrisome. It looked more and more like the threat of a riot was looming. So, Pilate turned to his officer and whispered an order to him. "The number of these religious authorities and their supporters continues to rise. Their anger and persistence worries me that they might start a riot. Have the Sargent at Arms assemble the Cohort, ready them for a riot, and deploy them inside the Praetorium, but most of all keep them out of sight. This angry crowd must not know about it. If they learn of it, it might ignite them into rioting."

Now, this was no simple veiled threat that Rabsaris made. Not being a friend to Caesar by implication meant you were his enemy and his enemies were punished severely or put to death by one of his assassins. Caesar's spies were to be found everywhere and Pilate worried they were probably in with the mix of these people already, or at least watching nearby. Of no doubt, if Rabbi Jesus walked, the Sanhedrin would report it to the emperor. This could result in him being recalled to Rome, or worse, bring about his own death.

As he considered what he would say to the chief priest next, Pilate was at a loss for words for the first time in a long time. In turn, Rabsaris felt like he was now in a position of power so that he could dictate his terms to the governor and he shouted at him saying, "We are no longer concerned with the proceedings of your Roman trial and your verdict. This man has been found guilty and our Law says he must die. You reserve capital punishment for yourself. Therefore, you must carry it out, or you are no friend of Caesar."

Though Pilate was deeply concerned about reprisals from Rome or Caesar, he knew that he did not have to do anything immediately. "Condemn him to death as many times as you like. But we both know that you have no authority or power to carry that out." With that said, he simply took his leave of them and returned to his headquarters and then he order the soldiers to have Rabbi Jesus brought there too.

Chapter Twenty-Six
The Judgement Seat

Now Pilate desired to release Jesus more than ever, but not while the Temple authorities were at his gate. They were much too worked up to let the Rabbi walk out safely and if he provided an armed escort for him it would end up in a crazed brawl. He hoped they would calm down and leave, but instead their crowd grew in size as workers from the Temple also joined them.

As he looked out his doorway to the gate his officer asked him, "Shall I send out soldiers to disperse them?"

Pilate simply shook his head no and looked down. He hoped that he could end his involvement in all this soon. Up until now he had been rendering his verdict from just inside of the gate, which was a very informal thing to do. This he did to accommodate the chief priests who refused to be received inside, formally at court. His tactics with them were failing and so he decided to do things differently, the Roman way. He invited Rabbi Jesus to accompany him, as though they were colleagues. Together they walked side by side from his lofty office to the foot of Gabbatha, the Judgement Seat. This was where he sometimes issued his decrees and court judgements. Normally a person charged with a crime stood below Gabbatha as their case was heard and the verdict was delivered. That was not going to happen today. Pilate had already found Jesus not guilty. So, instead he gestured to Jesus to go first and he climbed the highly polished stone steps. At the top Pilate seated Jesus first and he sat on the Judge's Bench.

This new tactic gained the undivided attention of all the religious authorities there. Pilate did this to show them that he was extending to Jesus the courtesy that he would any visiting Roman official, or a king. He did this with the full intension of mocking the chief priests, showing them that he was recognizing Jesus as their King. The chief priests knew that when the Roman governor issued his decrees and judgements from Gabbatha, it was the final word on any matter. After judgement from there was made the only thing they could do was to appeal to the senate or the emperor. That would take months or years if the Romans were even willing to hear their petition.

Pilate was in no hurry to pronounce his final judgement on Jesus then he would simply be repeating what he already said. He hoped to use the passing of some time to wear his opposition down, to discourage them and get them to leave.

Now as they leisurely sat together, his wife's personal handmaiden arrived with a soldier from their residence escorting her. She carried an urgent message from her mistress for the governor. The soldier passed word to Pilate's officer that this message needed to be delivered at once. The officer stepped forward and looked at his commander. Pilate took notice of him, but he made it clear that this interruption came at a very inconvenient time and that he was irritated by it. The officer came close to Pilate and whispered into his ear stating what the request was.

This kind of interruption was a very rare occurrence. His wife was not known for involving herself in his government's affairs, and he preferred it that way. Though irritated by the intrusion, he felt it was best to hear what the woman had to say given that it came from his wife and was deemed urgent by her. Pilate gave his consent for her to come to the top of Gabbatha to speak with him. The officer waved for the handmaiden to come forward. She walked very gracefully up the steps, looking down the whole time so that her eyes did not meet with Pilate's prematurely. She approached the governor, lowered her head, and then bowed low before him. She turned her eyes upward and looked into Pilate's eyes just as her mistress had done with her. "Sir, I am before you at the urging of my mistress. I am carrying her message to you."

Pilate acted arrogantly toward her and he wanted everyone to know it. In their residence he treated her in a more personal way and was grateful to her for her devotion in caring for his wife's needs. But here, she was out of place and therefore he needed to treat her this way. "Very well, you may convey your message to me."

Her words were simple and to the point, "My lord, my mistress begs you to have nothing to do with this man, Jesus of Nazareth. She states that she knows he is innocent. She has suffered much already today because of a distressing dream that came to her during the night."

He shook his head wondering what was going on with his wife and said, "How could she know these things?" Then he remembered when he was awakened in the night to first deal with this problem. His wife was sleeping then, but her eyes were moving rapidly about. He wondered if that was when she had this dream that her handmaiden was talking to him about. He dropped his head now and held it in his hand as he tried to rethink everything that had happened that morning. He looked to the slave and said, "That's it? That's the message?"

"Yes, my lord. That is every word just as she told it to me."

"Fine. But it has come to me a bit too late. I am already deeply involved with this man and how I wish it was over."

Pilate did not think much of her right then and he did not like what she said, whether it was from his wife or not.

He made the woman wait as she bowed before him. He wanted to inconvenience her as she had inconvenienced him by the message she brought. Then in a huff he spoke to her, "Well, whatever the devil are you waiting for. You have conveyed your message and fulfilled your mistress' instructions. You are dismissed."

Though he had handled her roughly, she displayed a very humble and gracious spirit before him. She now lowered her head still more, bowed still lower and then backed away from the governor.

At that moment he simply wanted to follow the advice of his wife more than ever, but things had gone too far for that. Now he was entangled in the case and it seemed increasingly as though he was without means of escape. His new approach for addressing Rabsaris and all his supporters now continued in the political arena rather than as a legal case in a courtroom. Pilate announced for all to hear, "Behold, here is your King!"

Now it was before the noon hour that this took place. Pilate's new tactic did not have the effect he had hoped for. It was as though he had just thrown a match on a highly flammable situation. All the people at the gate took offence at him and they cried out "Take him away! Take him away and crucify him! Let him be put to death!"

Now Pilate rose and looked at them as though he was taken entirely by surprise by their words. He played dumb to them as if in shock and was having trouble hearing them. He turned his ear to them and held his hand to it. He spoke as though he was very surprised, even shocked to hear them calling for his death. Pilate stepped closer to them as he said, "But this is your king! What are you asking for? Shall I send your King to his death? Am I hearing you correctly? Do you want me to crucify him? He is your King!"

The growing crowd was led by the chief priests there who coached all the people to shout out, "He is not our King. We have a king and he is the emperor. Our king is the emperor! Let this man be crucified." By making this claim they had, in essence, appealed to Caesar, not as citizens but as his subjects and as political rivals of the governor.

Pilate could not believe his ears and he shook his head in disbelief. But he had heard them correctly. They were claiming allegiance to Caesar Tiberius. It seemed more than odd to him that they did this. He opened his eyes up wide and looked at all of them standing outside his gate. They were now nearly out of control. He tried to talk to them, but the crowd no longer quieted down for him. Elamadad, Rabsaris and Kallahadad no longer bothered to listen to him. They would not even look directly at him. Then Pilate realized that he could no longer reason with any of them and the crowd they had assembled could begin rioting at any moment.

Pilate looked at his officer and closed his eyes, then he nodded. This was the signal to bring the cohort out from hiding. The officer looked at the Sargent at Arms who was standing nearby and ordered him to have a trumpeter blow his horn to call all the soldiers in the Praetorium to step forward and be seen. Eight hundred men in all, fully dressed for battle rushed out in one accord. From inside the headquarters, from behind every wall and door, from around every corner, out from the gate to the prison and from their barracks they rushed out. They stood in rank and file formation. Many surrounded the Judgement Seat of Gabbatha where Jesus and Pilate were. Archers also appeared on all the high places of every building there.

The crowd outside the gate quieted down, but only because the chief priests urged them too. None of them were intimidated by the presence of the soldiers.

Rabsaris looked with a scornful face and said, "Pilate, you know very well that if you put us to the sword the whole city will riot."

Pilate believed that by the presence of his soldiers he would get things back under his control. He stood up on Gabbatha, proud and with his arms crossed against his chest he pompously replied, "Do not think that I would do such a foolish thing! My cohort is here to give this innocent man protection and a military escort safely out of the city. Do not think so foolishly that I, a Roman governor, would do such a thing as attack you."

Now Pilate pointed out to Rabsaris his trumpeters, "If you think you want to incite a riot my trumpeters will call for all the soldiers in the city to rush here and they will crush any uprising that you might start. Now he tried to hide his smile and his pride, but it broke through his straight face. He felt again like he had the upper hand. He turned around to face his troops and raised his hands and pointed out their vastness. He tapped his feet to the ground as though he was marching and his men in turn stomped their feet in perfect rhythm. The loud sound of it was threatening.

The chief priests and their supporters stood in awe wondering if their lives were truly at risk. They wondered if they had lost their bid to have the Rabbi put to death. Then Rabsaris remembered his instructions from the high priest, "Remember that Pilate has a mind of his own. He will not simply accept what we have done as the final word. Do whatever it takes, and I mean just that, do whatever it takes and see this through to the end."

Then Rabsaris rallied his helpers and they resumed their protests with loud shouting and demanding the Rabbi Jesus be crucified.

Chapter Twenty-Seven
Their Voices Prevailed

Pilate let them go on shouting fully expecting that that they would wear themselves out and then quiet down on their own. When that did not happen, he raised his hands high and motioned for them to quiet down. Then he spoke loudly to them, "Crucify him? Why? He has done no evil. He is an innocent man!

But Rabsaris called out, "He is a criminal according to our Law! And for that he must die." He rallied all those with him and the crowd was again stirred up even more to the point that they were simply in a mad frenzy.

Pilate looked at his cohort, 800 soldiers, seasoned warriors, all ready for battle and more than willing to fight. Yet, for as threatening as they appeared, they no longer were intimidating to the chief priests and their supporters as he had expected. In fact, it had the opposite effect on the people and they grew increasingly hostile. Pilate reasoned, if I release him from custody there will be a riot and people will get hurt. Some may even die. They would certainly seize the Rabbi and stone him to death in defiance of his authority and then he would have lost their respect. If they riot, some of his own people would be hurt, maybe even killed. Rome would certainly hear about it and they would recall him and possibly sentence him death for incompetence. The rule of law was not carrying the weight that Pilate expected. The threat of a riot was no longer just looming, it was only moments away. He had his soldiers standing at the ready and when the rule of law was not observed civilly, then the right of might needed to be brought to bear.

Pilate spoke with his most eloquent and noble voice, it was the booming sound of a Roman aristocrat. "Your King is hardly anything now. You have seen that for yourselves! And you want me to crucify him? It would be a worse punishment to him, to let him live as a broken man. And you want me to condemn him to the cross? He may very well die this same day from the wounds I have had him afflicted with."

The chief priests cried out, "This man must die for his crimes." Rabsaris stood forward from the shouting crowd and rudely turned his back on Pilate. He looked at his supporters and raised his arms to lead them like an orchestra in a mad display of screaming voices. The sound of it was the sound of madness. They were crying out as if their very lives depended on this outcome. Their vile chorus grated upon Pilate's ears and sent a cold shiver down his spine. So intense was their outcry that he looked at them disbelieving they could create such an inhuman sound. Though they were known as dramatis, this was them at their worse. As Pilate looked on, he saw that their once familiar faces had become strangely alien to him.

Despite their display, Pilate maintained his highly dignified composure. He looked at the religious leaders and crossed his arms over his chest. He mildly chuckled to himself and shook his head. This he did to show them how little he thought of them. He turned and looked at the many stations, both high and low, in the Praetorium where his soldiers now stood. He was very impressed with their threatening appearance. He turned and looked at a growing crowd of madly shouting religious zealots. He used broad gestures of his arms to point out to the zealots the breath, width, and height of his cohort.

Still the madness of this crowd continued. He again looked at his soldiers and he smiled at them. Their presence gave him a sense of security and their weapons gave him a sense of power over the crowd. He smiled even larger at them and he stomped his feet for his men to see. His soldiers followed in his example and stomped their feet in a sharp unified beat which sounded as if they were marching in stride. This sound was well known among all the people of that day. It was made to remind the protesters that when the Roman legions marched, everyone had better yield the way. Pilate grinned widely and turned again to his opponents. He lifted his arms and swung them freely as if he was leading a band of drummers in a grand and glorious marching song.

Pilate's mind grew hypercritical of his opponents as he thought to himself, *'These religious sorts that I am always wrangling with, they are so obsessive about their views of cleanliness. They have taken from their religion and formulated their own sect of extremism about being clean and calling others outside their nation unclean.'* Pilate held them in contempt for it. He could even pick these ones out in a crowd simply by looking to see who had chapped skin from obsessive hand washing.

Now Pilate determined to use this practice of theirs to make a final point to them, one that he was sure they would recognize and take him seriously on. They loved to be dramatic so he would create his own drama for them to see. He ordered that a pedestal and a basin of water be brought out to the gate that separated him from them. As it was set before him, he looked the chief priests squarely in the eyes and called out to them. "Look! Before your eyes I am washing my hands of this matter!" His words carried with them all of his anger and resentment toward them. He lifted his arms high into the air and rotated his hands forward and back. Then he dipped his hands into the water and washed them thoroughly for all to see. He shook the water off his hands in their direction with the greatest disgust and dried them with the towel. Having completed his ritual, he shouted out with a new boldness. He reached out with his arms and making greatly exaggerated movements as he pointed toward the Rabbi, "Innocens ego sum a sanguine iusti huius." Which means, I am innocent of this man's blood. This, he was sure, would be something they understood without a doubt.

Now Rabsaris shouted back to the governor, "Yes! Yes! Then let his death..." then he used both his arms to point at himself and then at the others standing with him, "...let his death and his blood be on all of us and upon our children as well." He looked to the others for their approval and nodding his head enthusiastically encouraged them to join in. They all shouted, "Let his death be on us! And on our children too! May his blood be on us and on our children!"

Pilate had hoped that by putting that immeasurable burden of guilt on the priests, of sending an innocent man to his death, that they would bend under its weight, but to no avail, and worse, they welcomed it.

The priests and their supporters now joined in together shouting and chanting for the Rabbi to be crucified. Some of the people came forward and began to shake the gate to the Praetorium. That was a sign to Pilate that they were going to an extreme that he did not think was possible. Those that touched his gate were no longer concerned with maintaining their ceremonial cleanliness. Touching the gate made them unclean.

Pilate was suddenly dizzy and at that very instant everything ceased to move forward, and time was suspended. He could think but not move, he could look but not turn his head. The sensation of waves reverberated over him once again striking like the powerful waves of the sea as they crash into the shore. He feared to move and worried that he might fall. He feared this might, if it hadn't already had, overpower him. He felt that if he did not yield to their demands that it would turn into a bloody fight. He believed that it was at the very point where they would not be able to back down and that it would become a slaughter of the people. His heart beat fast and his eyes shook as he grew fearful of what he had created by his might. If they climbed on the gate or tried to break it down, the force of his Cohort would automatically fight, with or without his orders. That was their rule of engagement. He realized now that he had tightly wedged himself into this frightful position and that he could not escape it. He told himself that he needed to prevent another riot in the city like the one Bar-Abbas had led. He told himself that he needed to prevent the slaying of the citizens by his soldiers and therefore the lesser of all evils must be done. His head felt like it was about to burst, and he was to that point where he would say just about anything to escape this crisis. It was now that he had to either order his men to fight or he must turn the Rabbi over to the chief priests for crucifixion, there were no other options left. Quickly, he ordered his officer to have the men stand down and return to their barracks.

The stand down order was his last real order of the day, his last command decision. What followed was him reacting to the pressure of his opponents and defusing the volatile tension. As the pressure was relieved, he gave into them with his passive submission to do their will. He felt powerless and his thoughts were conflicted as never before.

He heard Rabsaris call out to him, "Pilate, you must crucify this man!"

Now the governor revealed a side of himself that was rarely ever seen outside of a military battle as he shouted back to them with the same vicious and bitter tone that they had used. As he spoke, he stretched out his right arm until it was as straight as an arrow and he pointed to them. Then in broad sweeping movements he moved his arm left to right and back again pointing to the lot of them. "I am tired of your unrelenting plague upon me. If you want this man put to death then you take him and crucify him yourselves! Now, do not involve me in your affairs any further."

The priests were a little surprised by the harshness of his outburst, but they grinned as it became clear they had won and were finally going to get their way. Chief priest Rabsaris snickered at the governor for his pale attempt at removing himself from guilt in condemning the Rabbi to die.

Pilate did not believe his ears for what he had just said. Yet he would not resend his order for fear of losing the last of his self-respect. His thoughts raced, and he searched his mind for the reason why he had impulsively given in. He felt tricked, that they had not just been wearing him down but grooming him for this very response. They had battered and backed him into the corner that he now found himself in. He told himself that he would simply give Rabbi Jesus over to them and then just simply not interfere with them having their own way. But, the truth was that for Jesus to be crucified it would require his own soldiers to carry it out. He had succumbed to what every soldier fears in battle, that they had found and struck him in the weak spot of his amour. But it was worse than that because there was a criminal irony in his actions. He was sending Jesus of

Nazareth to the cross to prevent a riot and he had freed Jesus Bar-Abbas from going to the cross even though he was guilty of leading a riot.

While he felt a pathetic sense of relief by having quelled a riot, he came to a second realization of what he had done. He was sending a man he had declared innocent to his death. He quickly turned to look at Rabbi Jesus and he feared for what he might see. A flood of emotions surged through his body. He recalled the look of those who he had tried and sent to their deaths before. How they looked so frightened, yet with a desperate glimmer of hope on their faces they pleaded for mercy and their release. He fully expected to see something like this as he turned to face Jesus. But as he looked at the Rabbi it was not at all what he expected. Jesus had already turned to face the gate that lead out into the city. He was not concerned with the injustice that had befallen him from within the walls of the Praetorium. It was as though he did not even notice the many chief priests and others who condemned him from without.

Jesus, as he had set his face to go to Jerusalem to be rejected, thrashed and put to death, now again set his face to go to the final step and die on the cross. He was not anxious about the pain and suffering that was ahead for him. He was not afraid or unwilling to go. He looked toward the gate, and with a determined look he was ready to go before anyone else was. He had the look of purpose and providence about him. This the governor had never seen before, no one had.

Pilate knew that he needed to issue the order for his crucifixion so that his soldiers would carry out what the chief priest had demanded of him. He did not want to say that order. He was too ashamed to give it in clear and simple language. Instead, he simply looked at this officer and said, "Well, get on with it and get it done."

Chapter Twenty-Eight
Behold the Passover Lamb

The Temple was filled to capacity and most of the people there had hopes of seeing and hearing from Rabbi Jesus. They had no idea of what the high priests had done to him. As they waited in anticipation their hope gave way to disappointment as the Rabbi did not appear. Then it came time for the high priest to make his grand entrance. It was at the top of the noon hour that Caiaphas appeared in the Temple and the Levites blew their silver trumpets to announce his entrance. It was an exciting occasion and the people were amazed to behold the man who was their high priest elaborately dressed in his high priestly robes. As Caiaphas appeared he waved his hands and greeted everyone with a great wide smile. He loved the attention and recognition they gave him.

That morning some of the chief priests had prepared the national Passover Lamb that the high priest would sacrifice. They had bathed him the day before and today they groomed his wool by minimally trimming his coat to make its contour flawlessly even. They polished his horns and hoofs to a high shine and made him look as perfect as a lamb could appear. They wanted him to smell sweet and so they had burned frankincense and let the smoke rise into his wool. They had also inspected him a final time to ensure he fully met the high standards that Moses required. He needed to be without spot, wrinkle or blemish, which he was.

As the cheering of the massive crowds quieted, the chief priests attending to the lamb brought it over to their high priest and handed the lead cord over to him. After they had cheered for some time, Caiaphas motioned for them to quiet down and he spoke in the most eloquent way, "Behold! The lamb that takes away our sins whose blood covers our doorposts so that the angel of death will Passover our homes sparing us from God's judgement on sinners."

Now the great crowd that had gathered cheered nonstop. The high priest waved at everyone and motioned to the lamb with his hand so that the people would admire it with great awe. Caiaphas let the people cheer for some time again. The Levites then lined up the people who wished to approach the lamb and allowed them to pass by and touch it, symbolizing the transfer of their sins onto the lamb. Many of those who came shed tears and held their hands in humble prayer. Others were in a joyous mood raising their hands in praise to God, singing, and some were dancing.

As this part of the presentation of the lamb finished the high priest prepared to leave the Temple with the Passover Lamb for a parade in the city streets. This was at the same time when Jesus left Pontius Pilate's Headquarters and was marched in chains to Golgotha. So, Caiaphas with the lamb in tow, along with Annas prepared to set out. Many chief priests, priests, and other national leaders also joined in.

As the high priest stepped out into the city streets the sudden appearance of the sun's bright shining light temporarily blinded him and he raised his arm to cover his eyes until they became acclimated. Then the day light suddenly dimmed as though a cloud had veiled it or when a sandstorm kicked up. Many looked up to see what had happened. But there was no apparent reason for it. Nevertheless, the parade commenced without another delay. As Caiaphas passed by the people gladly stood to the side and watched with celebration in their hearts as they saw their greatly honored high priest with the lamb pass them by. It was not allowed that anyone should touch the high priest, especially when he was dressed in these special robes. However, the lamb could be touched, and many people reached out to it hoping to be blessed by it. Everyone reveled in joy and cheered knowing that it was being sacrificed for them. This day was a day to live in the very remembrance of the night of Passover, as though it was reoccurring for them right then and there. They remembered when their ancestor's lives were spared as the angel moved over the land taking the life of every firstborn male of the nation that enslaved them. This was a time for reliving the memories of their ancestors, of how God delivered them from the bonds of oppression and brought them into the land promised to them long ago through their ancestors Abraham and Sarah. They imagined what it would be like to be free of their foreign oppression from Rome. But, as it was their festival, they made the most of their celebration regardless of the repressive bonds they lived under. As the parade continued, many people also rallied behind the high priest and followed him as he made his way through the city.

The parade lasted nearly three hours before Caiaphas made his way back to the Temple. Many people followed behind him and others were waiting for him at the Temple all hoping to be able to see their high priest sacrifice the lamb. They crowded into the Temple and into the courtyard where the lamb would be sacrificed because Moses required that it be sacrificed in front of the assembly of the congregation.

Chapter Twenty-Nine
To the Place of the Skull

It was nearly the noon hour when the soldiers and one officer hastily took Rabbi Jesus back inside the prison where they stripped him of the robe that they had put on him. It came off with some difficulty because scabs of his blood had clotted over his wounds and were also embedded into the fabric. So, taking a firm grip, one soldier took hold of it and tore it off of him. As this happened Jesus flinched backward as he was suddenly overwhelmed with pain and cried out, "E aaah..." as he fell to the ground in agony.

Now the officer ordered his men to bring out from their cells two criminals who were also sentenced to die. Then together with the Rabbi he ordered the three of them to pick up and carry the crossbeams that they would be crucified on. This was part of their punishment, to carry these to the place where they would be lifted-up. This practice kept them from becoming too much trouble along the way, because the beams weighted about one hundred pounds each. By the time they reached the place where they would be crucified, they were exhausted from carrying their own crosses. When it came time for them to be nailed to the cross that they would die on, they did not struggle nearly so much.

The soldiers stood by and watched as the men struggled to lift their heavy crossbeams. The two thieves managed with some difficulty to pick theirs up and place them across their own shoulders. But as Jesus bent over and tried to lift the crossbeam that was originally meant for Jesus Bar-Abbas, he couldn't raise it because of the great pain he was already suffering with. Ordinarily that feat would have been effortless for him, having been a carpenter he possessed great physical strength. But the thrashing that he received had robbed him of this. The soldiers goaded him thinking that he only needed to be threatened. Still, no matter what they did, it became clear that he needed them to lift it up for him. As the weight of it came to rest across his shoulder, it was excruciating for him and he cried out in pain as he grimaced, and his eyes rolled as he staggered under its great weight. He struggled to cope with the pain and held his breath for a moment. Then he let out several quick breaths as tears of agony welled up in his eyes.

This practice of having the condemned carry their own crossbeam was more than humiliating to them. Everyone they passed on the way to their crucifixion knew that they were going to be punished by this cruel and torturous death. In some particularly notorious cases, a sign was prepared that spelled out what their crimes were. Because Jesus Bar-Abbas had lead a bloody insurrection and committed murder Pilate had ordered a sign to be made for him. But now he gave an order that the sign should be written to say, 'Here is Jesus of Nazareth the King of the Jews.' And he had it written in Latin, Hebrew, and Greek, so that everyone who could read would know who he was.

But when Chief Priests Rabsaris, Elamadad and Kallahadad saw it, they strongly protested it.

Rabsaris demanded that the governor change the sign, "You cannot write that 'He is the King of the Jews'! You must change his sign to say that 'This man made the claimed to be King of the Jews.'"

Now Pontius Pilate had grown very weary of their never-ending demands. This one seemed especially excessive to him. He knew something about the lengths they had gone to have him condemned. He determined for himself that though he had yielded so much of himself to them, he would not concede this to them also. He looked at the chief priests and showed them his most stern face and shouted to them in no uncertain terms as his voice rose upwards, "I have already given you enough on this day! But what has been written is exactly what I wanted it to say and it will stay as it is, damn you."

Now Pilate looked at his officer and nodded to indicate that they should begin their march to Golgotha for the execution. A they began their march, Temple trumpets sounded loudly announcing to the city that their High Priest Caiaphas was presenting the nation's Passover Lamb to the people at the Temple. Soon he would be parading it through their streets for all to see. Then the chief priests and all of their supporters also rejoiced knowing that the lamb would be paraded through the holy city.

As the soldiers lead the way, their march to the place of execution almost resembled a royal procession as it had many of those elements. There was the sign announcing his title and it appeared as if he was being kept safe by his personal guard. As they set out of the Praetorium, the people on the street turned their faces away as they stepped aside to make plenty of room for Rabbi Jesus and those with him to pass by unhindered. But this was not a royal procession and the sign did not honor him as their King. It dishonored him. The soldiers were not there for his personal safety. They were the ones who were taking him to be executed. The people did not bow their heads to honor him, rather, in fear they turned their faces away and parents diverted their children's eyes away from the horrible sight.

Their destination, of which there were many possibilities because the Romans like to crucify their condemned where the local people would be sure to see was Golgotha. The sound of its name was ominous among the people and its meaning was even worse. It meant the place of the skull because it was a rocky cliff whose side resembled a human skull, with its sunken eye sockets and concave nose.

Along the way the crossbeam Jesus was carrying shifted and came to rest against the crown of thorns pushing it deeply into his scalp. He cried out with fearful pain and then he fell to his knees and dropped the crossbeam. The soldiers tried to force him to pick it up again, but he was unable to lift it. They tried to set it on his shoulders after he stood up, but when they did the Rabbi fell again under its weight.

The soldiers were very frustrated by all of this. They were not going to stoop to carrying it for him, that was beneath them. They looked about at the crowded street and saw a large strong man coming into the holy city and they asked him if he was a Roman citizen, to which he answered "no." So, they forcefully pulled him away from his family and pressed him into service against his many protests. He did not understand what they wanted from him and he feared that for some reason they were going to take him to be crucified. His family and the friends that he was traveling with also loudly protested what was going on as they feared for his life too. The officer explained to them that all he was being ordered to do was to carry the crossbeam for Rabbi Jesus. After he carried it to Golgotha he would be freed. The man's name was Simon. He had travelled all the way from Cyrene with his wife and their two sons, Alexander and Rufus, to worship at the Temple. As he was forced to march, he called out to his family to wait there for him.

As they made their way to the place of crucifixion, Simon felt strangely different. He did not recognize the sensations overcoming his body. He felt his hands going numb and his fingers were tingling. He was becoming nauseous and his head felt as if it was spinning. He found that his breathing was becoming very rapid and he began to panic. His arms trembled and he felt an irresistible force upon him as if he might need to run away. If not for his fear of the soldiers he would have run, but they would have restrained him and even beaten him if he ran. He prayed asking the LORD for strength to carry on.

Though Jesus was no longer carrying the cross, they made him march in front of everyone just behind the leading soldiers. They forced him to carry the sign that was inscribed for him and Simon was made to walk behind him. Simon kept his head bowed low for fear of being seen and then his face would be known as a criminal.

Jesus staggered in weakness as he led lead the way to Golgotha. As they approached the Damascus Gate, he heard some of the women of the city wailing. He stopped, turned to them, and called out, "You who have come after me, daughters of Jerusalem, don't weep for me any longer. Weep for yourselves and your children over what will come to be. Now the days will certainty come when the childless will be considered more blessed. For destruction will come and everyone will want to hide, but there will be no place you can go to where you will not be found. And all this will happen because of what is being done to me here.

Chapter Thirty
Mary, Your Son

Following his condemnation in the trial held by the lower court at the high priest's place, John knew that the trial by the full Sanhedrin was going to be a mere formality. When the guards marched Jesus out of the palace he simply left by walking out as easily as he walked in. He did not go to the Judgement Hall next to the Temple complex though. He took a different course. He made his way back to Zechariah's home where they had celebrated the Passover the night before. That was where Mary was staying.

On the street outside the home the early morning light was growing brighter with each minute that past. There he stopped to think about how he would break the news to his Master's mother. He had gone a full day without sleep and the cold night had worn him out considerably. The terrible news that he bore was very distressing to him. He wanted to go inside where it would be warm, but then he would have to answer their questions about why he was there at such an early morning hour and why was he alone. Because of his youth, he had never had to deal directly with the more difficult situations that mature men had to face. A horrible accident or a tragic death were hardly known to him. Dealing with the betrayal, the wrongful arrest, the nighttime trial and the condemnation of his Rabbi were far from his level of experience. He gathered his thoughts and his courage and went to the door where he hesitated. Then he spoke, "Hello" softly just before he knocked.

From within there was a voice who responded to him, "Whose there?" A small window in the door opened and a dimly lit lamp revealed a face. "Who is there? What is your name?"

John realized what he had just set in motion would lead to him having to share his news with Mary. "I am John, son of Zebedee. I am a disciple of Rabbi Jesus."

"What do you want at this hour of the morning?"

"I, ... I must speak with ..." he hesitated. He thought about their customs and how could he speak with Mary directly, especially about this? He knew he would need help doing it. "I must speak with your master, Zechariah."

"My master is asleep and is not to be disturbed. Go away and return later this morning. Then he will see you."

"Please, I beg you. This is most urgent. It cannot wait until then. I must speak with him now."

"Just a moment."

The servant was merely a youth himself and could not grant John's request. He had to go and wake Mikhail, the head servant.

Now Mikhail knew John and when he was told that he was at the door he hurried there at once and brought him in. "John, welcome. Come in please. Excuse our doorkeeper. He did not know who you were."

"Of course." Replied John.

He was led into the main room of the house. "Come and sit. May I offer you some food or something to drink?" It was the custom to offer hospitality to a guest and for the guest to accept.

In the urgency of the situation, John felt he must hold off on accepting the offer. Instead he shared what he had to say. "Mikhail, something terrible has happened."

Then Mikhail understood too that he must set hospitality aside and listen to young John.

"Yes, tell me. What can I do to help you John?"

"In the night as we settled in at Gethsemane, Judas came with chief priests and other officials from the high

231

priest. There he betrayed Rabbi Jesus to them. Their guards arrested him and took him to the high priest's palace. Peter and I followed him there."

Mikhail was in shock and speechless.

"They tried him during the night."

Mikhail remained silent and it appeared as though he was not hearing anything.

"I was there. I saw it with my own eyes. Mikhail, are you listening?"

Mikhail could only nod his head, so great a shock it was to him. Only hours before, he and the entire household there were honored to host Rabbi Jesus and his disciples for their Passover Feast. Now, he feared for what would follow and he dared not to ask. "I will wake my master at once. Please wait here."

As he rose, tears were welling up in his eyes. The news was quite urgent, and he rushed to his master's bedchamber. He composed himself so that he could relay the message without breaking down in tears. He knocked on the door loud enough to wake his master and then he waited.

Zechariah came to the door groggy and wondering what was going on at this early hour of the morning that could concern him. When he opened the door, there was his chief steward with an oil lamp in hand nervously waiting for him. He spoke softly and asked, "Mikhail? What is it?"

"Sir, Rabbi Jesus' young disciple John is here to see you and it is most urgent."

Zechariah was disturbed by this news and worried whatever could it be about. In his sleeping robe he immediately followed behind his servant. John was standing as he nervously waited. Zechariah hugged John with fatherly greeting and then they sat together.

"John what has happened that brings you back to my home at this hour?"

John tried to swallow, but his throat had gone dry. "Sir, as we settled in for the night in Gethsemane, Judas came with chief priests and other officials from the high priest, along with many Temple guards. He pointed my Master out to them. He was arrested and taken to the high priest's palace. The rest of us escaped into the night, but then Peter and I followed them to the palace. They tried him during the night."

Zechariah sat motionless as he listened in near disbelief. He was dreading what he needed to ask, "John, what was the outcome of the trial?"

John stared into the dark corner of the room as if he was detached from his surroundings. "He has been condemned to die for blasphemy." A tear, a single tear, rolled down his face and his countenance fell.

Zechariah also began to stare in the darkness. A moment passed, and then another before he spoke. "We must wake his mother, and somehow find the words to tell her what has happened."

The three of them sat in despair as Zechariah considered how he would break the news to his guest. He had never felt so utterly helpless before in his life. He did not know how to do what he had to do. Then in his hopelessness he led in a prayer, "Most Holy One. Before you we come frightened and with much worrying. How could this have happened? We cannot believe it and yet we know that it has happened somehow. We cry out to you for your aid so that we may somehow find in you the way to bring this news to his mother. By your mighty right hand lead us and by your mercy assist us to care for Mary. Amen."

Zechariah looked about and said, "Mikhail, please wake the cook and ask her to quietly prepare breakfast for us. Wake Gila and Nava and ask them to be in waiting should we need anything. John, I will wake my wife. We will need her help to do this. Please excuse me for a few minutes."

John sat down now that he was feeling more comfortable about doing this with the help he enlisted. Still, as the moment grew closer of when Mary would be told, he began to worry and shake from the great tension he was experiencing.

Soon, Zechariah returned with his wife, Samara, who had been in tears, but was now bearing up for what needed to shortly take place. "Samara, I think it would be best if you could wake Mary and accompany her to this room." She nodded to her husband and left.

Time could not have passed any slower as they anxiously waited for the return of the two women. As they came into the room, Samara showed Mary to a cushion that placed her between herself and Zechariah.

With all the grace he could show and all the maturity that he had come into over his years, Zechariah shared, "Mary, I have to tell you something."

Mary listened to him and her curiosity rose. She looked back at Samara who offered her hand for Mary to hold.

"After Jesus left here last night, he went to the Garden of Gethsemane. Then he was arrested by Temple guards and some chief priests."

Mary listened intensely, not turning away nor blinking an eye. She simply nodded to show Zechariah that he could continue. She held Samara's hand more firmly then.

"They took him to the high priest's palace and tried him on criminal charges during the night. John and Peter were there in secret to see what would happen."

Mary turned to John who nodded to her, assuring her that all this was true.

"Mary, they found Jesus guilty and have sentenced him already." Now as silence followed, Zechariah let the tragic news settle into Mary's mind. In his maturity he knew that when Mary was ready to know what the punishment was to be, that she would ask him.

Mary searched for the words that she wanted to use to ask the question that she feared more than anything in this world. "What …" she held herself back from crying, "… was he found guilty of?"

Slowly, Zechariah gave her the answer, "Mary, he was found guilty of blasphemy."

Mary did not need to ask the last question that lingered for a moment in her thoughts. She knew. Blasphemy had only one punishment, it was death.

There was another silence that followed. There had to be. What could any of them say at this time? There were no words for it. Time had become meaningless to them as they all slipped into mourning.

Then Samara asked Mary if she would have something to eat to keep up her strength, and Mary accepted. Together they left for the dining room and were followed by Gila and Nava who would wait on them. John and Zechariah also joined them in the dining room.

Soon the entire house was stirring, but only with the sound of muffled voices and quiet footsteps. Everyone had been alerted to the tragic news. Zechariah and Samara's children were kept upstairs for their breakfast so that Mary's needs could be attended to without any disturbances. The other women who travelled with Mary and supported her son were woken. There was Mary's sister Mari, John's mother Salome, Mariah the wife of

Clopas, and Mary of Magdala. Mikhail and his wife, Nizznah, who oversaw the female servants spoke to them privately telling them all that had happened. The women prepared themselves for the day and for whatever it might hold for them. They were waiting until they could join with Mary when she was ready to receive them.

At the table Mary asked John, "Please tell me more about what happened."

"As we were settling in for the night, Jesus was praying. The rest of us where having a hard time trying to stay awake with him. Then suddenly he called out to us, 'Quickly! All of you rise from your sleep and see what evil the darkness of this night has brought. The time of my trial now begins."

I rose to my feet and looked around. Then Jesus said, "'Look, all of you! I am betrayed into the hands of evil men.' I saw chief priests and other officials coming and behind them were Temple guards."

John looked at Mary to see if this was too trying for her to listen to. She was shaken by it, but her strength was more than evident and it was clear that she wanted to hear more.

"Then Judas came forward from them and greeted Jesus with a kiss. He did this to point him out to those with him. Peter and I even drew out our swords to fight against them. But Jesus stopped us and willingly allowed himself to be taken into captivity by them. The rest of us, I am heartbroken to admit, fled into the darkness of the night. I found Peter and from where we were hiding we could see them taking Jesus away. We followed them to Caiaphas' palace. I was able to get inside, and I learned that they tried Jesus there in the middle of the night. After that, they took him to the Judgement Hall of Hewn Stone. That is when I came here."

Mary's countenance fell as she heard this and she became weepy. She remembered when her son had escaped attempts on his life before. Now she knew that this was not going to happen this time because John had told her that he surrendered to them without resisting.

Though she continually followed her son to all those places his ministry had taken him, she and the other women had always remained in low profile. She had very actively cared for her son and those he called to be his disciples by washing their clothes, preparing their meals, and looking after their needs so that they could devote their full attention to their Rabbi and his teaching. Now, her hands gently shook, and her voice had acquired a soft quiver in it. She was hesitant in what she said and did. Mary asked for the other women who she travelled with to join her. She stood to greet them. Then they came and bowed in humility before her and offered hugs and words of comfort to her.

Salmone also turned to her son, John. She took him into her arms and hugged him very tightly and tears streamed down her cheeks. She needed to be comforted because her sons, James and John, had also come so close to danger in the night. She needed to comfort him also and offered him words of reassurance too, "You did the right thing John. I am sure it was very difficult for you to …" But she couldn't find the words to describe what he had gone through.

John replied, "Yes, mother. Thank you."

Zechariah now rejoined them in the room. "Earlier, I sent out two of my servants to see what they could learn. Just now one of them returned. He reported to me that Jesus was again condemned in the Judgement Hall." He waited for Mary to gather this in before going on with the rest, and she soon nodded to him. "They brought him to the Roman governor's headquarters so that his sentence may be carried out."

Mary had only one thought, that she needed to be with her son, "I must go to him. He needs me with him more than ever now."

Everyone in the room worried for her and cautioned her against leaving the safety of Zechariah's home.

Zechariah himself said, "Yes, Mary there are dangers in the city for all of Jesus' disciples and followers right now. Anyone of us could be arrested by the chief priests or the Temple guards. We may even need to quietly move you in secret to a safe house. You must stay here until all this passes."

But Mary would not be deterred, not even if she was risking her own life. "I am sure that what they do to my son is not more than I can bear as his mother and what I endured to bring him into this world. I will be with him in this, even if it means my death he means more to me that that."

Zechariah spoke to her again with the temperance of an aged father he cautioned her, "My servant reported that there is a large and angry crowd led by some of the chief priests at the gate to the Praetorium. They are arguing their case against your son to the governor. Please wait in my home until I receive word about the outcome. It is still possible that the governor will not confirm their sentence and refuse to carry it out."

All those with her agreed with Zechariah and pleaded with her to remain, to which she agreed.

Zechariah's two trustworthy servants took turns with each other as they stood watch near the governor's headquarters. They rotated bringing updated reports to their master for several hours, until at about the twelfth hour, they both came with their final report.

As Zechariah came into the large room where Mary and her companions were waiting, it was visibly clear that he was very shaken. The room fell silent and he told them, "I am afraid that ..." He nearly burst into tears but regained himself as he continued. "... that our Lord has been condemned to die and will be taken for crucifixion shortly."

As his words fell upon their ears, some broke out into weeping. Mary's sister, Mari, who was at her side held her and rocked her gently as the two of them wept over the tragic word about his fate that had come to them.

A few minutes had passed when Mary rose to her feet and said, "I must go to him now."

Zechariah cautioned her, "But Mary, it will be very difficult for you to see what they have done to him. It will be even harder for you to see what they will still do to him. I wish that you would not leave my home. Please stay with my family today. Let me send my servants there. They will bring us word of all that happens."

Mary paused and remembered the day when her infant son was presented to the LORD at the Temple. "No, I will not go into hiding. I knew this day would come. I knew it. When I dedicated my son in the Temple a man named Simeon came to us and spoke a prophecy. He said, "You must know, and forever remember; your son has a destiny that is set before him. He will bring about the downfall to destruction of some of our people and he will bring about the arising of many others in Israel to new heights. He shall be a sign to us all. But beware, he will expose the thoughts and secret intentions of evil men so that their hearts will be known. Then they will speak against him. They will oppose him and then they will reject him. When this happens, then shall the sword's long blade pierce your heart and soul though."

Zechariah now knew that he could not talk her out of going to be with her son, though he longed to extend his hospitality to her for what the day would hold. "Very well, Mary. Know that you are always welcome to return here, always."

"Thank you for your kindness to me. I will never forget it."

With that for their send off, Mary, along with John at her side set out to find her son. Following along close behind them were the women who had been with her for the last three years. They all walked quickly to the Praetorium to see if they could find her son there.

As they neared Pilate's headquarters John spoke to Mary and the other women, "Mary, they must not see you at the gate to the Praetorium. Please wait here, you and all the women, and I will go there. If I don't return, you must return to Zechariah's home and go into hiding."

At the gate to the Praetorium John did not see any Temple authorities or their guards. He called out to a soldier standing watch just inside the gate, "Can you tell me where Rabbi Jesus is?"

The guard acted as though he didn't even see John.

John spoke to him again, "Rabbi Jesus, Jesus of Nazareth, do you know where he is?"

The soldier did not know Aramaic and simply shook his head unknowingly and spoke back to him in Latin, "Nescitis quid vis stultum" which is translated to say, 'What do you want, your ignorant fool?'

John shook his head not knowing what the soldier meant. Then he tried again to see if the soldier knew something, "Rabbi Jesus? Jesus of Nazareth, do you know where he is?"

The soldier listened more attentively and tried to recognize what John was saying. He nodded and took on a solemn look and spoke to him, "Iesus Nazarenus transduco Goolgotda pro cruciarius." Which meant, Jesus of Nazareth was taken to Golgotha to be crucified.

John's heart sank low as he recognized a few of the words that were said to him. He fell to his knees and cried out loudly as his hope and faith for the coming of their Messiah's reign was dashed to this bitter end. He rose to his feet and returned. He spoke to Mary and the rest in fear and trembling as he uttered, "Mary, I know where they have taken him."

Mary listened and waited to hear the dreaded words that would follow.

John said, "It is not good. They have taken him to be crucified. It is outside the city walls. It is a place called the skull."

Her eyes welled full with tears that she was not ready to shed and looking to John one tumbled down her face, "I must be there for him. He cannot die alone, forsaken by his mother."

John nodded in agreement and they turned to make the journey there.

Now they all gather up their strength and courage to become witnesses to his fate as they set out. John took Mary and led her out of the Holy City's gate against the flow of pilgrims pouring in for the festival and took her to see what had become of her son.

Chapter Thirty-One
Nails Shall Pierce You Through

As Jesus neared the place of crucifixion he looked up to see the place know as Golgotha, the place of the skull. It was located just north of the Holy City on an east-west road. It was a large and imposing landmark, a large rocky cliff in whose side eerily appeared the image of sunken eye sockets with troubled eyebrows and a large hole for the nose. This place was very foreboding to all. A cold wind blew there constantly that day and there was no place for anyone to shelter in. Because of its location along a major road it served as a warning to all who passed, that lawbreakers in the empire would pay a terrible price for their crimes.

As Jesus and the rest turned off the road the soldiers began their preparations to crucify the prisoners. One of the thieves looked out to the far horizon. It was as if he was looking to see if anyone was coming to rescue him like Elijah, or perhaps he wondered where he could run to, if he could only escape. The soldiers were none too kind to him. One came up from behind and kicked him behind the knees forcing him to collapse on the rocky ground below. The other thief was so exhausted that he simply fell to the ground. In his weakness he was unable to break his own fall and as he hit the ground hard, he whimpered in pain and called out to the LORD asking for mercy.

Simon, the man who carried the cross for Jesus, was quick to lay it down. He stepped back and looked down and around him. The people traveling past squinted at him, some gave him dirty looks and insulted him as if he were a criminal. Still others looked at him with compassion knowing the cruelty of the Romans and the injustices that they carried out. Simon felt ashamed. Ashamed that he was mistaken for being a criminal. Ashamed that he was forced to carry Jesus' cross. Though it was hard for him to admit to, he sensed many deeper and frightening emotions surfacing in his heart. He felt compassion for Jesus, that no man, guilty or not, should have to suffer this excruciating fate for his crimes. He understood what would happen there shortly and he wanted nothing more to do with it. He wondered if Jesus and the other two with him were really criminals. Or were they just three unfortunate people who fell into disfavor with the Romans and were sentenced to die this inhumane death. It all made him shudder in fear for what this world and the people in it could do to a man.

As he looked about, his eyes made contact with the Rabbi's and then his heart fell low for what he had been compelled to do. He nervously squirmed about being unsure of what to do in that awkward moment. He looked up to the Rabbi and mouthed the words, "I am so sorry, they forced me to do this for you. Forgive me, I pray."

Jesus looked at him with compassion and whispered loud enough for Simon to hear. "I understand. Thank you for carrying my cross for me. I forgive you."

Then Simon closed his eyes for a second and when he opened them he nodded knowingly. He had a new sense of how he felt about having carried Jesus' cross. Forgiven of course, but also renewed, stronger and somehow blessed. He felt a new and deep love for his family too. He looked away and to the city, and then back at the centurion as he backed away in fear. He worried that they would compel him to do something even worse for them like force him to help in nailing the condemned to their crosses. The old guard looked at him and told him that he was free to go as he pointed with his arm at the road back to the Holy City.

Simon turned and began to walk away. He was in a hurry to get to the road where he could blend in with the people there. He quickened his pace because he could not get away fast enough. Soon he was running, but then he had to slow down and walk again because he was out of breath. He remembered how Jesus forgave him and the new feelings he had for his life and he could not wait to be reunited with his wife and sons again. They were exactly where he left them on the road. He quickly embraced them in overflowing love and the hope that he would never be separated from them again. Now, together, they continued their journey into the Holy City.

Back at Golgotha the soldiers continued their preparations to crucify the three men. They asked each other, "Which one do we hang first?"

To which one answered with a heinous laugh, "Royalty first?"

Another soldier replied, "Yes, but of course. How silly of us."

Now it was their practice to offer the condemned men a drink of cheap wine that they had mixed with myrrh and gall. It was a very bitter drink that would medicate them and relieve some of their pain. It also made the soldier's jobs easier because the men would offer less resistance being intoxicated by it. The criminals awaiting crucifixion also knew that the mixture would to help them bare the pain that they must endure. They offered it to Jesus first, but when he tasted it he realized what was in it and he refused to drink it. The soldiers then passed it to one of the thieves. He grabbed it and drank it hardily as some of it rolled down from the sides of his mouth and fell to the ground. He would have taken all of it, but one of the soldiers scolded him saying, "Hay, here now! Don't drink all of it! It is for both of you."

But the thief would not stop, so the soldier struck him in the head with his fist and he collapsed to the ground. The bottle fell and was spilling out on to the ground, but the other thief quickly reached for it and drank what little was left.

The soldiers stripped the men of their clothes. It was humiliating for them and they were left with just their loin cloths covering them. As they examined the garments that the two thieves had been wearing, they saw that they were ragged and torn and so they discarded them.

Next, they examined Jesus' robe and tunic and they saw that he was wearing the garments of a wealthy man. This pleased them greatly because whatever they might take from a condemned man was like the spoils of war and the riches go to the victors. These items they could keep for themselves or sell for the money. The purple robe that had been draped around Jesus was quite long. It was a finely woven robe and they knew it must have been very costly. All four wanted it for their own. So they decided that they would tear it into quarters and each would take a portion of the cloth. As they examined his tunic they found that it was an especially fine linen garment woven of one piece from the top down and having no seams. This was a very expensive piece of clothing. Again, all four wanted it, but to tear it would have ruined it because each piece of it would eventually unravel leaving them with only a pile of thread. So, they chose to cast lots for it for it. The soldier who won the tunic flaunted it to the others holding it up high and waving it before their faces. One of the soldiers took losing hard and was mad about it being flaunted in front of him. He was ready to turn on the soldier who won the gamble and fight him over it. But he knew he would not win and the other soldiers would also fight against him. So, he resolved to simply ignore the man and his taunting.

The soldiers removed the shackles from the Rabbi's hands but the ones around his feet were left on for now. Jesus offered the soldiers no resistance but neither did he help them. They marched him over to the cross that was brought there for him. Then one of the soldiers put his foot behind Jesus' feet and another shoved him to the rocky ground below where his cross was placed. His shoulders landed on the crossbeam and his head bobbed up and down in the air behind it. His muscles tensed up in pain from when he hit it. A soldier stood on the shackles that were locked around his feet and held them securely to the ground. Another held his left arm to the beam and the other one moved his right hand to the place where it would be nailed to the cross. Then another one came. He was the executioner. He was holding a hammer and three nails in his hands. This one stretched out Jesus' hand and examined it palpating the bones to find the location where he would drive the nail through. He did not hesitate but quickly placed his nail to his palm and pressed it hard into his skin. He looked at the other soldiers to see that they were ready. Then he lifted back his hammer, took aim and struck the first piercing blow.

The silence of the moment was shattered by the loud metallic ringing that sounded out as the cold hard metal of the hammer stuck the nail for the first time. It was as though time suddenly slowed and everything that now happened was in slow motion. As the nail was driven, the light of the sun flickered as though creation itself was in pain as the redemption from sin began its costly course. The executioner looked to the sky wondering if there were clouds setting in, but there were none. He looked across the landscape wondering if there was a sandstorm on the horizon, but there was none. There was no reason for it that he could detect, and he returned to his duty.

At the strike of the hammer's first blow, Jesus' muscles from head to toe suddenly grew tense and his body arched outward away from the cross as he cried out in pain.

The nail had pierced his skin and was being driven through his hand and into the cross. The nail caused blood to flow profusely out of his wound. It splattered on to the executioner's hands and he knew that it must have hit a vein or artery. Despite this, he would not stop, not until the nail was firmly set. With each blow the ringing sound of the hammer striking the nail was short lived as it was muted by the surrounding soft flesh of his hand.

Again, with each blow of the hammer the Rabbi called out even louder in pain. Then third time he stuck the nail and it was firmly set in place through the palm of his hand and into the cross. Jesus wept in anguish. The same was done to his other hand.

Then the executioner moved to his feet. One soldier held his left foot down on the ground. The other moved his right onto the cross, placing its sole flat against the beam. The soldier with the hammer examined the that foot to find the correct location for the nail to pass through. Then he placed a very large and long nail there, drew back his hand, and drove the nail into it. Jesus screamed out it pain and struggled to remain relaxed as the soldiers did their jobs. Now the two soldiers took his left foot and held it with the sole securely flat over the beam. The executioner grabbed the nail that was in his right foot and lined it up over his left one. The other soldiers held both his feet firmly in place. The hammer was now raised up high over the nail. With a powerful swing of his arm he struck down hard driving the nail into both his feet. Then he struck the nail again even harder this time driving it into the beam beneath it. Again, he struck it, once, then twice in rapid succession. Jesus screamed intensely filling and emptying his lung completely. His screaming carried with it the sound of the pain he felt, and the soldiers cringed in pain as they heard it. They wondered what manner of man this was that they could feel his pain too.

Jesus looked at them and tried to catch their eyes, but they never looked at him, not even once. Perhaps it was too much for them to look upon the eyes of those who they crucified. Then he looked heavenward and prayed, "Abba, my Father, forgive them, for they do not know what they have done."

Before they raised his cross, the officer called for the sign Pilate had made. He ordered that it be nailed on to the top of Jesus' cross so that everyone would know who he was. Then the soldiers tied ropes around the top of the cross and lined it up so that as they raised it up it would fall into the hole that it would stand in. So, lifting it up they guided it into place and it fell hard, down into its place. As it fell into the hole and hit bottom, Jesus body was jerked hard and he called out with an immense cry of pain. He felt the strong yank on his hands and feet causing them to burn deeply. The burning also passed into his legs and into his arms. His face grimaced as he clenched his teeth down hard and scowled. Tears welled up in his eyes and slowly rolled down his face. His head bounced back and struck the cross and the thorns of his crown were driven in deeply into his scalp. His eyes rolled back, and it looked as if the pain was so great that he might pass out from it.

Now when Jesus tried to take his first breath on the cross it was an immensely agonizing struggle. He tried to breathe in but was hardly able to. For him, and all the crucified, it was like trying to breathe just through your nose when you have a cold. That was because as he hung down with his arms above him, it forced his neck and chest inward. This in turn pinched his throat and closed his airway. Jesus, realizing that he was unable to breathe, looked about with a sense of great worry. His eyes searched about as he struggled to breathe and tried to think of what to do. His hunger for air grew and his face reddened. The muscles of his abdomen tightened and pushed hard in the hopes that he could breathe again, but to no avail. He tried to expand and contract his chest to breathe, but this was of no help either. His face showed an increasing sense of urgency on it. He began to tense up his arms and legs and move about straining for a simple breath of air.

Before long in his struggle he stood up on the nails and pulled with his arms to raise up and though it was a terribly painful thing to do, he found that this allowed him to breathe. This was required each time he took a breath because it relieved the narrowing pressure on his airway. But standing on his nail pierced feet was far worse than the torture he suffered when he was thrashed. Then someone else inflicted the pain on him. Now, he was the one who had to inflict this terrible pain on himself. He found that as he made an effort to standup, his natural reflexes reacted to the pain and caused him to stop instantly and he grimaced in the worst way. The nerves in his feet and legs felt searing fire in them. His feet and ankles ached deeply, as though they were severely sprained.

The soldiers then began to do the same to the criminals and Jesus looked on. He struggled to cope with the endless agony. His eyes were filled with compassion for these men as they suffered just as he was. As they attempted to throw the first thief to the ground he fought with them as best he could. He was bound with chains and shackles and was no match for these professional soldiers. They did not let him get away with resisting and two of them brutally struck him with clubs. Eventually, he collapsed onto the ground and wept for the pain was too much to endure. When he was raised up, the centurion called out his crimes. The other thief offered no resistance at all. He had fallen into a deep depression. He appeared to be strangely withdrawn from all that was happening to him. As they drove the nails into his hands and feet he merely muttered to himself in tears and retracted in pain as the hammer blows were struck. When they were raised up their crimes were also called out by the soldiers. As the second one listened he nodded, apparently admitting to them all. Then he also shook his head like he was denying them as well, or perhaps it was a sign of his regret over all that he had done. The first criminal cursed the soldiers as one of them read off his crimes and called them all fools

So again, he tried to rise up on his feet and overcome the unbearable pain. This took incredible concentration and determination. As he rose the second time he struggled with weakness in his arms and his legs. His hands cramped into a loose fist as though he was trying to grasp at something. He pulled first with his stronger right arm to rise up and then with his left continuing and back and forth. He pushed up on his feet against the weight of his body, against the pain, and rose up. This caused his feet to cramp and his toes to spread outward. Now he grimaced in so much pain that he thought he might pass out. Higher he pulled and pushed, until at last he could gasp for one breath. It made him think about what a man might experience if he were drowning in deep water as he struggled to use his hands and feet to try and surface and stay atop the water. That in the desperation of drowning, he had but one hope which was to stay afloat and breathe. As Jesus rose up he was able to breathe again, and he panted quickly to try and catch his breathe. Over and over again he struggled to do this because his life depended on it. It was an agonizing process that he had to go through because the starvation and hunger for air was greater than his intolerance to the pain. Finally, as he took another breath his face showed a small and short-lived sign of relief, but the mental and physical strain that he endured under quickly returned and erased that away.

Chapter Thirty-Two
Mock the King

The sun refused to give its full light during the hours Rabbi Jesus suffered on the cross. There were no clouds to be seen, no fog, or even a mild sand storm. Its appearance was a haze and it was unlike anything else they had ever experienced. Its light was too weak to cast a shadow and the temperature dropped. It was a divine action by God the Father who would not let the sun cast its brilliant light on what they were doing. He was condemning them in their sins and showing them that they were not of the light, but of the darkness when evil ruled.

Standing a stone's throw from the cross where Jesus was being crucified there was a large company of religious authorities. They were led by Chief Priests Rabsaris, Elamadad, and Kallahadad. Among their ranks were included scribal lawyers and many workers from the Temple. Though it was the calling of a priest to do it, none of them offered spiritual care to anyone that day. They made no effort to offer forgiveness for their sins, or the assurance of heaven. The scribes, who knew many of the scripture by heart, did not recite the Psalms or any of the Holy Scriptures, nor did any of them say so much as a single prayer for anyone. Still, they were a very vocal company of people and they were the most adamant of the authorities who wanted Jesus condemned.

Despite the extremes these leaders of the people had gone to, they did not bear up well if they looked at Rabbi Jesus as he suffered. They would glance his way from time to time and then it was always so that they could cast a terrible insult upon him with their words.

Now the three leaders from the ranks of the chief priests discussed amongst themselves privately their worries about the legal proceedings. Elamadad wondered, "What if it should become known among the people that we did not follow the Law to condemned him?"

Rabsaris quietly told him, "Our scribes are the best at what they do, they were there. No one can guide us better in the Law then them. They did not object to this. If there is a need to cast blame on anyone, let it fall on them."

Kallahadad pointed out, "They will not like that."

Rabsaris laughed quietly, "Then let the blame fall onto the Romans. No one likes them anyway."

Elamadad cautioned, "But the people talk. They will hear. And there will be rumors."

Rabsaris confidently responded, "Let them talk. None of them were there. Their talk is only speculation at best. And if there are rumors that we don't care for, then we will circulate rumors of our own that put us in a better light."

Elamadad worried, "You make it sound so simple."

Rabsaris did not like having to feel as if he needed to defend himself over what had already taken place, so he turned the conversation toward a new focus. He looked at Rabbi Jesus as he hung on the cross, and shouted out to him for all to hear, "Look at you Jesus! Are you the same man who was so bold as he taught in our Temple! For a man who was never at a loss for cleaver things to say, you certainly have met your match in us."

Sadly, it was not enough for these three that they had sent an innocent man to be crucified. They had to come and mock him and lead others to do the same.

Rabsaris looked at the other chief priests and the rest of them who were there with him, "How can you be so quiet?

Our plans have been successful! Look at this miserable thing before us. Say something!"

Elamadad rose up and shouted, "What was it that he taught in the Temple, about vineyard justice and it being taken away from us? What has always been ours is still ours you false prophet!"

Others joined in jeering him too. An elder shouted, "You wanted to be a King, so we delivered you to the Romans and they made you a King. And soon you will be dead!"

Kallahadad shouted out, "Who will be your subjects?! Only fools who will follow you to their own destruction!"

A scribe yelled out, "You wanted to be our King, so we turned you over to the Romans! You have your crown. How do you like being a King now?"

Another scribe stood forward and shouted, "This man imagined he could destroy our Temple, but he cannot. He said he would raise up another one in three days! Yeah, in three days he will be rotting in a common grave."

"I heard he had the power to work miracles, heal the sick, and raise the dead. But just look at him. He has no power here and there is nothing he can do to help himself escape death."

"Did I hear that you can walk on water? Why don't you walk on the air and leave the cross to keep yourself from dying?"

"You wanted us to believe in you? Why should we believe in you? So that we may share in your fate?"

"Show us a sign or a miracle from the cross. Then we will believe in you."

All these religious people who were gathered were well known for their respectable manners. But now they showed that they were capable of the most outrageous behavior known among people.

Another one called out, "You say you are the Son of God. Then why are you dying? God is immortal."

"They say this is the man who raised the dead. How can that be? He cannot even save himself from death!"

"He says he trusts in God and yet God does not save him from execution, so how can he claim that he is God's Son?"

"He deserves every bit of this punishment and more. He made himself out to be the Son of God, but God would never let this happen to his Son. He saved others from death, but look, he cannot save himself."

The soldiers also joined in mocking him. One stood up tall, gripped his sword, and with the other hand he held high his spear saying, "If you are their King, call on your subjects to fight against us so that they may save you from this fate."

Another soldier called out, "You have your crown? Where is your power? Are you unable to come down from the cross and begin your reign?"

There was a well-travelled road that ran next to Golgotha and many pilgrims were passing by as they made their way into the city for the festival. As they passed, they saw the religious authorities and heard them shouting as they mocked the Rabbi. It was a common practice to hurl insults at the condemned as they were dying on a cross. It was part of their punishment and some of the people were glad to insult the criminals. But none of them knew that this was the famed Rabbi they had heard about. So many of them followed in the example of the religious leaders as though it was a sacred obligation to them to insult him.

Through this entire time the Rabbi did not say a word of rebuke against them either, nor did he look their way. It was not that he turned a deaf ear to them. It was because he was dying for their sins including the very sins they were committing at that time by mocking him.

Chapter Thirty-Three
At the Cross, At His Feet

As they neared their destination, John pushed hard against the pilgrims hurrying to get into the city. He was leading Mary by the hand and trying to make his way against the wave of people who could not imagine why anyone would be leaving the Holy City as the festival was underway.

Mary followed closely behind John. Though her heart had fallen when she first heard the news of her son's arrest, she had been nurturing hope and praying for his release. But then when she learned that the governor had condemned him to die she knew there was little hope left for him. She allowed herself to believe that he might have escaped from his captors along the way to Golgotha as he had escaped death so many times before. As the two rushed as fast as they could, Mary hoped for another miracle to happen, but she feared the worst was going to happen. It had all come upon her so suddenly that it was hardly real to her. She wanted to hurry to her son's side, but not to be a witness to his death. She wanted to be with him so that he would know that though he had been rejected and condemned to die, that he was not rejected by his mother or his family.

There was following immediately behind Mary and John the women who had helped to care for the needs of the Rabbi and his disciples for the past three years. All of them were accustomed to traveling long distances, up to twenty-five or occasionally thirty miles in a day. However, none of them were conditioned for running and as they approached the place of his crucifixion they were exhausted.

John let his eyes look into the distance and he could see three men hanging. He was unable to see which one might be his Master, but it was all that he dared to view at that time. As they neared close to the three crosses, John worried about how Mary would react to the sight of her son. He tried to imagine what things would look like, but his thoughts stopped shy of thinking of him being hung on a cross to die. He could not bring himself to image anything more. He worried about how Mary would ever be able to endure this. "You must know that I will stay with you in all of this," he said to her. He paused to prepare himself for what he had to say next, to prepare Mary for what she would see. "Mary, this will be very difficult for you, to be there and to see what they have done to him."

Streams of tears now rolled down her cheeks and she thought to hide her face by pulling her veil up higher but as she reached for it, it fell to the side. She looked at John and nodded showing him that she was still going to follow him there to be with her son. In doing this she revealed to him one of her most private moments in life. She told him, "John I must be with him. I bore him and gave him birth and I must be with him in his death."

John was assured that he had done what he could, little as it was, to help her before they went any further. Their pace slowed, and the other women gathered in near to Mary and together they approached the place of the crucifixion. As they neared, a soldier stepped forward and pointed to the ground while yelling at them in Latin. They did not understand his words, but they knew that he was telling them how close they could approach Jesus. It was there that they stood. Their eyes had been glued to the ground for fear of what they might see. Now they let their eyes look up, cautiously, slowly. The saw the base of the cross, their eyes rose still more, they saw his pierced feet nailed to the wooden beam, and a slow crimson flow of blood dripped from them striking the ground below.

A mother knows her child and as Mary saw his feet so wounded any doubt that had been lingering in her thoughts was now vanquished from her. She knew this was her son and she became faint and began to fall to the ground. John reached out for her to brake her fall. Her fists pounded hard the rocky ground in rapid succession over what they had done to her son. Her cries came from deep within her and it was the sounds of violent protesting and deepest brokenness.

John knelt to her side to help her back up as she spoke, "No, no John. I can do this." She rose to her knees and prayerfully put her hands together. Again, she let her eyes look at the cross where her son had been nailed. She beheld his feet and taking courage she let her head tip further back and her eyes rose until she saw his face. Looking steadily upward, she saw her son and their eyes met. He was in torment and laboring to breath. He could do nothing more than offer her that momentary glance. Her thoughts tried to imagine what her son was enduring. She wanted to be there for him to support him somehow and not add to his distress by disclosing too much of hers back to him. The women who came to be with Jesus gathered in to stand as close as they could to Mary.

Mary gasped for breath as she was stricken again with the memory of what was said by devout Simeon when she presented her infant son in the Temple. "You must know and forever remember: your son, has a destiny that is set before him. He will bring about the downfall to destruction of some of our people and he is for the arising of many others in Israel to new heights. He shall be a sign to us all.

But beware, he will expose the thoughts and secret intentions of evil men so that their hearts will be known. Then they will speak against him, they will oppose him and then they will reject him. When this happens, then shall the sword's long blade pierce your heart and soul though."

She wept softly and her hands rose to her mouth to muffle the sound as she gasped from knowing that this recollection's fulfillment was now underway. From deep within her, the sounds deepest brokenness was heard as she prayed,

"My God, my God, from my heart I call out to you,
Yahweh, God of my ancestors, my heart has fallen low.
Why have you looked with disfavor upon my son?
His glory was once the miracles that he brought,
and in the hungry people that he feed.
Now he will be remembered for his death.
It was out of love for you that he did
great things for the people,
in compassion he took mercy
upon the poor and the weak.
Is there no mercy for him now?
How can it be that you have
turned your face away from him?
Did you raise him up only
to have him suffer this agony?
Why have you let the proud lift him up in this way?
Why have you turned a deaf ear to my child's voice?"

Mary's hands reached upward to heaven and motioned for God to hear her plea as she had prayed. Now silent tears rolled down her face as she hoped for an answer, for her son, that he would be delivered from this injustice. But this day, no answer came to her. She recalled how she had spent the last few days preparing for the great festival of the Passover and reminiscing of God's mighty deliverance of her ancestors from Pharaoh's fierce oppression. Now, this execution of her son had taken all that away from her, all of it. Just as the ruler of Egypt had ordered the murder of their people's baby boys, now another ruler had demanded her child's life. Mary reached for her son though she could not go to him. She reached for him as if she could touch him, motioning as though she was stroking his face to sooth him.

The other women joined in close around her. They struggled to provide their presence for their Rabbi and to comfort his mother. Their own need to grieve would come only after his needs and Mary's needs were met. They all agreed with each other that Jesus must not die alone and that Mary must not be there alone with him because they both desperately needed their support.

All the women present had been with the dying before, sitting in vigil with them in the hours leading up to their passing. It was always much to endure. This death was not like the others. None of those who had been gathered to their ancestors had died from being punished for crimes committed, let alone been crucified. Though all of them had seen a crucifixion, it was at a distance and only for the shortest of time as they quickly passed it by. Then they dared only to glance at it, so horror filled was it. Now, they could not avoid it and they were torn between wanting to look away, or even walking away, and not daring to leave his side, because they loved and believed in him so much.

None of them fully understood what Jesus was struggling through. How could they? The pain he endured just to take a simple breath was beyond comprehension. As they cast their eyes on him they wondered why he tortured himself by standing up on his feet and pulling himself up higher on the nails with his arms. Then they saw how he held himself up and gasped for air, breathing rapidly, two or three quick breaths. Then falling in exhaustion, he grimaced in a frightfully painful way.

As they watched, they hoped that he might look upon them, but his very survival depended on using all of his strength, the strength of his body and of his mind by concentrating fully to repeat the endless torturous exercise just to breathe. His great physical strength and insurmountable endurance was now being exhausted to its terminal end. The weight of his body seemed to grow as his muscles became increasingly weaker. His strong physique was being altered before their eyes. His feet and lower legs became swollen with fluid as his heart weakened. As his suffering continued, his muscles began to spasm from fatigue. They could now see the faint beating of his heart through his ribs.

With a sense of utter helplessness, Mary looked to John. Her hand rose to her forehead to hold her head up from a deep weariness. Her countenance revealed her sense of despair, of hopelessness and desperation. She wondered was there anything he could do? He was one of her son's apostles, the ones he gave special gifts to so that in his name they could heal the sick, cleanse lepers, and even raise the dead. What could John do? He looked at her knowing how great her suffering was as her son's life was being taken from him. He did not want to add to her distress or give her a false hope. He slowly shook his head from side to side and his eyes wandered as his mind searched in vain for a thought of what could he possibly do to help her.

Jesus, aware of this, struggled hard to rise again. His face was contorted with pain and he stood upon the nail in his feet. He clenched his jaw tightly as he turned his head from side to side to see his contracting arms as he stood tall. Catching his breath, he looked down upon mother, "Woman, look to him as you own son now." And his eyes moved to John, "From here on, now this is your mother." In earnest Mary listened attentively so that she could be responsive to everything he said in the hopes that it would give him some small measure of comfort. As that word came she recognized that her son was not asking anything for his own needs, instead he was providing for her needs. In her mind it first seemed strange. John was not old enough to have a family, or even take a wife yet, let alone support a mother. Still, it was John alone who had faithfully followed her son from his arrest, throughout his trials, and to Golgotha. Therefore, he was the one Jesus could trust with this important task. She accepted her son's instructions knowing that he needed to provide for her in this way so that he could leave this world.

Then there arrived a wealthy man, Joseph of Arimathea, who had defended Jesus in the Sanhedrin. He had secretly been a disciple of Jesus before this, but now it become known that he had stood up and defended him in the court proceedings. He was waiting for the Kingdom of God and had hoped that Jesus was the long-awaited Messiah. Joseph came to Mary and bowed to her, "Mary, I did everything I could to get Jesus released. I argued his innocence before the Sanhedrin, but to no avail. I'm so sorry that I could not have done more for your son."

Mary reached out her hand and he took hold of it. She squeezed his tightly saying, "Thank you" and she nodded her head to him in acknowledgement of all that he did.

Soon another secret follower of Jesus' came. His name was Nicodemus. He was a renown rabbi. He was the one who had come to Jesus by night. As he hurried along, he shook his head not believing what he was now seeing, but it was just as it had been told him. As he grew nearer to Golgotha he saw the images of three men on crosses. He quickened his pace, moving as fast as an old man could run. He had to fight against the people still coming into the city. Soon his eyes welled up with tears for fear of what would soon become fully apparent to him. He looked forward and then forced his eyes to look up. There at the base of that rocky mount were the three men in plain view. He looked at them and saw the Rabbi in the middle of the two others. His head dropped as he was overcome with grief and terror struck his heart. "Oh, dear God, how can this be?" he cried out. Now in the greatest reverence, he slowed down and walked at a mournfully slow pace as he came near to his cross.

He saw from the corner of his eye the chief priests and all those with them, but he did not acknowledge them with even so much as a glance. As he looked at the cross where Jesus hung, he saw Mary and John. He slowly approached them. As he drew near, Mary diverted her eyes from her son to see who this was. John also looked, and they greeted Nicodemus who then came and stood alongside them. Nothing was said. What could be said? It was simply understood that he was joining them in their great sorrow over Jesus' looming death.

It was not long before the cold of the darkened sky began to chill them. Added to that was the cold wind that blew relentlessly. So, they all drew in closely together for warmth and to shield Mary from the weather. John, who would not leave her side, wrapped his arm around her hoping to keep her warm.

At a distance, the soldiers also wrapped their capes around themselves tightly and they started a fire to warm themselves with. They gathered a large supply of dried out palm branches that had fallen to the ground, and some dried-out tree branches that had fallen nearby. Against the wind they had some difficulty getting it started and as the fire took hold, the kindling of it gave off a terrible scent of burnt leaves, one that harshly burned their eyes. As John looked at them, he was reminded of the fresh palm branches that countless people had laid at Jesus feet only six days ago as he paraded into Jerusalem. Now the rejoicing of that day became a painful memory for him as saw the smoke and soot of their kindling rise and vanish into the wind.

Some of the women who were there worried about Mary and all that she was suffering in. Mary's sister spoke to her in nothing more than a quiet whisper, "Mary, you do not have to endure this. Come with me to Joseph's home. It's nearby and he has opened it to us. We can wait there until this is over. Do not let yourself be burdened so greatly by standing here when there is nothing more that you or anyone else can do. Then, when he is buried you may return to see him."

Mary swallowed hard and John held her tightly with his right arm. She waited to answer. First she needed to think for herself and come to the realization of why she was there, or if it was better to leave. Then she could put words to what she was feeling. "He is my son. I will be with him in this. I will not leave him. I will not show my back to him. Let them take my life too, but I will not leave him here alone. I travailed to give him birth and in pain I brought him into this world. I was the first to hold him in my arms. I will be with him in his dying so that I may hold him again even though he will be dead." Mari looked into her sister's eyes as she spoke, and tears of sadness streamed down their cheeks. There was no question left to ponder, Mary would stay.

Now Nicodemus stood to the front of them and he began to recite from the Psalms and they all joined in as well,

> *"O LORD, rebuke me not in thine anger,*
> *neither chasten me in thy displeasure.*
> *Have mercy upon me, O LORD; for I am weak.*
> *O LORD, heal me; for my bones are put out of joint.*
> *My soul is sorely tormented, but thou,*
> *O LORD, how long must I wait?*
> *Return, O LORD, deliver my soul*
> *and save me for thy mercies' sake.*
> *For in death there is no remembrance of thee,*
> *And in the grave who shall give thee thanks?*
> *I am weary with my groaning,*
> *all the night long I weep great tears,*
> *And I covered my couch with my tears.*
> *My eyes are twisted dry because of grief,*
> *And have grown old because of all my enemies.*
> *Depart from me, all workers of iniquity,*
> *for the LORD has heard the voice of my weeping.*
> *The LORD has heard my supplication,*
> *the LORD will receive my prayerful cry.*
> *Let all my enemies be made ashamed and brought low,*
> *let them turn back and be suddenly humbled."*[9]

---

[9] Based on Psalm 6, KJV

Then in silence they waited. For what they were enduring there were no words they could find that could help. Time passed so slowly, and their bodies ached from the tension and the cold. They all knew that once on the cross there were no last-minute stays of execution. The Romans did not practice mercy at this point. Never before had they felt so helpless. Never before had they all felt so hopeless. What was there to be said? What more was there to do? Nothing, nothing at all.

Chapter Thirty-Four
Jesus, Remember Me

As the religious authorities were mocking Rabbi Jesus, one of the criminals took notice of them and what they were saying. It seemed strange to him that they were there at all. They were priests and scribes. Even more strange was what they were saying about the man who was hanging next to him. Then he looked to see his face and he recognized that he was the Prophet Jesus. He had seen once before. He had been performing miracles and healing the sick. So, he turned to Jesus and began to beg him, "You, Rabbi, I know that you are the Messiah. I have no doubt. I have seen your miracles with my own eyes. Why are you letting them crucify you? You have the power of God to stop them from killing us. Use your power and save yourself from death, and me, and the other man over there too!"

But Jesus did not answer him. He did not even look his way.

The other criminal who was on his left also joined with him and yelled, "Yes, he is right. I know what others have said about you and your power." Then his tone became very demanding, "Set us free from here! Take out the nails from our hands and feet and strike those soldiers down. Let them die for what they have done to us here. Deliver us from death. You must do it! If you do it, then everyone will know who you are, and they will all believe in you too, even these Romans." As he spoke, he struggled to pull his feet free from nails that held him to the cross. He pulled with his arms hoping to free them too as he pleaded with the Rabbi. But no matter how hard he tried it only created more pain and suffering for himself.

Jesus held up his head and looked at them both, but he did not answer either of them.

The criminal on his left continued to plead with him, "I know who you are Jesus. You are our Messiah, the King of Israel! Why haven't you put a stop to this and saved yourself? You can do all things, I know. How could you let them do this to you? You could have stopped it at any time. How long are you going to continue letting this happen to yourself and to us? Haven't we all endured enough agony? Stop this suffering for all of us and save yourself and us too." But his manipulations were not successful no matter how hard he tried to convince the Rabbi. But at the same time, it was increasingly clear that his only interest was in trying to save his own life and escaping.

The other criminal continued to shout at Jesus, "Look at how they mock you Messiah. Aren't you going to show them your power? Judge them according to their words and let them be punished instead of us. Save us from death before it is too late." He hoped that his words would move the Rabbi to action. But nothing he said made any difference. And still he became more agitated and demanding, "If you would be our King, I will join your army and fight for you if you will just save my life from this death." Then when all that he said to manipulate the Rabbi to save him failed, he joined in mocking Jesus along with the religious leaders that stood nearby. In bitterness, he screamed with vehement hatred, "You are no Messiah! You can't even save yourself. How can you possibly save our nation from these Romans! You are no King to me or to anyone. You are worthless and accursed. Look at you, pathetic thing that you are. Your crown of thorns suites you so very well."

The other man, the one on Jesus' right accepted that he was going to die, that all three of them would die. He thought about his sins and his crimes. He knew that he was being punished justly for all that he had done to break the Law and that he will certainly be suffering a worse fate in eternity for his many sins. He accepted that there was nothing he could do for himself, nothing. But he came to have hope that somehow Rabbi Jesus could save him from an eternity of punishment for all his sins. He remembered when Jesus was first nailed to the cross and raised up. He prayed for those soldiers that his Heavenly Father would forgive them their sins. This gave him hope that maybe even he could be forgiven his sins if only Jesus was to pray for him to his Father.

He looked at the other criminal and demanded of him, "Enough, I tell you! That is enough of your greedy pleas and manipulations! I have heard enough of you. Have you no fear of God? You and I are under the sentence of death here. We deserve to die for what we have done wrong. But he has done nothing wrong to anyone. He is innocent, and they are putting him to death."

Now this criminal that hung on the left side of the Rabbi, there was no one who came and stood in vigil for him. There was no one there to be with him in his final hours of anguish and despair or to grieve for him. In his darkened heart and demented mind, he was doubly deceived because he loved his own life in this world and he would keep loving it to his end. Then he would meet his bitter fate. Little did he know that he would be forever memorialized by the legacy that he was creating for himself on the cross. He was to be remembered, but only as a criminal, unrepentant, and dishonorable in life and in death. His life was fleeting in that terrible and fateful day and he would be forever remembered, forever unnamed, unsung and forever unwept.[10]

Then the criminal on the Rabbi's right side looked to heaven and resolved in his heart to repent of his sins. He wept for all that he had done and humbly cried out, "Lord God of Israel have mercy on me, a sinner!" Then he looked at Jesus and said, "Rabbi, will you remember me when you come into your Kingdom?"

Jesus said to him, "Tell me your name."

And he told him, "Elishuah."

Jesus said, "Yes, Elishuah. That means *my God is salvation*." Then Jesus strained to turn his head so that he could see him, so that he could look into his eyes as he spoke kindly to him, "Yes, Elishuah, today you will be with me in the paradise of heaven."

And by this he was forever changed, as his life was in the painful grip of death. He found peace with God and forgiveness for all of his sins.

---

[10] Influenced by *"Breathes there the man"*, a poem by Sir Walter Scott.

Chapter Thirty-Five
Into Your Hands

The sun that had not given its full strength upon the earth from about the noon hour and now it was obscured completely from sight. The land grew still darker. It was creation itself that was withholding its light in this hour as the powers of darkness strove to kill the Lord of all Creation. That great star's light had to be hidden because it dared not cast its light upon the dying Lord of its own making. There seemed to be a fog without clouds just overhead extending everywhere. One that was always just above the grasp of your fingertips. There were no shadows cast in those hours and the cold was felt everywhere. It was one that reached deep down and chilled to the bone.

Jesus, along with the two criminals at his sides, had agonized in excruciating pain on the cross for several hours. The Lord's suffering was intensified by the thrashing he had been given at the Praetorium. His back was stripped of its skin, and his muscles were torn so badly that some of his bones could be seen. His raw wounds were in constant contact with the ruff hewn beam of the cross and they rubbed against its course surface each time he struggled to rise-up and breathe. His reflexes, like a jerking knee, moved his body forward and away from the grating pain, but the nails held him back, pinning him to its relentless torture.

As the hours of his suffering took their toll, his muscles grew weaker and his breathing became shallower and less frequent. The nails that pierced his hands and feet inflamed his nerves multiplying his pain many times over. His arms went into painful gripping spasms as he struggled to lift himself up. Because of the nails impinging on his nerves, his fingers were forced into half-closed fists that could neither open nor close all the way. The muscles of his chest and abdomen were straining to exhaustion as he labored to take a breath. It was becoming frightfully clear that his strength was nearing its end. Even the spaces above his collar bones were retracting as he inhaled and the spaces between his ribs were drawn inward as he gasped hard for another breath. He struggled to rise on the iron nails that pinned his feet to the cross and each time he did his toes spread widely apart as he grimaced in pain. The muscles on the back of his legs were forced into prolonged cramps as they resisted the strains that he put upon them. As he took his breath, pain and fatigue overcame him and he helplessly fell back down scraping his back and his open raw wounds against the cross. His legs and arms were worked to exhaustion and his muscles everywhere cramped badly each time he rose to take a breath. It was apparent that it took every last bit of his strength and concentration to rise and take each breath.

He summoned every reserve of his strength to lift himself back up on the cross so that he could take a deeper breath. Then suddenly, with the sound of terrible desperation in his voice, he cried out, "Eli, Eli lema sabachthani!" which translates to, God, my God, why have you forsaken me? But his throat had grown dry and his tongue clung to the roof of his mouth so that his voice was muffled. To some it sounded as if he had called for the Prophet Elijah to come to his aid. They wondered among themselves if the prophet would come to take him down from the cross and save his life so some of them looked to the skies hoping for his arrival.

Now, Jesus, having taken care of the needs of his mother by giving her care to John, and knowing that his time of death was nearing, fought off the final exhaustion that was overtaking him. It was about three in the afternoon and despite being severely parched he struggled to speak clearly. He worked hard but was only able to weakly say, "I thirst." There was a jar soured wine there so the women sopped up some of it on a sponge, placed it on a tree branch and held it to his mouth. But there were others there who were insistent that they withhold the wine, so that they could see if Elijah would come and save him. Still, those who heard his plea spoke against their objection. They told them that the wine would not keep him from appearing. Then they went ahead and gave him this small comfort as they lifted up the wine and he sipped it.

Now Jesus collected his strength and courageously strained to rise-up on the nails and then he raised his head high. The beating of his heart that they had seen through his ribs was now no longer visible to them as his life was nearing the end. He strained to look upward to heaven, but all he saw was the darkness that had overcome the land. His face grimaced in pain as he closed his eyes for a moment. His head moved left to right and back again as he summoned the final measure of his strength. As he labored to draw in a breath the spaces above his collar bones retracted and even the flesh between his ribs was drawn back into his chest. As he drew air into his lungs he made an inspiratory sound like that of a muffled trumpet sounding off in the distance.

Jesus knew that all his Father had sent him to accomplish was completed and as he stood tall on the nails he cried out in a loud voice, "Abba my Father! I surrender my life into your hands."

As he said this, the silver trumpets of the Temple were heard blowing in the distance declaring to Jerusalem that the high priest had slain their national Passover Lamb. Jesus remained standing tall on the nails until his strength gave out for the final time and he collapsed and fell almost lifelessly back down upon the nails. His back scraped on the cross as he slid downward and as he exhaled he shouted, "It is finished." Having breathed his last, he bowed his head and his chin rested on his chest and his life was no more. Finally, at the last, his lifeless body hung down upon the nails. At that moment the Temple's silver trumpets sounded out for all of them to hear and they knew that it was the third hour.

Mary tore open her robe and broke down quietly weeping in the deepest distress, her arms falling lifelessly to her sides. Turning to John she buried her head into his side. John took hold of her in his arms as he too trembled in tears that were too many to be measured. For what she had also endured with her son, there were no words to begin to describe it. For John, there was nothing he could do or say to bring her comfort.

According to their custom, all the women tore open their robes as had his mother. Mary's sister fell to the ground, weeping loudly, and making lamentations to God. She reached up with her arms to the lifeless body of her nephew, calling to him, but it was to no avail. He was gone from this world. As she wept her voice resonated a deep inward groan that had welled up inside her heart. And with her was Mary Magdala who collapsed to the ground below her feet. Bitter tears streamed ceaselessly down her cheeks and fell into the rocky ground below. Other women had also come and were standing only a short distance away and they too wept bitterly over his death.

Standing far opposite of the chief priests, and next to the followers of the Rabbi stood Joseph. He was a follower of Jesus and lived in the hope of seeing the coming Kingdom of God. He was a member of the Sanhedrin, an elder among them. He had not agreed with the conviction of Rabbi Jesus and was against their plan to hand him over to the Roman authorities for execution. Standing with him was a venerated religious leader in their nation, Rabbi Nicodemus, who was well known and respected by all the people. He too was a secret follower of Jesus. He was the one who hand come to Jesus by night and heard about the need to be born again to enter into the kingdom of heaven.

Following Jesus' death there came a sudden blast of wind. It rose and surrounded everyone as it continued to grow stronger. It swept around them all touching everyone, not only the followers of Jesus, but of those who had condemned him as well. It was a forceful gale that stirred up all the sand around them and carried it away until the ground was swept clean. It pushed hard against all of them, so much so that they needed to brace themselves to keep from being pushed over by it. Even the warming fire that the Romans had started was blown out by it. Everyone looked about to see what was going on.

Then as suddenly as the wind had come upon them, there was an earthquake that began as a slight trembling of the ground. Just like the wind, it grew in strength until all the ground was shaking and anyone still standing tumbled to the ground. Some looked around hoping to somehow escape or find a place of safety. Then with a great cracking sound, the earth in front of Golgotha fractured open and the fissure spread from there toward the city in the direction of the Temple.

As the shaking ground calmed and the wind settled down, the soldiers who had been knocked to the ground rose to their knees and faced the body of Jesus. These men who had only three hours before nailed him to the cross, now looked at him in humility with great reverent fear in their hearts. Of all the men they had killed in battle, of all those who they executed, and of all those they had witnessed dying, there was never a death like this man's, ever. And they remembered his prayer for them when they had begun, "Abba, Father, forgive them for they do not know what they have done." So moved were they by all that had happened in Pilate's headquarters, by all that he endured, and by what he said, that they could only believe that he truly was the Son of God. It was now at the time of his death that they came to believe in Jesus. They looked at each other in silence, held their hands to their hearts, and nodded in agreement. Then the officer spoke for them all saying, "We have come to know that this man was truly innocent and we have come to believe with all certainty that he was truly God's Son and the King of all kings."

The religious leaders who had looked on and mocked Jesus before had all cowered in fear as the wind and the earthquake came upon them. They witnessed how the fissure had moved toward the city in the direction of their Temple. They cried out in fear knowing that it might have reached all the way to their Temple. Then most of them quickly left to see if it had been damaged. But those who had been the most opposed to Jesus' ministry, Rabsaris, Elamadad and Kallahadad stayed behind.

Only a moment before Joseph and Nicodemus spoke quietly with each other about offering to Mary the things that were needed for a proper burial for his body according to their practices. Joseph said that he was able to offer clothing and a burial shroud and the use of his tomb which was nearby. It had only recently been carved out of stone and had never been used by anyone. Nicodemus offered to

277

bring from his home a compound of myrrh and aloes along with other spices so that they could prepare his body for burial.

Then these two men went together to Mary. Joseph spoke softly to her, "Mary, my family has a tomb very near to where we are standing. May I offer it to you along with clothing and a shroud so that he may be laid to rest there?"

Nicodemus who was standing at his side also offered, "I can provide spices with aloe and myrrh for his burial as well."

Mary turned her head down and away as tears welled up in her eyes for the great kindness that these men were offering to her. She was already so very overwhelmed with her son's death she had given no thought to making any arrangements so that his body could be properly cared for in death. She spoke so softly that only John was able to hear her. John answered for her, "Mary says, 'Yes' and she thanks you for your great kindness to her in this way. She is very grateful, truly she is."

Joseph and Nicodemus nodded in agreement and then they went to arrange for all that was needed.

Chapter Thirty-Six
Sacrifice Synchronicity

Now as the hour of sacrifice had come, the third hour, Caiaphas and his chief's priests made their final preparations. They gathered around the lamb on all sides and took hold of it by pushing their hands deeply into its white wool and gripping it firmly.

It was then that on Golgotha Jesus was summoning the last of his strength to rise-up on the cross and he shouted, "Abba my Father! I surrender my life into your hands."

They secured the Passover Lamb among them with all their strength so that it would not move as his life was sacrificed. One chief priest now took hold of it at the back of his neck and he pulled taught the loose skin covering its throat. Another grasped it around its mouth and chin, pulling its head back and retracting it so that its neck was fully extended outward. Under the watchful eye of Annas, Caiaphas grasped the ceremonial knife by its silver handle and removed it from its sheath. He lifted the blades razor-sharp edge high for everyone to see and the people held their breath for the moment of its death had come. Caiaphas turned to face the lamb, drew back his hand, and rested the blade just a fraction of an inch from its neck under the lamb's right ear.

It was at this moment that Jesus cried out on Golgotha, "It is finished" and then he surrendered his life unto death on the cross.

The high priest in one swift and precise move, sliced open the entire width of the throat of the lamb and blood poured out. Then Caiaphas announced, "Our Passover Lamb has been sacrificed."

With that proclamation made, a long line of priests raised their silver trumpets in unison and blew them loudly. They were announcing to everyone in Jerusalem that the Passover Lamb had been sacrificed according to the commandments given to them by Moses in the Law.

When the lamb fell dead in their hands, the priests lifted it up high so that he could be bled out. As its blood flowed, they collected it in a basin. They formed two lines of priests. In the first row the priests held beautiful silver chalices that were inlaid with gold. In these they poured the blood of the lamb and then passed their cups down to the next priest in the line all the way to the Holy Place where they sprinkled its blood on the Altar. The second row of priests stood to pass the empty chalices back to the courtyard where the lamb was so more of its blood could be passed to the Altar until it was completely bled out.

Now as they carried this sacrifice out there arose a strong breeze that circulated around everyone in the Temple. This was followed by a sudden hard blast of wind that blew out many of the lamps in the Temple. All the priest's long robes were ruffled by it and many of the people were pushed about on their feet by its great power.

Before the wind subsided there came a gentle rumbling sound in the Temple and it trembled. As everyone looked about wondering what was going on, there came a great rolling sound and the Temple began to shake violently. It was a powerful earthquake that knocked everyone about until they were forced to the floor. It was as if creation itself insisted that they bow low in humility in this way because, unbeknown to them all, Jesus the Lamb of God had just died. Many cried out in fear as the shaking and the rumbling continued. The people feared that the Temple and its pillars might collapse on them. Others feared that the ground might open up and they would fall into a great fissure in the earth.

As the quake subsided, Caiaphas immediately made his way into the inner courtyard of the Temple. He examined the sacred furniture that was there to see if any had been damaged. The Temple shook again with several milder aftershocks. The high priest turned to examine the veil that concealed the Holy of Holies were the Ark of the Covenant resided. He worried that the Ark might have been tipped over but he was prohibited by the threat of death from entering in there. He was only allowed to go in on the Day of Atonement and only then with the blood of a lamb. He struggled terribly, wanting to somehow ensure the safety of the Ark and still not break the Law of Moses regarding its care.

His thoughts now turned to the great curtain that separated the Holy Place where he was standing from the Holy of Holies. This curtain was more than a foot thick being made of densely woven blue, purple and scarlet linen. It was so heavy that if it was to be moved, it would take over a hundred of priests to carry it. As he looked upward he grabbed his robes and was prepared to tear them in anger over all that had happened. He could see the top of the curtain, which was some sixty feet up in the air. He could see that it was not shaken loose from its place or torn by the powerful quake that had just ended. He was greatly relieved to see that it was undamaged and he breathed a sigh of relief. Then he saw what he could not believe. He saw it wrinkle, as if two hands had laid hold of it at its top. The wrinkles spread out immediately to the right and to the left. Then at its center, where no man could reach, it was suddenly torn in two. The sound of it ripping was an unbearable noise to his ears. It was split completely in two from the top down all the way down to the floor.

Now the priests there along with Caiaphas cried out in fear. This was beyond their belief, but they could not deny what their eyes revealed to them. Many of them covered their faces and rushed out of the courtyard. They feared that they might die if their eyes should fall upon the Holy of Holies and the Ark of the Covenant.

Chapter Thirty-Seven
This is My Body, Given for You

At Golgotha, after Jesus' death, many of the chief priest's supporters left. Of those remaining, they no longer continued to mock Rabbi Jesus in his death, neither did they mock those who were there to be with him in his final hours. Even though jostled by the strong blast of wind and shaken by the earthquake, the chief priests showed no sign of remorse or regret over what they had done to him. It was painfully clear now that he was dead they did not want to let his body out of their sights, not until he was taken down and dumped into a common grave.

As they had planned, Nicodemus and Joseph went to the centurion overseeing the execution and Joseph spoke with him privately. "I would like to be granted his body so that I may burry him."

But the centurion shook his head and made it clear that he would not release the body to him. "Sir, I have been given my orders. I must carry them out exactly, just as they were given to me. His body, along with the other two, will all be buried in that common grave over there, once they are all dead."

Joseph shook his head in disbelief that this should happen. He was already deeply grieved beyond what words could say. Though he had listened carefully to all that the officer said, it was hard for him to comprehend that Jesus would be buried in a common grave. He couldn't have imagined it in the first place, not by any measure that Jesus would be crucified. Now, this horrible tragedy was about to be followed by a second one. It was unacceptable that the Rabbi should have to share in a common grave meant for the outcasts of their society. He must be properly prepared for burial according to their ways. The words of the officer slowly started to have their impact on his thoughts and so he determined to do whatever he must to properly burry his body.

Joseph spoke to Nicodemus, "I will go to the governor and ask him to release the body to me."

Nicodemus agreed and said, "I will assemble all that is needed."

Then Joseph turned to his servants and to one he said, "Return to my home and bring back with you clothing and a shroud for his body. Also bring a briar and water to wash him with." To the other he instructed him, "Go with Nicodemus and help him carry the things we need." His men listened attentively and then they went on their way to make all things ready. Joseph returned to John and said, "All things are being arranged. I will return shortly." He turned and rushed off to the Praetorium.

Once he arrived at Pilate's headquarters he noticed that some of those Temple authorities, who had been at Golgotha, were at the gate talking to Pilate. He overheard them asking Pilate to order his soldiers to break the legs of men who were crucified. This was requested to hasten their deaths so that they could be buried before sundown which was the beginning of the Sabbath. To have them hanging on the cross would be a sacrilege of their holy day of rest. Upon hearing that, Joseph's heart trembled and sank. He could not let them break the legs of Rabbi Jesus, he couldn't. Then Pilate issued the order and his soldier left for the place of the crucifixion.

Quickly approaching Pilate, Joseph spoke out, "Governor, I am Joseph of Arimathea."

Pilate looked at him, "I know your name. Have we ever met?"

"No. I am here about Rabbi Jesus who was crucified."

He spoke with a foul tone, "What a rancid affair. What is your involvement in all this?"

"I am asking for you to release his body to me so that I may give him a proper burial in a tomb, not in a common grave."

Pilate hesitated. He wished more than anything that the entire mess would just simply end, but with each passing hour something more came up to complicate the execution.

Joseph spoke with urgency in his voice, "Sir, the night will soon be upon us and I wish to place him in a tomb before the sun sets. This is our way."

"What are you saying? Is he already dead? I find that hard to imagine."

"He died just a short time ago."

Pilate first shook his head in disgust and he looked at Joseph, nodded and said, "As you wish." He ordered a soldier to accompany Joseph to Golgotha, "Tell the centurion there that he may release the body of the Rabbi to Joseph of Arimathea." The soldier stood at attention, saluted the governor and stood by Joseph.

Now Joseph was under a great burden of grief and filled with much apprehension. But now he felt a sense of relief, small as it was. Neither did he want to worry about how or where Jesus would be buried. He wearily looked at the governor and nodded his head in agreement with him. With that, he turned and hastily made his way back to Golgotha.

Pilate was left exhausted from all the troubles of the day so he took his helmet off. It had been weighing heavily upon his head. He looked down and shook his head. He wanted nothing to do with this entire situation. But it would not go away. Not even now that this Rabbi was dead. He knew that it was his quest for rank and place in Roman politics along with his lofty ambitions that brought all this down on him. He turned and walked away from the gate. He lifted his head and looked to the sky as he spoke out loud to himself, "Will there ever ... be an end ... to this, ... this ... eternal ... man's ... life and death?!"

Chapter Thirty-Eight
In a Rich Man's Tomb

The soldier arrived at Golgotha with Pilate's orders to break the criminal's legs and hasten their deaths. He relayed this order to the centurion there. So, he in turn ordered his soldiers to break the legs of the first man, the one who had repented, and the legs of the other one also. When they looked at Jesus' body, they already knew he was dead. There was no need to break his legs. But, the soldier who carried the order from Pilate to break their legs objected to their decision. Because of his insistence one of the soldiers who was there took his spear and stood before his body. He raised his weapon, and with the precision of a professional warrior, he took aim and thrust it hard into the chest of the Jesus' lifeless body. As soon as it pierced his skin out rushed a flood of blood and water onto the rocky ground beneath his cross. Some of it flowed into the hole that his cross stood in and the rest of it flowed into the what remained of the fissure in the rock caused by the earthquake.

As the spear pierced his skin, Mary felt a sudden and sharp pain. She bent over grasping her womb and wondered why this should happen to her at the same time as her son's body was pierced. Then she knew that this was the fulfillment of the prophecy spoken to her long ago by devout Simeon when he foretold, "Then shall the sword's long blade pierce your heart and soul though."

At that same time, Joseph returned from having met with the governor. The soldier with him relayed his order to the centurion there, "The governor has ordered that the body of the Rabbi be given to this man for burial." So, the soldiers removed their helmets and slowly went to the cross where they genuflected before his feet. They stood at its base and ever so carefully lifted his cross from the hole that it was standing in. They slowly lowered it down until it gently came to rest on the ground. Joseph and Nicodemus went immediately to Jesus' body, removed the crown of thorns, and covered his head with a large white linen. This was also a custom of theirs, that the face should not be seen until the body was prepared for viewing. Then the soldiers used their tools to tenderly remove the three nails that had held him in place.

As his body was freed, Joseph and his servants moved him to a burial brier and carried him a short distance away. All those with them were greatly conflicted. Their grief was so heavy a weight upon them that they did not want to bring themselves to do what they must now do. But he must be attended to, and quickly because the sun was setting and with that the Sabbath would be upon them. So, they worked in haste to complete just the necessary things so that the tomb could be closed before the nighttime came. Joseph's servants had brought several jars of water and they quickly washed the dirt and blood from his body and dried him off. Then they lifted him up as a burial shroud woven of very fine linen was placed beneath him on the bier.

Nicodemus had brought about one hundred pounds of spices in baskets to prepare his body for burial. The women along with the men anointed his head with olive oil and applied myrrh to his many wounds and wrapped them all in strips of cloth bandages. They also covered him with the aromatic spices and frankincense. Following this they clothed him in the tunic and robe that had been brought there from Joseph's home. Then they placed more of the spices and frankincense all around him. They quickly wrapped his body in the shroud that Joseph provided and sewed it shut, all but the portion around his head.

Having done all this, Mary viewed his face for the final time. She knelt alongside him on her knees and looked at her son, Her tears streamed down her face and fell gently onto his. She held his head with both her hands and kissed him on the cheeks and forehead before stepping away. So also, all the women knelt to their knees to be at his side. Some of them whispered prayers or quietly recited Psalms. Now they completed the preparations as they wrapped a white linen cloth around his head and tied it under his chin. Then they sprinkled spices about his head and, last of all, the shroud was sown shut.

Nicodemus stood to lead the way, as a Rabbi should, and with him stood Joseph. At the four corners of the briar the servants bowed, took hold, and in unison lifted him up high and carried him on their shoulders. Behind the bier there followed Mary, with John at her side. Following close behind them were the other women who had been there for him to the end and they weep aloud.

They painstakingly made their way to the garden where the tomb was, and their weary hearts grieved deeper than they could understand or described. The weight of his body which seemed at first very heavy, became lighter once it was upon their shoulders and their legs never tired and their feet never grew sore. Together in unified steps, they carried him back into the city. Earlier, the road that led to Jerusalem was filled with large crowds going there for the Passover. Now it had dwindled down to just a few people here and there.

For all who were in the city it was a day of great rejoicing. But for this small number who were on their way to the tomb, it was deeply emotional for them. It was a time of untold mourning and grief. For Mary and John in their fatigue they did not notice much along the way. Not the city's walls or its gate, nor the soldiers standing there. The houses they passed seemed more like one endless wall of impersonal windows and doors. Though the delicious aroma of roasted Passover lambs was everywhere, they took no notice of it.

Now they neared the cemetery, it was called the Garden of Jerusalem. There was a newly cut tomb there. One that had never before been used by anyone. It belonged to Joseph and his family

The garden had a wall around it. They passed through its gate and came to the large tomb. Joseph and his servants now rolled back the stone that sealed its entrance. Nicodemus and Joseph went in first. The men carrying the brier followed in as well and they set the brier down beside the stone bed where he would be laid. They lifted his enshrouded body and gently laid him onto the bed. The men knelt and stayed a moment to be with him, their Rabbi. Then they left, all but Nicodemus. Now entered Mary with John at her side. He was worried that she might faint from exhaustion, but she showed a resilient inner strength that could have only come from the LORD. Also coming into the tomb were the women who had been with him all this time at Golgotha. Mary now sat by her son on the side of the bed. She clasped her hand tightly together and wept softly for her son. The other women also wept quietly. Then the women came out as they were ready, but with the hopes of returning after the Sabbath to further care for his body.

Still in the tomb, Mary now held her son's shrouded head with one hand and stroked his cheek with the other. She leaned forward as if to look into his eyes. Her tears fell onto his shroud as she spoke to him. "My son, my son, my son! I am so sorry that they did this to you. I would have given my life to save you from this suffering. I would join you if I could even now, but I must abide here. May you find comfort as you wait for the resurrection of the dead and the life to come. I love you most dearly, my Jesus."

Mary reached out her hand to John and he took hold of it. She looked at him, revealing her devastation and crushed heart. So intense was it that John wanted to look away and be spared the burden of it. But no, that would never do. His Rabbi had given him charge of his mother's care and he would not fail him in this duty. He looked at her knowing that there were no words on earth that could bring her comfort at this moment. He looked directly into her eyes hoping to show that he knew and understood something of her sorrows. He knew that what he was now witness too was a very private part of her life. He was honored to see what was meant for no one else. Then Mary, with John, came out of the tomb.

All of them were anxiously watching the sun as it began its final descent into the western sky warning them that the Sabbath would soon begin. They stood together, somber and in silence as the finality of sealing the tomb took place. Most of the men were needed to help roll the stone down its channel. They slowly rolled it down a grooved channel until it came to rest in front of the entrance to the tomb. As it was rolled it made a grinding sound like that of a millstone rolling to crush wheat. And when it settled into place it made a hard-clasping sound, like the sound of thunder off in the distance. Then the men stood back while Joseph inspected it to be certain everything was sealed properly in its place.

Now everyone gathered in front of Nicodemus as he recited a psalm.

"God is our refuge and strength,
a very present help in trouble.
Therefore, will not we fear,
though the earth be removed,
and though the mountains be
carried into the midst of the sea;
Though the waters roar and be troubled,
though the mountains shake with the swelling.
There is a river, whose streams
make glad the city of God,
the holy place of the tabernacles of the Most-High.
God is in the midst of her, she shall not be moved:
God shall help her, and that right early.
The heathen raged, the kingdoms were moved:
he uttered his voice, the earth melted.
The LORD of hosts is with us,
the God of Jacob is our refuge.
Come, behold the works of the LORD,
what desolations he has made in the earth.
He makes wars to cease unto the end of the earth;
he breaks the bows, and cuts the spears asunder,
he burns the chariots in the fire.
Be still and know that I am God.
I will be exalted among the heathen,
I will be exalted in the earth.
The LORD of hosts is with us,
the God of Jacob is our refuge.[11]
Amen"

---

[11] Adapted from Psalm 46 KJV

Nicodemus would have liked to offer more of the traditions they normally observed at funerals, but the day was almost over. All of those gathered would have also lingered longer, and though they longed with deep pining in their hearts to tarry there, but just as their Lord was taken from them, so also was this time. They needed to hurry back to their homes and to where they were lodging before sundown. This made their sorrows still greater. They knew that they would not be able to return the following morning but would have to wait until the day following the Sabbath.

Joseph spoke quietly with Nicodemus and then they approached Mary and stood humbly before her. For the moment they said nothing. That was their custom. They made eye contact and their expressions let her know how truly sorrowful they were and how much they cared for her estate.

Joseph broke the silence, "Please come and spend the Sabbath with my family. My home is not far from here and you are so very weary."

John replied, "Joseph, you have done so much already. How will we ever repay you for all that you are doing for us?"

"There is no need to worry about that. Please come, won't you?"

Mary was relieved to be invited to a home close by. Her soul was heavy and she was well beyond what she could endure. She simply nodded her head in agreement as she took her place at John's side and they both left with Joseph.

Chapter Thirty-Nine
Sabbath Unrest

They rushed as swiftly as they could, it was a pace just shy of running, to get to Joseph's home before the night sky set in and the Sabbath began. Once everyone was inside the door Joseph locked it securely. He gave instructions to his chief servant Gamalah, who was there waiting for him, "Lock all the entrances and shut all of the windows on the first floor as well."

His servant asked him, "What is it? Has something happened?"

Joseph found it hard to say the words. It had not really sunk in yet. He had not had to tell anyone what had happened. "Gamalah, it is the Rabbi Jesus."

Gamalah was silent as he worried about what he might hear next.

"Rabbi Jesus was arrested last night and ..." His voice could not produce the words he needed to say. Up until now it was surreal, saying it would make it real to him, and then he would have to begin to face his deepest sorrow. For now, he needed to keep his wits about him. He could not breakdown. He had to provide for Mary and his other guests. His tears would have to wait. He shook his head to clear his thoughts and bring his mind back to Gamalah. "... he was arrested and sentenced to death."

His servant's thoughts raced. Maybe there was something they could still do, something, anything.

"Gamalah, they crucified him. We just laid him to rest in the tomb."

He was in shock as he heard this unbelievable report. Joseph looked at him and then his eyes moved to the guests that he needed to provide for. His trusted servant knew that there was much to do for them and so he nodded to his master. "I understand. I will take care of securing the doors and windows and see to the needs of our guests as well."

As Gamalah left he quickly alerted the rest of the household staff. Many of them came to the entryway welcoming their guests and washing their feet. Then Mary and John, along with the others, were taken into a well-furnished parlor so they could sit and rest. Gamalah's wife, Adah, joined him and shared with everyone, "Joseph will be with you again shortly."

Joseph had gone upstairs to the hallway that was his family residence. In his bedroom he met privately with his wife, Ziphorah, to share with her the tragic news. As she heard what her husband said, she broke down into bitter tears and buried her head into his shoulder. He held her tightly as she wept.

Then she stepped away, wiped her tears, and listened to him. "We laid his body to rest in our family tomb. I have invited his mother and the others who were there to stay with us. I am worried there may be other arrests. I have had all the doors and the windows downstairs locked. We must somehow keep the Sabbath and provide hospitality with our guests."

Joseph tried to imagine how he would keep the Sabbath when this dark shadow had fallen on all their lives and upon his home. He and Ziphorah decided that they would wait until morning to share with them of the Rabbi's death. Rather than hosting a large meal in their dining room, they would share the meal with their children in their private family room upstairs. Ziphorah instructed the children's maid to make the arrangements with their kitchen servants.

Now the couple gathered their strength and went downstairs to greet their guests. As they entered the room they saw how exhausted John was. Mary was seated next to him and was very tired as well. With them were several of the women who had traveled with the Rabbi and cared for his needs and all the disciples as well. They were exhausted.

Ziphorah spoke first, "Our friends, welcome to our home. My husband and I are both deeply sorry for this terrible loss that has come into your lives. We want to assure you that you are very welcome to stay with us and that you are safe in our home. We have rooms for you to stay in where you can rest. Our servants will help you with whatever you need."

Joseph then shared, "I am having a Sabbath meal prepared for you if you wish to eat in our dining room."

John spoke up, "Thank you."

"I will ask my servants to provide supper for you. I hope you will all eat at least a little food for your strength. Now, forgive me for leaving you. My wife and I will be observing the Sabbath alone with our children this evening. The children are very young and they would not understand the circumstances we find ourselves in this evenings. In the morning we will share with them about Rabbi Jesus."

Ziphorah then shared, "Gamalah and his wife, Adah, will see to your needs. Please let them know if they can do anything for you."

There was a silence that everyone shared in. There was nothing more anyone could say. Then Mary softly spoke, "Thank you for taking us into your home and so kindly offering us this hospitality."

Joseph and Ziphorah bowed in humility and left the room, but the head servant and his wife remained. Outside the room were other servants. Joseph had given them instructions to bring in food and drink for his guests right away. He also asked them to double the night watch for fear of the Temple authorities. Because they had illegally arrested Rabbi Jesus during the night, he worried they might come to his house seeking to arrest him or anyone of his guests. He also instructed a servant to stay awake in the hallway where his guests were staying. If they needed anything at all during the night he did not want it to be difficult for them to get the help they needed.

Together the couple now went upstairs and tried as best they could to put this aside so that they could celebrate the Sabbath with their two young children. This was a very difficult experience for them because the combination of any festival day falling next to the Sabbath day made it a very high and special occasion. The joining of the two days multiplied the joy of the occasion for everyone. Sadly, the reverse of this seemed to be in effect because this great tragedy fell on this occasion making the depth of their morning far beyond any measure.

Now Gamalah led them in the observances that began their sacred day of rest. While it did not entirely seem fitting to do this while they were in such grief, it was something they could not simply skip doing. Gamalah found words that seemed fitting as he began, "What God has made as a day of rest cannot be altered anymore than we can change his creation, because this is part of his very creation."

Servants brought in plates of food for them to eat and they quietly shared in their evening prayer traditions.

As all of Judea and people of faith everywhere were joyously closing out their Passover festival, they were suffering with Jesus' death. After some time had passed Mary spoke again, "I think I need to lay down and rest now."

Adah then softly spoke, "Yes, let us show you all to your rooms. With all that has passed this day you must be very tired. Even if you cannot sleep you must lay down and rest." Then she brought everyone into a part of the house where they were all given guest rooms to spend the night. "If you need anything at all just ask. There will be a servant here in waiting for you throughout the night."

Young John was the last to go into his room that night. He felt very alone. He was used to being with his Master and the other disciples, or at the very least with his brother James and Peter. The three of them were part of an inner circle with their Rabbi. Now, his constant companions were somewhere in hiding and his Rabbi had been crucified. A new charge had been added to his life, the care of Mary, who he was to provide for as would a son for his own mother. He was burdened by the great weight of all this and he wondered what his life would become like. He needed to sleep but so much had happened and difficult as it was, he wanted to reflect on it. He forced himself to lay down and wait until he fell asleep even though it came hard to him. His mind was overcome with images of his Master's dying and superimposed on that was the face of Mary and all that she suffered as they endured his death together. He could not clear his thoughts or his mind's eye from all that he was witness too. It was out of sheer exhaustion that he fell off to sleep late that night.

Chapter Forty
Pilate's Imperial Seal

Now, early in the morning on the day of the Sabbath at first light, the two High Priests Caiaphas and Annas met. Together they discussed the case of Rabbi Jesus and his death.

Caiaphas brought up another one of his many worries with his father-in-law, "Do you know what worries me now?"

"I know that too much worries you. It is going to make you grow old before your time."

"Remember that the people claimed the Rabbi raised Lazarus of Bethany from the dead? Supposedly he was four days dead and in his tomb."

"I remember the claim that he did this, but I do not believe that he actually did it. I think the whole thing was a hoax. But how can it be proven or disproven now that it is long since past. Anyway, the people will only remember it for a short time and then they will forget it."

"Do you remember that the Rabbi said he would rise on the fourth day too."

Annas corrected him, "Yes, but he said it would be on the third day."

"Just like this first deception, that he raised this man from the dead, his followers could steal his body away and then claim that he is risen from the dead."

"Pilate granted them his body. That would make it very easy for them to do that very thing." Annas thought for a moment and then asked, "What shall we do about that possibility?"

"I will send Rabsaris and the others to the governor. They will ask Pilate to seal the tomb and have it guarded for a few days." Then Caiaphas sent an order to the chief priest asking him to gather his supporters to go to the Praetorium and request it.

As it was on the day before, along with the three chief priests came a company of scribal lawyers. Once they arrived at the gate to Pilate's headquarters they requested an urgent meeting with him.

The governor thought he had been through enough trouble with them the day before. He had fully expected that his troubles with them over the Rabbi had ended when he had died. This was the one his wife had urged him to have nothing to do with. But on that count, the only thing that he and his wife had agreed on was that he was innocent. Today he expected that because it was their day of solemn rest that he would not hear from them about anything, especially this. He wanted nothing more to do with the matter and he absolutely did not want to hear from the Temple authorities so that he too could get some rest himself.

Upset and disturbed by their arrival, Pilate walked out to see them, but he was in no hurry. After his last painful ordeal with them he felt that any contact with them would be too soon. He wondered if having a sword put to his side would be more tolerable then their manipulating. So, he did what he could to make the event more pleasant for himself by doing something he rarely ever did. He stopped on the way to the gate to look around, see the sky, and smell the air and he enjoyed doing it.

The company of men waiting for him were impatient and irritated by his casual manor. As always, he offered to invite them in, and as always, they took offense at his offer and then refused him. Pilate knowingly nodded and then paused giving thought to what on earth could be so important to bring these men here on their Sabbath day.

He looked at them. "I should just put some chairs and tables out there for you and a few in here for me and my officers for our little meetings. That way we could all sit, albeit at different tables, and have our meetings. After all, they are becoming daily occurrences. What do you think? The bars of the gate would be in our way, but that would not be a new problem would it?"

They did not answer him. They looked brassy and stern. As it was they did not like his little joking around and treating them so informally.

"Now, correct me if I am wrong, but aren't you breaking your Sabbath requirements by being here this morning? How far did you walk to get here? And could it be that you are, by definition, working if you are here on matters related to your duties as priests?"

The company of men simply stood still with their arms crossed, stone faced, and not at all humored by Pilate's offer, or his accusations against them. Neither did they offer him any answer for his question about their Law.

Pilate had a chalice of wine in his hand and throwing back his head he drank it down in one swift gulp. Then he passed his chalice to his attendant saying, "I will be needing more of this." His attendant sped off to do as was asked of him. Pilate turned to face them straight on, "So, here we are again and isn't this pleasant?" His voice was thick with sarcasm. "I had thought that giving you the death of that innocent man yesterday would have kept you happy for longer than this. So, what is it now that you are seeking from me? Do you have more unreasonable requests of me? Do you want him back alive or something like that?" His attendant return with his wine and placed it in his hand and

301

Pilate looked at his reflection on its surface. Then he swirled it around as if he was trying to entertain himself with its image.

Rabsaris spoke out with a cutting edge in his voice, "I do not take this matter so lightly that it can be made into a joke and neither should you governor. Soon you will find that your attempt at humor is in especially poor timing this morning." He waited to speak further expecting that Pilate would offer an apology for his comments. None followed, nor would one be offered. The chief priest when on, "I have been reminded that one of the lies this man told his followers was that he would be rising from the dead in three days."

Pilate had just taken a sip of his wine, which was very poor timing on his part. He nearly choked on it when he heard their claim. He looked as if he was going to either choke on it or spew it out of his mouth. However, neither of those responses were fitting for a man of his distinction. The priests were not humored by his joking and he was not humored by their claim that the man would rise from the dead. No one rises from the dead after having been crucified to death and then having a Roman spear thrusted into his heart. He looked at them unbelieving their claim about what the Rabbi said and unbelieving that he could rise-up given the death he suffered. He told them, "Death by crucifixion is not that kind to anyone. Thrashing can leave a person half dead, but crucifixion does not leave them half dead. Not even a strong man can survive it. Your Rabbi died on the cross. My soldier speared his chest to assure that there was no room left for doubt. Believe me there is no reason for you or anyone to believe that his body will rise-up alive again. Ever." He took a gulp of his wine and looked into his chalice. He wanted to see his reflection in the surface of the wine again. Then he looked at the priests, "So what is it with your religious superstitions here? I am told that your Sadducees don't even believe in an afterlife but your Pharisees do. Of which school are you?"

Rabsaris spoke, "Sir, don't take our concerns the wrong way like that. We don't believe that he is going to actually rise from the dead and walk among us again any more than you do. However, we are seriously worried about his followers. We fear that they will go to his tomb and secretly open it to steal his corpse away. That way they can bring a greater deception to the people with a false claim that he has risen from the dead. Then this deception of the people will become worse than it already is."

The governor was already exhausted over this case from the day before. Now he wished more than ever that it would just go away entirely. A dead person had never been such a problem to him as this one. He resolved that it was simply best to just give these chief priests what they wanted, again. That way he could get rid of them quickly and put this nightmare to rest once and for all. His patience, which was already thin, was now gone and he was in a foul mood, "So what do you propose that I do for you, kill him again?! Do you expect me to try and round up all of his followers and place them under lock and key?"

Rabsaris spoke out, "Governor, may I offer a simpler solution than that? We want you to send a company of your soldiers to his tomb to secure it by putting your imperial seal on it and have them watch over it until after the third day passes. That way his disciples can do nothing. Then the man's memory will simply fade away from the people's minds over time."

"Why should I send my soldiers to resolve your problem? You have your own guards. You have an abundance of priests. Use them to do this thing if it worries you so much."

Elamadad explained, "Governor, our priests are forbidden to come so close to a corpse and being in a cemetery will defile them and make them ritually unclean. Our guards also serve in the Temple. They would also be defiled."

"Then, however do you burry your dead?"

"With this the priests cannot assist and those who do are unclean and must go through a cleansing ritual that takes seven days to be completed. That is why we cannot help and that is why we cannot use our own Temple guards."

Pilate laughed, "Very well if it will get you to leave here and put all this to rest. If that is what it takes, then very well! We Romans will oblige you." The governor called for his officer. "I want you to take four soldiers…"

Rabsaris objected, "That is not enough. He had many followers you know. Thousands of them."

He reiterated himself, "Take four soldiers and place them at the tomb of this Galilean Rabbi to stand watch over it. They must ensure that no one opens the tomb for any reason especially to steal away the body. The tomb shall be sealed with clay and embossed with my imperial seal. Now see to it." Pilate smirked at the religious authorities, "There, now are you satisfied? Is there anything else I need to do for you?"

Rabsaris answered, "This should be enough for now. We will go with your soldiers and see that it is done properly."

He sneered at them, "Yes by all means please go with them. All of you go and then leave me alone. Stay there with them for as long as you like." Pilate exaggerated his bow to them as he left. He bowed for the sake of appearing polite but added a certain flare to it to mock them as well and then he walked away into his headquarters.

None of the religious authorities liked being treated this way, but they got what they wanted in the end. When the officer and the four soldiers were assembled they followed them to his tomb. They went straight to the tomb of the Rabbi which was in the cemetery known as the Garden of Jerusalem. The chief priests did not enter the cemetery. Instead they looked on from a distance.

Once there, the officer oversaw the soldiers who opened the bucket of clay that they had brought. They applied it thickly to the entire base of the stone that covered the tomb's entrance. They also applied the clay to the top of the stone and to its sides, left and right. Deep into the clay they pushed ropes to secure them tightly in place and crisscrossed them over each other in the center. If for any reason the stone was moved the seals would break and the ropes would fall to the ground.

Their officer stepped in and closely examined their work and assure that it was properly done. Then he used a large signet to impressed Pilate's own Imperial Seal into the surface of each of the four clay seals. He stepped back and saw the image of a Roman eagle with a laurel wreath surrounding it.

The seal stated "Pontius Pilate, Imperial Governor of the Provence of Judea." The laurel wreath was a symbol of victory. The eagle was a symbol of the strength of the legion and imperial rule. Oddly enough, the eagle was also a funeral emblem, symbolizing the ascent of a person's soul to heaven.

Then he charged the soldiers with their orders, "You will all remain here until relieved. Only one of you may sleep at a time. Two of you shall be standing at all times. You will not remove your clubs or swords from your sides for any reason. Your shields and spears shall remain secure at your sides or between you and the tomb at all times. No one is to approach you or the tomb. Warn them if they do. Beat them off with your clubs if they try to get near it and if they attack you with weapons of their own, fight them with lethal force. They must not interfere with your work or attempt to open the tomb. These are the orders of the governor."

There the Roman soldiers stayed. Then came the night and they lit their lantern and started a fire to keep warm. Then they waited for the mornings light.

Chapter Forty-One
The Day of the Sabbath

In the morning, at dawns first light, John woke with an alarming start. He had jumped out of bed and was ready to fight before he realized that there was no one there. His heart raced as he stood in readiness for action. He looked around but saw no one, and so he breathed a difficult sigh of relief. He tried to gather his thoughts and look around the room that Joseph had provided for him. It was strange and unfamiliar to him. Then it all came back to him in a flood of horror. That day, the feeling of helplessness, the tragedy and Jesus' cruel death. His head suddenly swelled, giving him a pounding headache. The room started spinning and he quickly sat to the bed and held his forehead in the palm of his hand. It had come back to him like a terrible rushing storm and he wept uncontrollably. He did not want to be heard and so he covered his face with a pillow as he wept and felt fearful of the endless depth of sorrow than overcame him so suddenly.

He thought, *'I cannot do this. I cannot let myself do this. I have to control myself.'* His weeping was disturbing to him. He told himself, *'I don't want to cry this way, I am a man. I must be there for Mary. I don't need to do this.'* But his thoughts about containing his emotions were worthless to him and he finally yielded to the unremitting flow of tears. He found that they took over his entire being and they were flooding out of him like a raging river. He missed his dearest Master more than he could imagine and he loved him so much. His body nearly convulsed as he sobbed, and he laid down and allowed it all to happen.

He remembered that when he was at the cross he had focused on only two things, the dying of his Master, and the care of Mary. He had not attended very well to his own needs to grieve as Jesus was dying. Now as the weeping and the flow of his emotions continued, his mind was stricken with flashing memories of it all. From the arrest in the garden, to the trial by night, and the crucifixion. It was flowing past his mind's eyes. When it came to an end he was left doubly exhausted and he was overshadowed by the worry of not knowing what to do with himself.

His tears subsided and as he lay there he wondered if he could go back to sleep. He hoped that would bring him relief because in sleep all this did not exist, or so he hoped. But sleep was evading him as his room continued to brighten with the dawning of the morning sun. He sat up and saw that someone had taken his clothes and put out a freshly washed tunic and robe for him in their place. There was water and towels for him to wash with. So, he rose and took care of his needs and begin the day. He ventured out of the room, thinking that he needed to find out how Mary was and to see if she needed anything. He had no idea where she was though.

There was a servant sitting in the hallway who rose to his feet as John entered the hallway. "May I help you?" he asked.

"Where is Mary?"

The man replied, "Mary and the others are still sleeping quietly."

John nodded and went downstairs where Gamalah was waiting. "Master John, good morning." He whispered. "Only a few servants are up right now."

John nodded, "Where is Mary?"

"Mary is upstairs and still asleep. My wife is outside her door where she spent the night."

John nodded again, "Thank you for caring for her."

"If you are hungry, I can get you a little something to eat right now."

"Thank you, but not for now. Later perhaps. I'll be in the courtyard."

John ventured outside and sat in the open air. In part he needed to be alone and he wanted to face the Temple as he said his morning prayers, as this had been his lifelong practice. But this morning was unlike any before and everything was changed. When he first followed Jesus and then became one of his disciples his life had been remade in every way. It was remade to revolved around the life of his Rabbi and his teachings. Now, he wondered, what was his life to consist of? His thoughts only slowly came to him. His prayers in the past had been about serving as a disciple for his Rabbi and the work of God that he was doing for the people. That was over. It all suddenly died when his Lord died.

As he bowed his head to pray, he could not find the words to say. With his eyes closed he could only remember what he saw and heard when his Rabbi had so desperately called out from the cross, "My God, my God, why have you forsaken me?" It startled him and his body shivered as if a cold wind had passed over him. He felt desperate, overwhelmed and uncertain of his faith. Since God turned a deaf ear to his Master, why would he hear the prayers of one of his disciples? He wondered, my Master was a faithful servant of the Most High God for all these years. He was given the power of God to do miracles beyond number and beyond compare. But he was rejected by the chief priests and abandoned by God. So then, where did he stand before his Maker?

He was obligated as a man of faith to pray in the morning, but what had become of his faith? It wasn't just disillusionment, it was worse. He could not get past the point of fearing that if this could happen to his Master, his judgement could be at hand too. If he called on the name of the LORD and God looked down on him, he would be held to account for his life. His mind would let him think no further. He jumped up quickly and as he looked back to where he had been sitting it was as if he could see himself still there for a moment. It was a glimpse of himself, the empty corpse of his self, as if he too had died along with his Master. He did not like what he saw. He did not like being who he was, and he feared his own death could be near at hand.

He thought about how all his life he could go to his grandfather or his father for their wisdom and advice. He could go to his older brother equally well. In the past three years as Jesus' disciple the mysteries of creation were opened to him and all the answers he could have imagined were explained to him. Now, here was the greatest and worst of mysteries and there was no one he could turn too. He felt very much alone. He had taken in enough of the courtyard as he could stand for and without a single prayer spoken or even thought, he charged toward the door and reentered the house.

Mary had great trouble falling asleep Friday night. It was hours before her exhaustion overcame her grieving heart and let her fall into a fitful slumber. When she woke her thoughts immediately returned to the death of her son. Saturday mornings were a time for her to wake early, wash and put on her best clothes and go to the synagogue for worship and hear the word of God. She had been greatly looking forward to the combined remembrance of the Passover Feast and the following Sabbath. This had given her warm feelings in the weeks leading up to it. Now the sorrow she bore has stolen all it away. If she had any comfort that morning, it was that she had been able to be with her son to show her love to him as he suffered and died.

In the midst of that memory she wondered how she could imagine that it was any kind of comfort to her. Her son was dead and the memories of it were a horror to her. Her heart was broken and the dread of it felt to her as if the world had ended. Less than a week ago her son had entered the city to the high praises of their people in a wonderful palm branch parade. It was irreconcilable that course of her son's life could have fallen so far that he was condemned and put to death by their religious leaders at the hand of that Roman governor in less than one week's time.

Mary did not want to get out of bed. It was her way of not having to face the others. But she knew she was a guest in Joseph's home, who was she to sleep this hour away? She slowly rose to her feet and looked around. Her garments were not there. She wondered what was going on? She saw a bowl with water for her to wash with, and next to it was a fresh set of clothes that had been set out for her to wear.

At the sound of her stirring, Adah softly called her name, "Mary?"

She had been trying to not be heard by anyone. She was frightened and was not ready for company. Mary had never been accustomed to having a servant care for her. She did not want to be noticed. The servant called her name again. Mary paused and wondered if she should she say something? She didn't want to answer, but that could become a problem too. She didn't want the servant to worry or alarm anyone. Out of necessity she answered,

"Yes. I am just washing up a little. If you could wait until I am done, please."

"Of course. I have put out fresh clothes for you to wear. Yours will be washed for you after the Sabbath. Let me know if I can do anything for you."

Mary had spent the last three years of her life caring for the needs of her son and his disciples in this way. She didn't want to be waited on now. That would add to her grief. She wondered if she should slow her pace and delay the start of her day. But what good would that do? It would not really make much difference. She was going to have to face what the day had to hold for her sometime. Having washed and put on the fresh clothes she invited the servant in.

"You must be hungry. I can bring you some food, or there is a table that is being set in the dining room. My master and his family are also just beginning their day. They have invited you to be with them for their breakfast."

Mary needed a minute to think about what she felt best about doing. She did not want to hear anyone offering their condolences for right now. It was hard enough to face the day without that. She remembered the day before and how Joseph and his wife had already offered their empathy to her. He and his wife along with his servants had been so helpful the night before, she felt comfortable being with them then.

"Yes, thank you. I will join them and eat."

"Is there anything else I can do for you? My master has asked me to be in waiting for you today so that you will have need of nothing."

"Thank you. That is very kind of you. I don't need anything right now though."

"Then I will send word to let my master know that you will be joining his family soon." The servant bowed as she left the room.

Mary felt a sense of relief that it had not been too overwhelming for her up to this point. But everything she would now do was an awkward first for her because she was doing it in the aftershock of her son's death. She ventured out of her room and waiting for her were the other women who had served alongside of her during his son's public ministry. They all greeted her with warm hugs and made eye contact with her in a show of love.

Other than that, there was no great show of emotions by Mary and the other women followed her example.

They all ventured downstairs and made their way to the dining room. As they passed by the kitchen they saw the servants preparing breakfast. Mary wanted to busy herself by helping them. This was what she was accustomed to doing. But it was the Sabbath and there was nothing for her to do. All the food had been prepared the day before and they were merely putting it in bowls and platters to bring into the dining room. And, she was the guest of a wealthy benefactor who she knew would not hear of her helping in this way, especially while she was in mourning.

In the dining room Joseph and his wife were quietly waiting with their children as the ladies entered. His family all greeted the women warmly and his wife offered a caring hug to Mary. She invited her to be at her side for the meal.

Then Ziphorah looked around, "Where is John? Has anyone seen him this morning?"

They all looked around wondering why he wasn't there and then they worried that he had not been given an invitation to join them. Joseph excused himself and hurried off to find him.

John had returned to his room and was sitting in silence. He was looking out a window with a blank expression on his face when Joseph knocked on the door. He did not answer. Joseph called his name, "John?" There was no answer and he knocked again as he spoke, "John, are you in there?"

John had to rouse his thoughts and wake them from their idleness as he tried to speak. It was in a weak voice that he said, "Yes." But then he cleared his throat and spoke again more clearly, "Yes, I'm ... ah, I'm here. Please come in."

Joseph worried about him and looked around to see if anything was unusual before he spoke, "John, please come and join us for breakfast."

John was in a passive state and did not know what he really wanted to do. He was not hungry, but it seemed appropriate to accept his invitation rather than reject it for no reason. He quietly rose and stepped toward the door.

Joseph, still worried about him asked, "How are you? Are you ...". He did not know how to phrase his question without bringing up the tragedy of Jesus' death.

John politely responded right away because he did not want it brought up just then either, "I'm fine, just fine. Let's not keep everyone waiting."

In the dining room Joseph offered a blessing to the LORD and they began their meal. Many of them did not feel hungry, but as the food was set before them they all seemed to find an appetite. The children were very subdued at the meal. Their parents had explained to them that the Rabbi had died, and that the meal would likely be a quiet one. Mary especially enjoyed the children's company, even though very little was said between them during the meal.

All over the city synagogue attendance was typically at a high point on this Sabbath day because it followed the Passover. Joseph debated in his mind whether he should bring his family out into the city to attend worship or not. He worried about everyone's safety, especially of his guests and so all the first-floor windows remained shut and the doors locked. Joseph decided they must go to prevent undo attention from falling on them due to their absence on this special occasion. He did not want anyone finding out that he was secretly hosting Mary and John at his home. Though it was difficult for his family, they presented themselves there as if all was well. Joseph timed their arrival so that they entered the synagogue as worship was just to begin and they sat in the back. He also left immediately at the close of their worship and returned directly to their home.

Because it was the Sabbath and Mary was in mourning, it was necessary for her to practice customs that were very restrictive. She was allowed to go to evening prayers in the synagogue and then she had to return home, all without interacting with anyone. In worship she was expected to be entirely silent. This was to be done for at least seven days. At home she must practice prayer at the seven appointed hours: sunrise, midmorning, noon, afternoon, early evening, evening, and bedtime. This was required for the first three days as she lived in isolation. She was also not allowed to work for seven days. None of this would be a problem for as so many of the other women were there to support her in these customs. They also joined in observing them as well. Though some from Joseph's household did go to morning worship at their synagogue, many stayed home. They wanted to be there to attend to the needs of Mary, John, and the others too.

Mary returned to her room after breakfast. She felt like she needed to be alone, but the truth was, she did not really know what she needed, or what could help her as the day was unfolding. Upstairs there was a hallway window overlooking the street that had been opened. She did not feel safe near it and so she veiled her face and passed by it quickly. In her room she opened a window that overlooked the home's inner courtyard. John was out there, but she did not want to disturb his privacy, so she drew the curtain and sat down to rest.

Now that she was alone again, tears slowly rolled down her cheeks as she considered the loss of her son. Shortly after that, Mary Magdala knocked and asked to come in. Mary rose and washed her face to conceal her tears and then went to the door and welcomed her in. Mary sat and wondered what they might talk about, but the very thought of this was overwhelming to her and she was overcome with weeping. The other Mary came to her side and held her in her arms.

Mary told her, "I took care of him all of his life. I knew he would never take a wife, so I remained with him to care for him, washing and mending his clothes, and cooking his meals. I lived for him. When he traveled I went with. We were together so much and his life was a blessing to me." A moment passed and she cried, "Now I am a widow without a son." She gasped with tears, "I have become like one who is childless, only it is worse because I have survived my son. But, now it seems like my life has ended with his." Mary dropped her head and held her face in her hands as she wept. The other Mary sat at her side and held her in a loving embrace for a long time, but for them time had somehow lost all meaning. As Mary regained her composure she wiped away her tears and said, "I must look like a mess."

Mary Magdala found a brush that was on a chest of draws and then began to attend to Mary's hair. There were a few tangles that needed to be worked out and having freed them, she gently brushed Mary's hair from her scalp down to their ends.

Mary Magdala shared with her, "When I was a child my mother would love brushing my hair for me. It felt so good and it told me that she loved me. It always made me feel better, especially on sad days."

Mary found comfort in having her hair brushed. It was soothing and by it Mary Magdala showed her how much she cared about what she was going through. The tension in her shoulders lessoned and she became sleepy. "Thank you," she said, "I feel better now, and this helped me relax. I think I need to lay down and maybe sleep for a little while." Mary Magdala knowingly nodded for her Lord's mother to see and left her side.

It was after their noontime meal that Joseph asked John to come with him into his private office. They both sat on pillows and enjoyed the comfortable furnishings that Joseph's well to do life offered him. He calmly waited to speak wondering if John would say what might be on his mind first. After about a half a minute of silence, Joseph sensing John had nothing pressing on his thoughts, spoke first, "John, there are many concerns I have for Mary and yourself, as well as my other guests."

John nodded as if he knew what Joseph was about to say but he did not have a clue about what those concerns might be.

With a relaxed and calm posture, he slowly spoke, "I don't know if it is safe for you or Mary to go out into the city. I just don't know. If the Temple guards have been given orders to seek out and arrest any of Jesus' followers they will find you out there."

John was disheartened by such a thought and looking down he gave a slight nod of his head. "Thank you for taking Mary and myself in. There was nowhere for us to go last night."

"You and Mary are very welcome guests in my home. However, I worry it may not be safe for you to stay here. I have posted a lookout on my roof to watch for guards or soldiers should they come to my home looking for you two or any of Jesus' followers. There is a secret passageway out of here. If they come for you and Mary, you and the others must leave that way."

John was increasingly worried as Joseph spoke on. It was fearful enough to worry about falling into the hands of an angry God as he had imagined that morning. Now there was this added burden, that the Holy City of Jerusalem was a dangerous place for them to be. His muscles instinctively tightened and his body jerked. His new fears had taken him to the edge of panic and his thoughts raced within him as his eyes darted about the room wondering what to do.

Joseph had been watching for whatever John's reaction might be. He did not want to alarm him, but at the same time he needed to prepare him for this contingency. He spoke softly, "John, John, stay with me now. There is no reason for you to worry so. I don't want you to leave my home in secret and without my blessing for your travels. I will be able to keep you and Mary safe and get you out of the city if it comes to that."

John's racing thoughts were overtaken by Joseph's soothing voice and he refocused his attention on him. "Yes, thank you."

Joseph was a wealthy man and had many business dealings throughout the middle east. "If you wish, Mary can stay on in my household indefinitely. Or, she can live with my relatives back in Arimathea. They will gladly welcome her into their home."

"No, that doesn't seem right to me. Jesus gave me charge of her. She must come with me when I leave your home."

"Have you given any thought to what you will do?"

John had given no thought to what he would do now. His mind, now alerted to his circumstances, returned to his former occupation as a fisherman. "Why, yes, of course. I think that I will look for my brother, and Peter too. Then I will make my way north to Galilee, or Capernaum and take up fishing again."

"You know I have business dealings among the Jewish community in Egypt. Mary could travel there, along with you, and the two of you could stay there for her safety."

John was feeling a little intimidated by this man of great wealth and influence. He knew Joseph meant for the best and that he could trust him. He did not want to disrespect him. He had done so much for them in past two days. Still, he did not feel like a foreign land was the right place for them. Cautiously he answered back, "Thank you very much. You have done so much for us. I worry that because I don't know anyone there and am unaccustomed to their culture, that I will not be able to resettle there."

Joseph smiled all the while, not wanting to give John any sense that he was displeased with what he was saying.

For John, he was suddenly having to take on the role of an adult and think about what he must do to provide for Mary. This was new to him and he had not been certain he could discuss it without simply giving into someone who could easily take his new responsibility away from him. But he did rise to the occasion and the prospect of his new future gave him a small sense of purpose that he must fulfill.

John's material needs had been met for him by others over these last three years. Jesus' ministry purse was able to provide for all the disciples. However, now there was no purse for him to draw funds from and it left him with the uncomfortable thought of asking for help from Joseph. "There is something I would like to ask for help with from you." John was very nervous about what he had just said and he felt like it was very out of place for him to say such a thing.

Joseph continued to listen and maintain a very constant focus on his interactions with John. "What may I do to help you? Just name it."

"Thank you for all that you have already provided for Mary and myself."

Joseph nodded.

John was nervously shaking as he spoke his request, "Can you provide for our trip to Galilee? We will need money, clothing and supplies, perhaps even a donkey. When we get there, we will need money for housing and startup money for a boat and fishing nets. I may even need to take on one or two workers to help me." John was surprised at how easily the words just rolled out of his mouth. He was direct, just as he needed to be. He had worried he might sound demanding or proud in his manner, but clearly, he made his request with all humility and respect. He did realize that he was not able to look directly at Joseph as he spoke, but now as he looked into his eyes he was delighted to hear his answer.

Joseph wanted to be like a father to John and guide him in this need for planning. He hoped to offer him whatever help was needed. He was pleased John had made up his own mind about the future and Mary's care. Now, he was delighted to grant John's request and provide for his needs.

"I see that you have given thought to what is needed to bring about your plan. I will give you all that you have asked for and when the time comes I will send you out with my blessing as well."

John was amazed and relieved that this had gone so well. He took a moment to enjoy this time with Joseph. It was like getting a new start in life after all the upheaval that had come into his life. Even still, he found that he was easily exhausted by even the simplest of activities that day. So, he as well as the others rested quietly that afternoon. Sometimes they would talk about Jesus' death, but even that was limited because it quickly overwhelmed them.

Chapter Forty-Two
Sun Fall to Sun Up

As the evening sun began its descent, Joseph's family and his guests began to gather in the dining room for their evening meal. Late in the afternoon as twilight drew near, Joseph called his two young sons to his side and whispered to them. He asked them to go out into their courtyard and watch the sky for the appearance of three stars, which they excitedly rushed off to do. The Sabbath ended when night began, which was marked by the observation of three stars in the sky. With the setting of the sun, the time of the Sabbath was over and so also ended the constraints of the day, or so it would seem. The days that followed the Sabbath had their requirements too. Sunday was a day that was lived in the immediate shadow of the Sabbath and to lessening degrees Monday and Tuesday were also lived in remembrance of the Sabbath. In contrast, Wednesday, Thursday, and Friday were in increasing degrees lived in anticipation of and preparation for the coming Sabbath.

When the nighttime began, a final meal was eaten which brought to a close their day of rest. It was not long before the two young children reappeared and went directly to their father and announced together, "Father, we have seen three stars in the sky and so nighttime has come to us again." The young children beamed with joy to be able to do this task because their announcement told everyone that the Sabbath had ended. Now they would eat and then celebrate the Havdalah ceremony marking the beginning of the workweek.

As the meal began, Joseph's wife Ziphorah lit an oil lamp to show by its light and the shadows it cast how that the Sabbath day had ended. The light showed them how the greater light of the sun separated the day from the night and the lesser light of the moon. With the passing from day to night, they passed from the holy time of the Sabbath into the ordinary time of the weekdays. As she lit the candle she recited this text from the First Book of Moses.

"And God saw everything that he had made,
and behold, it was very good.
And the evening and the
morning were the sixth day.
Thus, the heavens and the earth were finished,
and all the host of them.
And on the seventh day God ended his work
which he had made,
and he rested on the seventh day from all his
work which he had made.
And God blessed the seventh day,
and sanctified it because in
it he had rested from all his work
which he had created and made.
These are the generations of the heavens
and of the earth when they were created,
in the day that the LORD God
made the earth and the heavens."[12]

The meal was served in formal fashion as Joseph was a man of great wealth he employed many servants who waited on his family and their guests in their dining room. He did not want any of his guests to want for anything. He had instructed his servants to be very attentive to their needs and sensitive to their moods because they were in mourning. Though mealtime was normally a place for

---

[12] Genesis 1:31-2:4, adapted from the KJV

much conversation, there was not much said because everyone was still suffering from the death of their beloved Rabbi.

As the food was removed from the table, the things needed for the Havdalah were brought out and set before Joseph; a large Kiddush cup of wine, a box of sweet smelling aromatic spices, and three candles. As people of faith they celebrated this at the close of every Sabbath and at the end of every major festival. This Havdalah brought to a close both the Passover and the Sabbath. This ceremony was also a transition from the Sabbath into the ordinary time of the six days in which God created the heavens and the earth. They would observe four special blessing that reminded them of the differences between days that are Holy to the LORD and the other six days of the week. It would remind them of the difference between common things and holy things.

As the entire household, including the servants, were gathered, Joseph rose to lead everyone in the service. He invited those still reclining for the meal to rise for the short ceremony. His two children were at his sides as he spoke, "Our Torah reminds us to remember the Sabbath and keep it holy. Now as night divides the day, so also, we begin our period of six days of work. God created the heavens and the earth in six days and on the seventh day he completed his work and rested. Now, the first day of his creation had returned for us to live in, so also, we again return to our work and in the continuance of his ever-renewing creation."

Some of those gathered heard a more monotone voice than was typical of Joseph and they were not sure that his words, though meant to bless them, didn't make them more sorrowful in their bereavement.

With that said, he took the cup of wine in his hands and held it up for everyone to see, sanctified it and blessed it, singing this verse over it,

"Barukh atah Adonai, Eloheinu, melekh ha'olam
"Blessed are you, LORD, our God,
sovereign King and Ruler of creation.

borei p'ri hagafen, Amein."
You are the Creator of the fruit of the vine, Amen."

He felt very self-conscious knowing that wine was a symbol of joy in life. This occasion, more than any, was not a joyous occasion, it was obligatory. He knew that Jesus had changed all of their lives, twice. First by bringing them the hopes that he was their long-awaited Messiah, and then when died so tragically on the cross. It was as though they died with him. As he returned the cup of wine to the table he was glad that part was over, knowing that it did not bring joy to anyone that night, but rather it reminded them all of their bereavement.

As this part of the Havdalah unfolded, John was reminded of Passover meal that he had celebrated with his Rabbi. It was then that he remembered the ten plagues, the suffering of his ancestors and their great deliverance from slavery, and bondage to Pharaoh in Egypt by the mighty hand of God. Jesus added to that ceremonial meal by offering them a cup of wine. His thoughts remembered those words that were spoken by his Rabbi, *This cup is the new covenant of my blood which is shed for the remission of your sins. Drink of it, all of you. For I tell you, I will not drink again of this fruit of the vine until that day when I*

325

drink it anew with you in the coming of my Father's Kingdom. Do this for the remembrance of me.

John struggled to understand what it was that Jesus meant by it. He had tears in his eyes as Joseph offered up the cup of wine that not only failed to bring joy, but it added to his sorrow by reminding him of Jesus' suffering.

Joseph continued as he took the box of rich aromatic spices and held it up for everyone to see saying, "In the celebration of the Passover we ate bitter herbs to remind us of the hard lives our people led while they were slaves and serving Pharaoh in Egypt. Now we enjoy the sweet aroma of these spices because we live in our own nation's lands and serve our God in holiness. Then he offered the second blessing as he sanctified it, singing this verse over it,

"Barukh atah Adonai, Eloheinu, melekh ha'olam
"Blessed are you, LORD, our God, sovereign King and Ruler of the creation.

borei minei v'samim, Amein. "
You are the Creator of all the spices, Amen. "

Then he held the aromatic box under his nose and inhaled its rich scent. "We sniff the aroma of these spices to remind us of the sweetness of the Sabbath day. We remember how God blessed the seventh day and rested from all his labors. So from the Sabbath to the first day of God's creation we share in his rest until we resume our responsibilities and return to our labors." He took in a deep breath and smelled its sweet scent and then passed the box so that everyone could enjoy its aroma as well.

When the box was passed to Mary of Magdala, she and the women who helped to prepare Jesus' body for burial had a very hard time. Its aroma quickly reminded them of the spices they used then. Tears rose in their eyes and a few of them sobbed briefly.

As the box was being passed, Joseph picked up the three tall slender candles and held them over the large oil lamp that was on the table in front of him. He used its flame to warm the wax of those candles and then he braided them into one single stick with three wicks so that the three flames would appear as one. He lifted them up high for everyone to see, sanctified them and blessed them, singing this verse over them,

"Barukh atah Adonai, Eloheinu, melekh ha'olam
"Blessed are you, LORD, our God, sovereign King and
Ruler of the creation.

borei m'orei ha'eish, Amein."
You are the Creator of the fire's light, Amen."

He held the candle up to the oil lamp and lit the three wicks and then put the oil lamp out. He held the Havdalah candles up high so that it shed its light on all the people. Everyone responded by raising their hands up high and covering the light that came to them to create shadows. Then as they lowered their hands they turned to those near them to see the light of the flame reflected in their eyes. They did this to see the distinction between light and darkness which marks the closure of the Sabbath day and the beginning of a new day. The light of the Havdalah symbolizes the light of the first day of the creation week and it is a sign to tell them that with the rising of the morning sun, it will be time for them to work again in God's creation.

The final blessing that Joseph gave reminded them of the separation of things according to God's creation. As Joseph sang these words he seemed to be able to express himself better and his words brought life and hope to everyone there.

"Barukh atah Adonai, Eloheinu, melekh ha'olam
"Blessed are you, LORD, our God,
sovereign King and Ruler of creation.

hamav'dil bein kodesh l'chol
Who separates between sacred and common,

bein or l'choshekh bein Yis'ra'eil la'amim
between light and darkness,
between Israel and the nations

bein yom hash'vi'i l'sheishet y'mei hama'aseh
between the seventh day of rest and
the six days in which we may labor

Barukh atah Adonai
Blessed are You, O LORD,

hamav'dil bein kodesh l'chol. Amein."
who divides between sacred and common. Amen."

Joseph passed the candlestick to his eldest son to hold and then he lifted high the cup of wine again and took a sip. He passed it around the room and each person of age took a sip. As the cup returned to him, Joseph took it and used the Havdalah candle to relight the oil lamp and then he extinguished the candle in the remaining wine.

Joseph announced, "Our household continues to be in mourning. I do not believe that it would be right for us to share in any of the traditional songs of joy that …". His voice trailed off as he held back his tears. Everyone understood exactly how he felt and some simply nodded their heads in silent agreement that it would not be right to sing at that time. Joseph looked around the room and he felt very self-conscious. As the head of the household, he had never displayed such personal feelings so openly to anyone but his immediate family. He regained a bit of his composure and then excused himself and retired to another room. Normally the evening would have concluded with the men enjoying a discussion about the Torah. However, this night most of the household shared with Joseph in his grief over the death of Rabbi Jesus. They did not want to discuss much of anything, and some did not feel up to socializing.

It was at that time that there came a knock at the door. While that was not entirely unusual for someone to call upon them after the sun had set, given their circumstances the entire household was on edge because of it. Joseph himself went to the door and opened a small window to ask who it was that was calling.

"Joseph, it is Peter. Please let me in. I am alone."

Joseph knew his voice well and immediately opened the door for him. As he came in a servant washed his feet and Joseph asked, "Have you eaten? Are you hungry?"

"No, I'm fine. Yes, I ate."

Having heard the sound of Peter's voice John came to the door to greet him. The young apostle asked him, "Where have you been these past two days? I was very worried about you."

Peter's head dropped as he remembered having denied his Lord three times. It was then that he had fled from Jesus' presence and abandoned John's company. He was uncertain if the younger apostle knew about what he had said. It was such a traumatic memory for him that he did not want to relive it or discuss it.

Peter was frozen in his thoughts as John asked him again, "Peter, where have you been staying since Friday?"

Peter shook his head to clear his thoughts, "I just couldn't stay there any longer. I had to leave so I returned to the upper room where I met up with a few of the other apostles. They arrived under the darkness of the night after the Lord's arrest in the garden. We are fearful that there may be more arrests. That is why I waited until dark to venture out in search of you and Mary. Is she here?"

Joseph answered him, "Yes. She and some of the other women have been here since Friday."

Joseph and John met with Peter privately and shared with him all that had happened over the past two days. Peter also visited with Mary and the others during the evening. Since the hour was late and they continued to be in fear over what the authorities might do to Jesus' closest followers Joseph asked Peter to stay the night.

The women who were there continued in their traditions of bereavement and its restrictions. Mary Magdala was particularly anxious to go to the tomb where they had laid Jesus. She planned to leave at first light. Her heart, along with everyone's, was deeply wounded and she remained confused about how his life could have ended this way. She hoped that visiting his body would bring her a bit of comfort.

Because the preparations of Jesus body for burial were done so hastily, Mary wanted to do more for him.

Therefore, she had asked Joseph for permission to use his household stores to prepare more spices and anointing balm for his body and bands of cloth to wrap him with.

She and Mary, the mother of James, along with Salome and Joanna worked together in the kitchen to prepare them. With pistol and mortar in hand they ground the compounds, myrrh, frankincense, cloves, cinnamon and more, into a very fine powder. They also made a balm of aloe and olive oil to anoint him with and they prepared bandages from white linen cloth. They would use these to wrap his wounds with and to wrap his limbs into a resting posture so that they would lay evenly and in their proper positions.

With that done the women returned to their guest rooms and went to sleep. Not only for Mary Magdala, but for some of the other women, it was a fitful sleep. They agonized over the loss of their Rabbi and took it very hard that he was made to suffer so greatly. They were shaken that the Temple leaders had unjustly tried and condemned him. They were very unsettled by it all.

Now, very early that morning Mary, was the first one to wake up and it was still dark outside. She could stay in bed no longer and as she stirred so did the other women who had helped her prepare the fresh spices. They washed and dressed quietly and then gathered downstairs near the entrance. It was still dark, but because they had seen the first light of the dawn they gathered up their baskets and set out. They had given no forethought to the danger of going out at that hour or to inviting a man to chaperon them. As they made their way to the garden they grew a little weepy knowing that they were going to visit his body. They tried to take courage but grew increasingly weepy knowing what laid ahead of them. Their hearts were still very tender, and they longed to find some comfort in being close to him.

331

They wanted to carry out these final measures for him as he slept awaiting the resurrection at the end of the age of all the ages.

Carefully and slowly they made their way in the dark remembering that because his funeral was carried out so quickly that there was no one who had sang a funeral dirge or recited a lament. What little they had done for him remained incomplete and they went to bring it all to fulfillment. They reminded themselves, and found some comfort in knowing that he was not condemned to be buried in a common grave with criminals like an outcast of their society.

As they began that very early Sunday morning it was truly in the shadow of the Sabbath as the first light had only just appeared. They entered the Garden of Jerusalem where his tomb was. They had given no forethought to having some of the men accompany them to roll the stone away. This was a dreaded realization for them. It meant they would have to return to Joseph's home to ask for help. The thought of this delay was a painful frustration to them, making them feel very overwhelmed by this setback.

Now, inside the garden, the day had lightened enough for them to see a little more clearly. As they neared the tomb, there was without warning a great earthquake that struck, and the women were forced to the ground. Looking at the tomb they could see the soldiers there also falling to the ground and they looked incredibly frightened.

Mary Magdala looked at the tomb fearful that it might be damaged by the earthquake. Suddenly, before her very eyes, the stone covering the entrance began to roll away from the doorway. She feared that the tomb was also in danger of collapsing and she gasped and broke down into tears for what she saw. The other women were also overcome saying, "This is absolutely dreadful! Why has this happened to our Lord? That he should suffer so greatly in life, and now in his death to have such a tragedy befall his body!" And great flashes of light, brighter than lightning shone, blinding them and they were seized with fear.

www.ingramcontent.com/pod-product-compliance
Lightning Source LLC
Chambersburg PA
CBHW070748280626
47162CB00018B/2665